TEAMMATES

On Ice

BY

ALISON SOMMER

BENTON HOUSE PUBLISHING

Benton House Publishing

bentonhousepublishing.com

Cover art by Predrag Markovic
Copy editing by Lessa Lamb

ISBN 978-1-952057-20-5 (Paperback)
ISBN 978-1-952057-21-2 (eBook)

For more information about the author and upcoming books, please visit the author's blog at alioffthemark.com

This book is dedicated to the Women's Hockey Association of Minnesota and all my amazing teammates, past and present.

Special thanks to Ethan for being an incredible partner not just to me but to all my imaginary friends as well. I love you.

On Ice

Fitz

Saturday, March 11th

"I'm going to leave soon for hockey," Patricia 'Fitz' Fitzpatrick called to her husband, Tom, from the doorway of his den. "I likely won't get home until late…"

Tom nodded, but he didn't raise his eyes from the phone in his hand. Fitz lingered, running her fingers over the molding of the door frame and chewing on her bottom lip. Did she need to explicitly *say* that she wanted him to put the kids to bed?

Fitz regarded her husband as he sat in his chair, still as a portrait. The yellow light from the reading lamp made his sandy blonde hair shine warm and golden. Tom was a handsome man: tall and athletic, with a strong jaw and the most expressive storm-gray eyes. When he smiled at her—*really* smiled—Fitz could feel her heart glow. But he didn't smile much anymore; these days when he cast his eyes toward her, all she saw there was disappointment, annoyance, or just plain *boredom*.

Tonight Tom wasn't looking at her at all; his jaw was set firmly, his eyes fixed in concentration on his phone. He could sit that way for hours, seemingly oblivious to the workings of the home around him. *He should know when to put the kids to bed, but will he remember?* Fitz loved her husband, but he rarely noticed when she needed help—the care of their home and children *was* her concern, after all, not his—except for nights like tonight, when Fitz got to escape her life to play hockey. *If I don't remind him, I'll just worry.* Today's game was important. Fitz wanted to enjoy it; and she wouldn't enjoy it if she was thinking about Tom and the kids.

"You'll need to get Tyler and McKayla to bed yourself," said Fitz, caving to her doubts.

1

"*Fine*," Tom replied, not looking up.

"I expect that I'll probably go out with my teammates after the game, at least for a little while, so—"

"Patricia," Tom cut her off sharply. He glared up at her, his face tight with irritation. "I get it. You do it *all the time*."

"Okay, well... thank you." *Maybe I shouldn't have reminded him about the children, but he didn't need to react like that. Twice a week over the winter is hardly 'all the time.'* Fitz quickly turned to leave before his irritation could rub off on her. *Hockey will lift my mood.*

However, once Fitz arrived at the rink, she began to worry that today's game might *not* lift her spirits quite like she'd hoped. Her team, the Hot Shots, had been a little on edge lately but today things seemed poised to boil over. The atmosphere in the locker room, as they all donned their gear, was eerily quiet, with none of the usual light-hearted banter—no joking around or smack-talking the other team to get themselves psyched up for the game. The Hot Shots just seemed out-of-sync, somehow.

As the game got underway, Fitz's fears were quickly confirmed. This was not going to be the smile-inducing, gratifying experience she usually had in the rink with her teammates. This game was *intense*—and not in a good way. The Hot Shots were immediately at each other's throats. The game *was* important: they were at the end of the regular season and needed a win to make it into the playoffs. But that didn't seem like a good enough reason to act the way some of her teammates were acting tonight.

"Tessa! What the hell are you doing? Go *get her*! Skate!" Jackie screamed at her own teammate as she hopped the boards onto the ice.

"God, what's up Jackie's ass?" Michelle muttered to Fitz. "It's just *hockey*."

"Don't let her hear you say that," Fitz replied with a wry smile for her linemate.

Truth be told, it wasn't 'just hockey' to Fitz either; but she kept her focus on her own performance, and tried not to let the tension on the bench get to her. The game was hard enough as it was. The Hot Shots were only down by one goal, but the opposing team was controlling the play. *We're never going to score if we don't get any shots on net,* Fitz thought as she watched from the bench. Again and again the Hot Shots failed to maintain possession of the puck.

"We need a shift change, they've been out there *forever,*" Michelle complained.

"They've been stuck in our end for a while," Fitz reasoned. "It's not like they've had many chances—"

"Whatever, it's been over *two minutes* and Jackie's still trying to *skate* it. Like, come on. Dump it and get the fuck off," Michelle griped, gesturing to the ice.

"Oh, Jackie's just hungry for a goal. I'm sure she'll get off soon," Connie, the team captain, commented from down the bench.

"Yeah, at least she *wants* to score," Cindy, Connie's right-hand, added.

"Yeah, it's not like *I* want to or anything," Michelle muttered sarcastically.

"We *all* want to score," Fitz said.

"Do we though?" Cindy laughed bitterly. "You wouldn't know it to look at the scoreboard."

"Don't worry, baby girl." Dawn patted Cindy's shoulder. "There's a lot of game left."

But the first two periods of the game seemed to fly by, with very few chances for the Hot Shots. Fitz managed one nice pass to Tessa up high, but Tessa's shot went wide of the net. The opposing team had better luck, putting another one past the Hot Shots, and ending the second period with a two-to-nothing lead.

The team moved to huddle up during the short break before the third period. Fitz felt her heart skip a beat as Jackie stormed down the bench toward Tessa, face almost purple with rage. Jackie had never liked Tessa; she'd made that abundantly clear all season long. The feeling was mutual. Tessa had even taken to calling Jackie her 'nemesis'—although never to her face. Most games, the

3

feud between the two women was contained to a few snippy comments from Jackie and sullen glares from Tessa. But today it seemed Jackie was determined to have it out with her.

"Could you *maybe* try and hit the *net,* Tessa?" Jackie snapped.

"It's not like I *tried* to miss," Tessa growled through clenched teeth.

"Fitz won that face-off right to you! You had an actual *chance!* We can't afford to give those away." Jackie leaned back. "I don't know if you noticed but we're not exactly *winning* here."

"We do need to make the best of any opportunity we get, you know," Connie said in her measured Minnesotan lilt. "We're not out of this yet, but we need to get some goals, you know."

"And we can't get goals if we don't get shots *on net,*" Cindy added with a smirk in Tessa's direction. Fitz looked sympathetically at her friend and defenseman. Tessa didn't say another word, her face was stone-still, a picture of frustration.

"Let's just fucking play hockey. Okay?" Michelle scoffed. "Who cares if we lose—"

"*I* care!" Jackie snapped. "If we lose this game our season is *over.* If we win we could make the play-off tournament. I can't believe you're all ready to just give up on that."

"Nobody's giving up, boo-boo," Dawn said calmly. "Let's just try and stay positive."

"Dawn's right, we can do this," Fitz nodded, trying to project as much optimism as she could muster. The confrontational atmosphere on the bench lately reminded Fitz more of her marriage than her hockey team, and she didn't like it. She went to hockey for exercise and escape, not drama.

The team circled up for a quick cheer and the third period got underway. If anything the Hot Shots had even fewer chances to score. And the more Jackie screamed at Tessa, the worse Tessa played, and the worse Fitz felt. When Tessa missed a second open shot, Fitz tensed, bracing for Jackie's reaction.

"That's it, Tessa, you're done!" Jackie howled when Tessa returned to the bench. "Don't even bother going out again! You're not doing us any good!"

All eyes turned from Tessa and Jackie to their captain, Connie. To Fitz's surprise, Connie nodded.

"Yeah, Tess, why don't you take a little break," Connie said, her sweet tone at odds with what she was doing.

"You're really going to *bench* her?" Fitz blurted out before she could stop herself. She normally made a point not to get involved in team politics, but this was unprecedented.

"Aren't you sick of giving her the puck just to watch her throw it away?" Cindy asked acerbically. Tessa looked at Fitz, her dark eyes full of frustration and hurt. Fitz shook her head but said nothing.

"What the fuck's going on? What did I just miss?" Michelle asked as she got off the ice and sat down next to Fitz.

"Connie and Jackie just told Tessa she couldn't play anymore," Fitz mumbled, her gut twisted in a knot just saying it out loud.

"Are you shitting me?" Michelle asked, aghast. "This is fucking old-lady-hockey. What the hell?"

Michelle was right, nobody got *benched* in this league. *It's supposed to be recreational, for crying out loud.* But there wasn't anything Fitz could do about it. Connie was the captain, Jackie and Cindy were her friends; Fitz and Michelle were Tessa's friends, but none of them had Connie's ear. Fitz glanced back at the bench. Dawn might have a chance at talking their captain into easing up on poor Tess. Fitz's eyes moved to the game clock. *There isn't time.*

"Let's just get it over with, alright?" Fitz gestured for Michelle to join her on the ice. With a couple more mumbled curses, Michelle complied. The puck dropped, and three minutes later, it was all over. The Hot Shots lost their last game of the season and their only chance at making the play-offs.

"I can't believe Jackie actually made you sit out," Fitz whispered to Tessa as they changed after the game. Tessa's eyes flitted across the locker room to where Jackie was changing.

"I don't call her my 'nemesis' for nothing," Tessa muttered under her breath as she pulled on her maroon Hot Shots hoodie and refashioned her thick bottle-blonde hair into a messy bun. The young woman looked so unhappy.

If anything is excellent or praiseworthy, think about such things, Fitz recited to herself; it was the last line to a Biblical passage, which she often turned to when she caught herself focusing on the negative. *There has to be something good about today.* Fitz pulled on her own matching hoodie.

"Hey, cheer up, Tess," Fitz nudged her friend. "At least we still have the Dart. Come on, first round's on me."

Tessa sighed. "That sounds perfect."

The Dart was an old dive bar a few blocks from the rink, home to their most dearly held hockey tradition: post-game beers. Every time Fitz stepped through those heavy green doors, and smelled the familiar scent of fried food over stale beer, she felt something inside her relax. *Home, sweet Dart.* Today was no different, although it was bittersweet—with the hockey season over, this would be the last evening spent at the Dart with her friends until next fall.

It's a shame I can't play hockey year-round, Fitz thought wistfully as she and Tessa settled into their customary seats.

The Dart was long and narrow, most of it dimly lit by the neon beer signs, flatscreen TVs, and flickering fluorescents lights. But at the front of the bar, a few tables were bathed in the evening light that shone through the bar's tall windows. The one in the middle was "their" table: Fitz, Tessa, Michelle, and Dawn, the four Hot Shots who still went out to the Dart after games.

Fitz stretched, shaking any remaining post-game soreness from her limbs, and tried to read Tessa's expression. She and Tessa were different in almost every way possible—outside of their love for hockey. Tessa was a true native Minnesotan; she had grown up watching Gopher hockey and skating on frozen lakes. Tessa was born to play; Fitz had fallen into it by chance.

Fitz had moved to Minnesota from North Carolina when she married Tom. She was athletic—an accomplished lacrosse player—and she enjoyed watching NHL games with Tom, but it wasn't until her children started playing that Fitz gave hockey a try. She'd immediately fallen in love and quickly connected with her teammates. She'd been able to find a type of friendship with them that went beyond anything she had out in her lonely suburban life. Hockey was a gift from God, and made Fitz feel incredibly blessed. Tessa didn't look as though she felt particularly *blessed* at the moment. *Let's see what we can do about that.*

"Two *Coors Lights*, please," Fitz ordered without hesitation when the server appeared. Tessa smiled gratefully at her.

"Thanks, Fitz," she said.

"You deserve it, you took way too much of a beating today..."

"So say we all," said Dawn as she dropped heavily into the seat across from Tessa. Her light brown skin was flushed and her posture slack; she looked exhausted, but no worse for the wear.

"Hey, Dawn, how's your leg doing?" Tessa asked.

"Yeah, that blocked shot in the third period was..." Fitz winced and sucked in air between her teeth. Dawn rubbed the back of her calf.

"Just part of the game, boo-boo." Dawn laughed. "You gotta do whatcha gotta do, you know?" she rasped. "Hey, you guys want to split a basket of fries?"

The server dropped by with their beers and took Dawn's order. Fitz's stomach gurgled at the thought of the Dart's thick, golden fries. She hoped her friends would stay out long enough to order real supper. Fitz was in no rush to return home.

"Hey, bitches!" Michelle, last to arrive as always, dropped her purse on the table and slid in next to Dawn. Michelle didn't look like she'd just played a hockey game at all. Her chestnut-brown hair seemed straight out of a salon, not a helmet; even her eyeliner was still pristine. She made the rest of them look scrubby by comparison.

"You already have beer?" Michelle pouted, eyeing Fitz and Tessa's glasses.

"Yes, ma'am," Fitz took a big exaggerated gulp; Tessa picked up her own and with a sly grin at Fitz, did the same. Michelle hated being late on the drink orders, and it was fun to tease her about it. Michelle turned on Dawn.

"Did she take your order already too?" she asked.

"Yeah, just did," Dawn admitted.

"Ugh! I always get my beer last!" Michelle whined. She peered at Fitz's glass, narrowing her eyes. "Not that I'd call what you're drinking *beer.*" *Here we go again.*

"You're just jealous that we have drinks, and you don't," Tessa rolled her eyes.

"Jealous? Of your, what? Fucking *Coors Light*? Hardly," Michelle scoffed. "That is, at best, a beer-adjacent beverage." She turned up her nose.

"Maybe," laughed Fitz, "but after skating hard, I like my beer-flavored water, thank you very much." She lifted her beer and swallowed another couple large mouthfuls, mostly for effect.

"Slow down there, don't drink all of your 'beer-flavored water' before I get my *actual* beer," Michelle admonished. "We need to toast the end of the season properly."

"What a rough note to end the season on, though," groaned Tessa.

"No shit," said Michelle. "That game sucked donkey balls. We lost, but I don't think I even broke a sweat." She shook out her soft, wavy hair.

"I sweat if I so much as look at my gear," Tessa said. "But yeah, there were so many skaters I was cold every time I got on the ice. No wonder I played like shit."

"You played fine," said Fitz. "Jackie just—"

"At least you touched the puck enough to fuck up," Michelle interrupted with a laugh. "I don't think I did *anything*. It's like, did I even *play* hockey today?"

"I feel you, baby girl," Dawn agreed. "Sometimes it seems like I barely even participate when we're getting dominated."

"I only *participate* when being *dominated* in the *bedroom*," Michelle said with a wink. "If you know what I mean."

"I would prefer not to," Tessa shuddered. "Today was bad enough already without *that* mental image." She shook her head. "I just don't get how Connie runs this team."

"It is a little frustrating..." Fitz chewed her lip.

"A *little* frustrating? It's some serious bullshit, and you know it," Michelle snorted. "Connie needs to grow a pair and cut some of these bitches. The team is too damn big. *Fifteen* women on one bench? It's no wonder we're such a shitshow—Jesus."

"Do you think Connie would kick people off the Hot Shots?" Tessa said, eyes wide with fear.

Would Connie actually do that? Just the thought made Fitz sick. All of the in-fighting made her sick, and it just seemed to get worse and worse.

"Naw. Connie would never kick people off the team. She hates drama," said Dawn.

"Helloooooo, are you talking about the same Connie I am?" Michelle asked. "Were you at the game today? This team is dramatic as fuck, and Connie doesn't give a shit. In fact, if she *did* hate drama, she'd've kicked Jackie to the curb, like, yesteryear."

"Yeah right, she'd be more likely to kick *me* off," Tessa grumbled.

Fitz furrowed her brow. There was a feeling growing inside her, an inkling of something she couldn't quite put her finger on yet.

"Did you guys hear the rumor that Jess isn't coming back next year?" Dawn asked.

"What?" Fitz felt her jaw drop. Jess was the Hot Shot's top scorer. *Is it because of the drama?* The nagging sensation inside Fitz intensified, as if her insides were doing cartwheels trying to get her attention—trying to tell her something.

"I heard that she was looking for a full-time spot on a higher-level team," Dawn added.

"That sucks, but maybe she has the right idea," Tessa sighed.

Fitz looked at Tessa. She was just as good as Jess—when she wasn't being screamed at. *Maybe Tessa should move up with Jess and find a team without a nemesis.* Fitz frowned; the thought of losing Tessa was surprisingly painful. *Doesn't she deserve better? Don't we all?* The odd tickling feeling inside Fitz was forming into an actual idea. *Would it be possible?*

"Earth to Fitz!" Michelle snapped Fitz out of her thoughts. "Come on. We need to toast." Michelle raised her beer. "Here's to another season dead and buried! May the next one exceed our ever-lowering expectations! Cheers, bitches!"

"Hey, y'all, I have a thought," said Fitz, when they'd all set their glasses down again. "It might be crazy, but...I think we should make a new team."

"Yeah, right," said Michelle with a snort.

"No, seriously, I think we should put together a new team," Fitz repeated, looking around at the group. "Come on, y'all, you said it yourselves, this team is too big. There's too much drama... And then we could all move up a level."

"Move up? Are you crazy?" Michelle drained her beer and belched softly. "We can't even win consistently at this level!"

"With a new team, we could," Fitz insisted.

The three stared at her, waiting like they were expecting a punchline, but Fitz was dead serious; something had ignited in her chest the moment she said the idea out loud. *We're meant to do this.*

"We who?" Tessa asked slowly.

Fitz could see in Tessa's wide-eyed expression that she was truly considering it.

"Us. The four of us at this table." Fitz looked pointedly at Tessa. Fitz had grown immediately attached to the concept, but she felt like it all somehow hinged on Tessa's approval. *We need to do this together or not at all.*

"So, like, quit the Hot Shots?" Tessa swallowed.

"Yes." Fitz unconsciously held her breath as she waited for Tessa to react.

"Well..." Tessa began slowly. "We'd need a goalie." Tessa smiled and Fitz exhaled in relief. *She's in.*

"Do you know any goalies?" Fitz asked.

"Um... Oh! What about that one sub goalie, what's her name, with the short hair and the orange pads?" Tessa said, perking up. "AJ, right? Didn't she just graduate or something? I think she was looking for a team for next season—"

"Wait!" Michelle threw her arm across the table. "Hold the fuck up. Are we really talking mutiny here?"

"Not *mutiny.* We wouldn't hijack Connie's team. We would build our own," Fitz said.

"That sounds like a hell of a lot of work." Michelle tapped her nails on the rim of her glass. "And move up?"

"Yes! I think we have the skills," said Fitz. "You're super fast, Michelle. And Dawn's got the quickest hands—"

"I can't shoot worth a damn though," Tessa muttered. "Apparently."

"See?" Michelle pointed to Tessa, as if that one self-deprecating comment could change Fitz's mind.

"We could practice shooting," Fitz countered, shaking her head. "You don't even need ice—"

"Okay, wait, before you start giving us a workout routine, baby girl," Dawn chimed in, "remember: this is old-lady hockey. Emphasis on *old.* We have jobs and lives and stuff. I hope you aren't hearing *Eye of the Tiger* and having visions of a Rocky-esque training montage going on here."

"No, no, I know, sorry. Forget the practice, we don't *need* it. I truly think we can do this. If we're all in it together, how much work could it be?" Fitz put up her hands. "Trust me, I can't even imagine the look on my husband's face if I told him I was going to spend even more time on hockey." Fitz shuddered; she *really* didn't want to think about how Tom would react. But this wasn't about him, this was about her and her teammates. Fitz put Tom out of her mind and stared hard at Michelle. "Don't you want to get away from the drama?" she asked.

"Do you really think you wouldn't have 'drama' on a new team?" Michelle let out a bark of laughter. "Trust me, you will. Women can't *exist* together without drama. You'd just be trading in Jackie and Cindy and all that shit for some other new shit." Michelle crossed her arms and sat back. Fitz clenched her jaw; this new team may be purely theoretical, but she found that she was already fiercely defensive of its potential.

"Women *can* be together without drama," Fitz said tersely.

"Well, I've sure as hell never seen it," said Michelle.

Ever think it might be because you're so dramatic, Michelle? Fitz would never say a thing like that outright. Instead she refocused on the point she was trying to make.

"We *can* build a new team. One without drama. But we can't unless we try, and I want to try." Fitz looked pleadingly at Michelle but her defiant expression didn't soften.

"I want to try, too," said Tessa.

"Dawn?" Fitz asked. "Will you join us?"

"Are you sure you want me? I'm not getting any younger, you know." Dawn rubbed her short hair, where her dark curls were starting to go gray.

"Are you kidding? I don't know what we'd do without you! We need our mama-bear!" Fitz said earnestly. Dawn was one of the most caring, thoughtful people Fitz had ever met. If anybody could set a 'no drama' tone, it was Dawn.

"Alright, boo-boo," said Dawn after a beat. "Alright, if you're really going to do it, I'm with you."

Fitz returned her gaze to Michelle, who was still sitting back, arms crossed. *If we decide we want to do this, we can do it without Michelle. It might even be easier that way.* Sometimes Fitz wasn't sure why Michelle even played hockey. She complained often and loudly; she didn't take the game very seriously; and if her life outside of hockey was half as *glamorous* as she made it sound, there was certainly nothing for her to be escaping from. *She's part of the group, and we'll need skaters*, Fitz reminded herself. The question was how to hook her. Something clicked and Fitz grinned.

"Michelle," said Fitz sweetly, "if the rest of us leave the Hot Shots, who's going to go out to the bar with you?"

"Well, shit, you've got me there." Michelle sat up. "Alright, it's fucking insane, but I guess we're doing it."

Michelle

Saturday, March 11th

Michelle's keys jingled as she opened her front door. She took a deep breath. *Fuck, it's good to be home.*

Michelle *loved* her apartment; it was spectacular. It's old industrial charm and sleek contemporary finishes were a welcome relief to her senses after hours at the dingy dive bar. Michelle loved the Dart, but this was her oasis.

Michelle slipped off her shoes. The polished cement floor felt smooth and cool under her feet as she walked into the open living space. The apartment was dark, save for the flickering light of the TV. Her husband, Ben, was sitting on the leather sofa watching *Archer* and eating cheese. *Because of course he's eating cheese. When is Ben not eating cheese?* He looked up at her.

"Hey, babe."

"Hi, there." Michelle straddled his legs and sat down into his lap. She paused the TV. Michelle liked *Archer*, but at the moment, she was in the mood for a little *attention*. She kissed her husband.

"Oof," Ben pulled away. "I hate to tell you this, but babe, you smell like hockey."

"*Obviously.*" She shook out her hair with a flourish. "I just *played* hockey." She could feel the lingering effects of exertion; it felt good.

Ben gave her an expectant look.

"Fine," she conceded and slipped off his lap into the seat next to him. "Ella's asleep, I assume?"

"*Obviously,*" he mimicked her.

Ella, their three-year-old daughter, was going through a difficult phase when it came to the bedtime routine. Michelle was

15

glad to have had a night off from that shitshow. Ben was better at it anyway.

"It only took four books, two songs, and then, *poof*," he snapped his fingers, "she was out like a light."

"My man!" Michelle gave him a high-five.

"You seem like you're in a good mood. How was the game?"

"Super fucking terrible!" Michelle chirped cheerfully. Ben raised an eyebrow.

"Oh?"

"Yeah, we lost hard. We played shittily, so we deserved to lose, but still... Overall, it sucked a big dick."

"I hear some people are into that kind of thing," said Ben suggestively. Michelle flipped him off with a grin. The fact that he shared her sense of humor, that his mind was as dirty as hers, was part of what made him not just her husband, but also her best friend in the whole world.

"So if it sucked so very much dick, what's with the good mood?" he asked with a laugh.

"We went to the Dart after, *obviously*, and while we were there, Fitz suggested we ditch the Hot Shots and put together a new team. Like seriously, a *new* team. It sounds like a fuck-ton of work, but I guess I got swept up in the excitement." Michelle tapped her nails together thoughtfully. *How did I get sucked in, anyhow?* It had all happened so fast. One minute she was just trying to keep her drinking buddies, and the next she was *participating* and promising things. *Fucking hell.* Michelle sighed. "I may have volunteered to front the startup money."

"Cool." Ben didn't mind. Why would he? They could afford it; it was no skin off his back.

"And obviously, I'm going to have to be the one to bring the *Fireball*," Michelle added. *Fitz got me into this over booze, so booze is what she's gonna get.*

"Obviously," Ben agreed.

"Hopefully it's not a total clusterfuck..." Michelle looked around the apartment. "Hey, why are the blinds down?" she asked, squinting at Ben.

"The sun was in my eyes." Ben shrugged.

"Sun's been down forever, dumbass." Michelle hit the remote, and the motorized screens started to lift, uncovering the apartment's floor to ceiling windows—revealing a breathtaking view of the city at night. "That's better." She leaned against her husband and pulled her bare feet up onto the sofa. It was more than better: it was *perfect*.

"I could probably program the screens to go back up automatically after sundown," Ben offered.

"Oh, God, no!" Michelle squealed. "Can you imagine if we were, like, *fucking* and suddenly half of Minneapolis could see your pale ass going to town? Ha!"

"When's the last time we fucked out here?" Ben smirked.

"I'd say about three years," Michelle said, glancing significantly in the direction of Ella's room. "But you never know! And I do walk around naked sometimes, so it's not a risk I'm willing to take."

"Fine." Ben yawned. "It's getting late, babe. We should go to bed."

"Yeah." Michelle stood and stretched. "I have an ass-ton of work to do tomorrow."

"How much work is an ass-ton, exactly?" Ben asked, following her to the bedroom and watching as Michelle began to take off her clothes.

"An ass-ton is more than a shit-ton but not quite as much as a fuck-ton. *Obviously*." Michelle took her time stripping down; she knew Ben was enjoying the show.

He is one lucky bastard. She admired herself in the mirror. She ran her fingers across her stomach, taking a moment to appreciate the curves of her well-toned muscles. *Because I am one sexy bitch.*

She glanced back at Ben; she loved the look of hunger in his eyes. *Shower first.*

"There's at least a few hours worth of shit I have to get done before Monday," Michelle continued, keeping her tone light and casual. "But I'd probably still have time for a run or bike or something. It's been super warm lately, might as well take advantage of it." *I think he'd like to take advantage of something else too*, Michelle thought as she sauntered toward the bathroom.

"Does your new team have a name?" Ben asked.

"Oh my God!" Michelle popped back out of the bathroom. "No! We didn't even talk about it! I have *got to* text those bitches." She grabbed her phone and immediately shot off a text.

Her phone chirped as her friends texted back. She read the screen and sighed.

"Tessa says we should get a goalie first." *Details, details.* "And Fitz says once we do we should 'reconvene IRL.' She doesn't want to plan it all over text." Michelle rolled her eyes. "Personally, I think she just wants a new excuse to get out of her house now that the season's over."

"Or maybe she just hates group texts. I know I do," Ben said.

"Whatever." Michelle tossed her phone onto the bed and returned to the bathroom for her shower.

When she stepped back out into the bedroom, all clean and wet, Ben perked up, the phone in his hand apparently forgotten as he watched Michelle stroll naked across the room. She smiled coyly, deliberately teasing him as she dropped the towel and opened her dresser drawer. When she pulled on a nightshirt Ben began to pout. *Aw, no more tits al fresco? Poor baby.* It took effort to keep from laughing.

"You got more texts," Ben said, his tone of voice registering his disappointment in her *attire*. Michelle glanced briefly over the texts.

"Mm-hmm." She turned off the ringer and hopped onto the bed. Ben drew her into his lap. "I'll deal with it tomorrow." She kissed him. "I really do think Fitz just wants to get out. Like, get a break from her family and her tool of a husband."

"What about you? Do you go to hockey because you just *need* to get away from me?" Ben pulled her in closer.

"*Obviously.*" Michelle kissed him. *Mmmmm.* She kissed him again. "Can't you tell how much I hate you?" she whispered between kisses.

"Totally." He ran his hands up under her nightshirt. She pulled them down. He nuzzled at her neck, nipping at the sensitive skin.

"Not in the mood?" he asked. He knew that she was totally in the mood; her body was practically writhing with desire. Michelle groaned. The practical part of her brain was wrestling with her more base instincts.

"Mmmm. It's late, and our sweet progeny doesn't understand the *concept* of sleeping in on the weekend." She moaned. He kissed his way up her neck to her ear; she moaned again. Ben pulled his head back for a moment and looked at her. She smirked.

"Oh, fuck it." She pulled the nightshirt off herself. "Sleep is for the weak anyway."

Tessa

Sunday, March 12th

Tessa pulled off her goggles and wiped the sweat from her forehead. She sighed as a light breeze brushed her damp skin. The weather was warm for March—the air cool, but well above freezing. Perfect for paintball. She was sad to be done playing, but it was going to be dark soon and she still had work waiting for her at home. Tessa tossed her goggles into the bin and trotted off after her best friend, Dragon, who was limping his way through the parking lot toward his old beat up Chevy. You'd think he'd actually been *shot* the way he was acting.

"It can't really hurt that bad," Tessa teased when she caught up to him. "Don't be a baby."

"Do I need to drop my pants and show you the *welt?*" Dragon rubbed at his inner thigh where he'd been hit by a paintball pellet at close range. Tessa shook her head violently; she had nothing against looking at bruises—she saw her fair share of those in the hockey locker room—but she didn't need the visual of Dragon in his underwear; they weren't *that* close.

"No, thank you," Tessa said, making a sour face. "I don't care what it looks like, you're still being a baby. I took a slap shot to basically the same spot last week, and you didn't see me hobbling around."

"Trust me, this is worse," Dragon said as he eased himself down into the driver's seat of his car.

"How would you know? When's the last time you took a puck to the leg?" Tessa dropped into the passenger seat beside him and buckled her belt. "I mean, if you really want to test that theory, I could take a shot at you. You know, for comparison."

21

"I'm going to have to pass on that." Dragon shook his head and chuckled. "Besides, I can't trust your aim. Didn't I hear you can't even hit the net?"

"Shut up." Tessa punched him in the arm. "Why do I tell you things?" Dragon laughed as he pulled the car out onto the road back to her parent's house.

"So, are you really going to ditch the Hot Shots for this new team?" Dragon asked as they drove. She'd told him about the whole plan earlier that day. Tessa looked out the window and shrugged one shoulder.

"If Fitz is serious, then yeah. I'd already considered moving up a level and playing with Andy, but last I talked to them they didn't like their team all that much. Besides I'd miss my friends," Tessa said. The thought of playing on a new team with Fitz, Dawn, and Michelle was incredibly exciting, but she was wary of getting her hopes up; it seemed too good to be true.

"If Andy's team is terrible, are you gonna invite her to join your new team?" Dragon asked.

"*Them*," Tessa corrected. "And yeah, I think I will ask them. We play really well together." In addition to the founding four, if they could recruit Jess, Andy, and get AJ to be their goalie, they might have a shot at this new team idea. Tessa had already texted AJ but she made a mental note to text Andy, too, when she got home.

"I wish I could see the look on Jackie's face when you tell her you're quitting," Dragon laughed. He came to enough of her games to recognize Tessa's 'nemesis,' and was a loyal enough friend to hate her.

"I don't," Tessa shook her head violently.

"Come on. Wouldn't it be fun to finally tell her to go to hell? You've been holding it in long enough," Dragon said with a grin.

"Nope, nope, all the nopes. I don't need that fight. I'd rather slip out quietly in the off-season and hope to God I never see her again." Tessa shuddered at the thought of an actual direct confrontation with Jackie. Tessa liked to think of herself as tough and stubborn—the kind to stand up for herself—but she also knew how to pick her battles. Fighting with Jackie outright wasn't worth it. *It's just old-lady hockey, after all.*

Dragon dropped Tessa off at her mailbox; she waved goodbye and grabbed yesterday's mail before turning and walking down the gravel driveway toward the small blue rambler she shared with her parents. Tessa could have afforded her own place—she was nearly thirty, and a fully employed mechanical engineer—but she liked coming home to her familiar basement apartment, her mom's home-cooked meals, and the company of her parents. Now that her dad was mostly retired, they were almost always around, and she knew they could use the money she paid each month in rent.

It wasn't a perfect arrangement; Tessa's commute to work was a pain in the ass. Her parents lived far outside the Twin Cities, amongst the farmers who hired her dad to repair their equipment. But commute aside, Tessa liked the quiet of the countryside. No neighbors to pry into her business, only gently rolling fields and wide open sky—a sky that was now tinged pink and orange by the setting sun.

Tessa stepped inside her apartment and immediately began to peel off her muddy, sweaty clothes, dropping them on the floor as she made her way toward the bathroom. She needed a shower. Badly. As the water warmed up, Tessa looked at her reflection in the mirror. There were red marks where the paintball goggles had dug into her high round cheeks, and dirt smudged on her nose. Her tan skin was still flushed from her walk through the cool evening air, and her hair was a wind-swept mess, half falling out of its ponytail. She pulled out her hair tie and shook out her thick, dye-blonde hair. She scowled at her long dark roots.

Why do I bother to dye my hair if I do such a crap job maintaining it? Tessa looked at her reflection and sighed. She knew *exactly* why she dyed it. Because being a short, young, *female* engineer in Minnesota was hard enough; blonde hair, even obviously *fake* blonde, helped her fit in with her largely Scandinavian peers. And some days Tessa felt like she needed all the help she could get. Tessa pictured Fitz's naturally light strawberry-blonde waves with a pang of envy. Life certainly would be easier if she looked like Fitz: tall, fair, and so pretty... Tessa shook her head. *What do I care about being 'pretty'?* The mirror began to fog up and Tessa turned away from her reflection.

I should text Fitz too. Tessa sent off a few quick hockey texts before jumping in the shower to scrub off the mud and sweat of an afternoon at the paintball course. Once clean, she dressed in sweatpants and her Hot Shots hoodie and trudged up the stairs that led to her parents' kitchen, intending to deliver their mail and hopefully score some leftover dinner.

"Hi, hun," her mom greeted Tessa when she stepped into the kitchen. Tessa took a deep breath; the kitchen smelled like ham, and her stomach began to grumble. Her mom gave her a knowing look and produced a plate of cheesy scalloped potatoes and ham. Tessa grabbed a beer from the fridge, and after thanking her mother, began to shovel the delicious meal into her mouth.

"How's Dragon doing?" her mom asked as Tessa ate.

"Same as always," she answered through a mouthful of food.

"Still no girlfriend?" her mom asked. Tessa groaned and rolled her eyes.

"No, not that I know of, but you *know* we don't talk about that kind of stuff," Tessa said. She took a few gulps of beer.

"Oh, I just thought since I hadn't seen him around as much lately..." her mom trailed off suggestively. *Why does she care so much about Dragon's love life?* Tessa suspected her own complete lack thereof might have something to do with it.

"It's been hockey season. I'm sure I'll see him more now that it's over," Tessa reasoned.

"He used to go to all your games though, didn't he?" Tessa's mom flipped her long gray braid over her shoulder and looked questioningly at Tessa.

"He still does sometimes, but I've been going out to the bar with my teammates more this season," said Tessa. Dragon had come out to the Dart a couple of times, but the teasing had been too much to bear. Her teammates insisted on calling Dragon 'man-friend,' and Michelle was always insinuating all sorts of lewd things. Tessa shuddered. Her relationship with Dragon was strictly platonic and that was never going to change, which she was sick of explaining to her teammates.

Tessa's dad shuffled into the room.

"Hey, Tess. What's new in the security world?" he asked, his voice gruff but warm. He always loved hearing the latest details of her projects at Hill House Security.

"Not much, Dad," Tessa answered. Technically that was true, most of the engineering on this latest project was done. All that was left was to find a way to make her idiot coworkers listen to her so that she could actually *implement* her solution. Tessa drained her beer and stood up from the table. "Actually, I do have a lot of work I need to get done tonight," she said as she cleared her plate. "If I make coffee this late, will the smell keep you up, Mom?"

"No, that's fine. I'm going to read for a bit before bed anyhow," her mom answered. "Just don't stay up too late, Tess."

"Fully grown adult here, Mom." Tessa pointed a thumb toward herself and grinned.

"I know, I know." Her mom gave her a quick hug; her dad did the same.

"Good night, Tess. You lock that work down tight," he chuckled.

"Night, Dad." Tessa turned and went back down to her apartment. Before settling into her work, Tessa read through the texts she'd missed while upstairs with her parents. She grinned as she sent a group message to Fitz, Dawn, and Michelle.

Tessa: AJ's in! We have a goalie! And I think Andy will be interested. We could actually do this!

Fitz: Jess is in too!!!! And I KNOW we can do it!!! Dawn, call Connie and tell her the news. We're leaving the Hot Shots for real!!!

Dawn: Alrighty then, baby girl. I'll call her tomorrow and let you know what she says.

Dawn

Monday, March 13th

When Dawn returned home from another long day as a labor and delivery nurse, she was ready to crash and crash hard. She let out a half sigh, half grunt as she flopped down onto the squishy brown family room sofa. *Gods it feels good to be off my feet.* Dawn kicked off her shoes, unhooked her bra, and pulled it off through her shirt sleeve. *Ah, that feels better.* Upstairs, one of her kids was listening to music too loudly. Dawn was about to shout at them to turn it down when James, her fourteen-year-old son, walked into view at the top of the landing.

"Hey, go turn that music down. You know the rule about music late," Dawn said.

"It's not my music, it's Mari's," he protested. "And it's not even late."

"It feels late to me." Dawn stretched. *Everything* hurt. *Ain't getting old grand?* She looked at her son. "Go up and tell your sister to turn it down."

"Why do *I* have to?" James slumped his shoulders and stared up at the ceiling, managing to look both massively annoyed and incredibly bored at the same time. It was one of the twins' favorite expressions.

"Because I said so, mister!" Dawn pulled her bra like a slingshot and sent it flying at him. He turned and it bounced softly off his backside, landing at his feet. "And because if you don't, I have a stinky sock here with your name on it," Dawn added.

"Geeze, fine." He stomped off up the stairs.

"Thanks, sweetness! Love you!" Dawn called after him. She lay motionless on the sofa for a bit, enjoying the relative quiet. There was something nagging at the back of her mind but she couldn't quite put her finger on what it was until her phone buzzed.

DAWN

Fitz: How did Connie take the news?
Dawn: Sorry, haven't gotten to it yet. I'll do that now.

I suppose now is as good a time as any. Dawn wasn't exactly looking forward to the conversation with her captain and old friend. Dawn wasn't surprised that she'd been asked to do it—to take on the most emotionally heavy task on the team's to-do list. She knew Connie, and Fitz knew *her*; she was the "mama bear," the one with the natural instinct to protect others from pain and discomfort—in this case the discomfort of a difficult conversation. *The curse of excessive empathy strikes again.* Talking to Connie was going to be awkward at best, and Dawn didn't want to think about what it could be at worst.

Isn't hockey supposed to relieve stress, not cause it? That was why she had started playing hockey to begin with: to take a break from the stresses of her life, and maybe get some good cardio. *And that's why we're starting a new team, to step away from the drama.* This call may be hard, but somebody had to do it, and if that somebody had to be Dawn, she might as well get it over with. Rip off the bandaid, as it were.

"Hello?" Connie answered on the third ring.

"Hi Connie, it's Dawn, from hockey." Dawn didn't know why she'd said it like that. Connie knew her well enough, she didn't need the context. *Oof, why am I so nervous?*

"Oh! Why hello there, Dawn, how's it going?" Connie's Minnesotan accent sounded even stronger on the phone. It wasn't quite Fargo material, but it wasn't that far off either.

"Oh, fine. And you?" Dawn replied.

"Can't complain." There was a pause. Dawn sucked in a deep breath. *Just do it.*

"So, Connie," Dawn's voice came out in a nervous squeak as she exhaled. "The reason I'm calling is that a group of us are planning on leaving the Hot Shots to start a new team, and I thought I really should let you know right away. So, that's why I called." The line went quiet. *Did that make sense? Should I say something else?* She waited.

"Oh... well... that's *interesting*," Connie said slowly.

That's a bad sign. Crap. 'Interesting' was a pretty harsh word in 'Minnesota Nice' terms.

"Thank you for the heads up, I suppose," Connie continued. "Who all are you talking about?"

"Tessa, Fitz, and Michelle," Dawn answered.

"And you." It wasn't a question.

Dawn winced. *Don't be mad, please.* "Yeah, and me," she confirmed softly.

"That is interesting," Connie said again.

Two 'interestings'? Double crap. She is mad.

"I'm sorry," Dawn said reflexively. "We were just thinking: the team is so big... not that there's really anything wrong with that... We were just thinking of trying something different. Sorry."

"Oh, that's okay. I suppose it's not too surprising. I know *some people* were getting a bit agitated at that last game, fer sure."

Some people. Presumably Tessa, or maybe Michelle. *This must be a shock coming from me. Shoot.* Dawn didn't want to sound like she was criticizing the way Connie ran her team.

"Yeah, sorry. But also, we wanted to try moving up a level."

"Well, good for you." Connie's tone was so sweet it made Dawn cringe.

Why did I mention that? I hope she doesn't think I'm saying we're better than her. Although, we kind of are. Dawn felt bad for even thinking it.

"You know Jess is leaving to move up, too. Maybe she can join your little team," Connie added.

"Yeah, uh, we'd thought of that," Dawn admitted.

"Oh, well, Jess really *should* move up," said Connie. "We will miss her, though."

Dawn tried not to read too much into Connie's words. Jess was an excellent player; any captain would miss her. That didn't mean Connie wouldn't miss the rest of them. *The rest of us...* Dawn counted them all up.

"Sorry, I guess that makes five of us leaving. I hope it doesn't cause too much of a problem for you." Dawn felt like a jerk.

"Oh, don't worry, I'm sure we'll be *fine*. Thank you *so much* for letting me know."

"Of course," Dawn took a deep breath.

"Just let me know if you change your mind," added Connie.

Dawn promised that she would and ended the call. *'If you change your mind'? I wonder if she thinks we will. Would she take us back if we did?*

Dawn was glad she'd talked to Connie, even if it had been hard—even if it left her feeling all sorts of guilty. *At least it's over with.*

Dawn looked at her watch. Now it really *was* late. *Time for the ol' bedtime routine.* Dawn heaved herself off the sofa and ambled down the hall to the room she shared with her wife. Sharon sat on the bed, twirling a pencil and glaring at the sketchpad in her lap. Dawn smiled. It was good to see Sharon busy with her work: a children's book she was writing and illustrating, *Sammi the Squirrel.*

"Hey, sweets, I'm going to say goodnight to the kids. Care to join me?" Dawn asked.

"Oh, I didn't even realize you were home from work, baby," Sharon said. She looked down at the sketchpad; she screwed up her face into a cute little scowl. "I might as well quit for the night too. Gorram squirrel isn't behaving anyway." Sharon dropped her work and followed Dawn up the stairs to say goodnight to each of their four children—Ian and James in one room, and James's twin sister Mari and their eldest, Annabelle, in the other. They tucked in little Ian, and reminded the teens of the bedtime rules before walking back downstairs.

"Oof," Dawn winced as she stepped down the last step, "my whole body hates me today, but I think my knees hate me the worst of all." She rubbed her kneecaps—not that it helped. Years of long days on her feet were starting to catch up with her. "I'm gonna get some ibuprofen. Want anything from the kitchen?"

"Mmmm, yeah," Sharon said.

"Well, what do you want?"

"I don't know what I want, just that I want *something*." Sharon sat down on the sofa and leaned her head back to make a sad puppy face at Dawn, "Something yummy?"

"You're so much trouble, woman." Dawn laughed.

Dawn bumped Sharon as she returned to the sofa. Sharon nudged her back.

"Thank you," Sharon said in an exaggeratedly sweet voice as she took the trail mix Dawn offered. Dawn sat down beside her.

"Anything for my needy-but-beautiful wife," Dawn said, running her fingers through Sharon's soft gray hair.

"What do you want to watch?" Sharon asked, turning to the TV.

"Something I don't have to think too much for; I'm tired." Dawn yawned. She was exhausted from the post-work crash compounded by the stress of her conversation with Connie.

"*Buffy*?"

"Perfect." Dawn had each episode practically memorized—no thinking required. "So, I told Connie about the new team thing," Dawn said as the show started up.

"Woah, really?" Sharon raised her eyebrows. "How'd that go?"

"I don't know... fine, I guess."

"*Fine*?" Sharon asked, voice raised skeptically.

Dawn shrugged. The whole conversation had been awkward, Connie's reaction polite but vague. Dawn looked at her wife. Sharon had a way of reading a lot into a very little, and would certainly have her own take on the situation. Sharon, too, could be empathetic to a fault, but she often leaned heavily on Dawn to help her manage that emotional load, and Dawn didn't have the energy for that right now—she was tapped out. Dawn turned back to the TV.

"Hey, this is the '*cuppa tea, cuppa tea, almost got shagged, cuppa tea*' episode!" Dawn said, pointing. Sharon gave her an I-know-you're-avoiding-something look, but she let the matter drop and settled into watching *Buffy*.

DAWN

Sitting with her woman and watching her show made Dawn feel all light and warm inside. She and Sharon were both big geeks; they'd met at a sci-fi convention and bonded over their shared geekery before falling in love. Four kids and many years later, they still made time to enjoy their fandoms together. For Dawn, there wasn't a happier place in the 'verse than on that old sofa, snuggled with her wife, watching something like *Buffy, Firefly,* or *Battlestar Galactica* together. Although hockey might be a close second. *I really hope this new team thing works out.*

> Dawn: I told Connie. I guess it's official
> Fitz: Thanks Dawn!! Hey, y'all, let's get a date on the calendar to get together for more planning
> Tessa: A Friday happy hour maybe?
> Fitz: Perfect!! Next Friday?
> Dawn: next friday isn't good, one after that?
> Tessa: Can't, sorry busy couple weeks. Is April 14th too far off?
> Fitz: Works for me! Michelle???
> Michelle: You said HAPPY HOUR. I'll be there.
> Dawn: ditto

Fitz

Thursday, April 13th

"I'm going out with my friends tomorrow evening," Fitz mentioned casually over supper. Tom stopped eating and looked at her expectantly. "Don't worry," she hastened to add, "I know you have plans. I already got the kids rides for everything, so there won't be anything for you to do. I just wanted to let you know."

Tom resumed eating.

"It's just some ladies from hockey," Fitz continued. "We're going to meet at Annie's restaurant, Global Leaf. Remember that place?"

"Sounds nice," Tom mumbled. He seemed to have something on his mind. He'd barely spoken a word to her or the kids, and he kept glancing at his phone. *It's probably work stuff.* Tom rarely talked to her about work unless she pushed.

At the table next to them, Tyler and McKayla were eating as fast as they could. They wanted to go back outside to play for a while longer before bed. Fitz twirled her fork. Sitting there with her family, she felt almost invisible, her presence known but not seen. As if she were no more notable than the furniture. The kids were barely looking up, they were eating so quickly. She handed Tyler a napkin to wipe the orange-red pasta sauce from his chin. He took it, wiped his face, and put it back down—all without a word. Fitz poked at her food.

She hadn't mentioned the new hockey team to Tom yet. She knew he wouldn't care, but it was almost always on her mind. She'd spent the last few weeks doing research, checking league rules, and trying to find an opportunity to get the team on the ice over the summer. Today she'd found the perfect thing: a tournament. Fitz had never played in an off-season tournament before. She was so excited, she just wanted to *talk* about it. She didn't much care if anybody actually listened.

"We're meeting because we're starting a new hockey team for next season," she said. Tom didn't react. "It's a few of us from my old team," Fitz went on. "We're going to try and play in the next level up. We still need more players, but I was thinking that if we can get enough for this summer tournament I found, that it would be a good chance to—"

"Patricia," Tom interrupted sharply. She stopped. There was a heartbeat of silence.

"Mom, I'm done!" Tyler stood suddenly, almost knocking over his chair.

"Me too!" said McKayla, her mouth still full of food.

"What do we say?" Fitz reminded them.

"May I be excused?" the two said in unison.

Fitz nodded. "Clear your places, and you can go back outside." The kids scrambled to pick up their plates and silverware. Fitz cringed as she heard the dishes clank together in the sink. "But you need to be back on time to get ready for bed. I don't want to have to be hollering all over the neighborhood for y'all. Understood?"

"Yeah, we know!" McKayla called over her shoulder as they ran for the door. Fitz shook her head. Her mother would never have put up with anything less than a polite 'yes ma'am,' but Fitz could never seem to get that behavior from her kids. *Northern 'manners' just ain't.*

Tom stood up. He began to walk in the direction of his den.

"The tournament is at the beginning of June." Fitz rose and began to clear the rest of the dishes from the table. Tom paused at the edge of the room.

"Do you need something from me? Why are you telling me all this?" He looked bored, bordering on irritated.

"I just wanted to let you know about the new team, is all. I'm excited about it." Fitz tried a small smile, but Tom only tilted his chin and frowned deeper. *He doesn't care.* Her smile fell. "And to tell you about the tournament."

"*What* about the tournament?" he asked sharply, looking up at the ceiling then back at her.

"Nothing really..." Fitz suddenly considered that she might not want to make a big deal of the new team. Tom was still frowning, his forehead creased. *It might be best if he doesn't notice the change.* The only thing worse than silence between them was fighting.

"Do you *need* something from me?" he asked, his eyes narrowing on her. Fitz shook her head. She didn't want to fight.

"No... It might cost a little bit, but not much. Under a hundred dollars, I promise." She chewed her bottom lip.

Tom grunted. "Okay, that's fine, I suppose. Now, I have work I need to get done. If that's all...?" He looked at her. She nodded. Fitz watched him walk off before getting down to the business of cleaning up from supper.

Fitz didn't see Tom for the rest of the evening; he stayed secluded in his den, as she cleaned, got the children to bed, and started her own nighttime routine. Fitz was sitting in bed, reading when Tom slipped wordlessly into the room. When Tom entered a room these days, an air of tension seemed to enter with him. He began getting ready for bed, taking off his cufflinks and setting them on the dresser. Fitz watched him over the top of her book. The silence between them was deafening. In that silence, the strain in their relationship seemed amplified. Fitz hated it.

"How was your day, Tom? You seemed busy this evening," Fitz noted, trying to make conversation; anything to break the silence.

"It was *work*," Tom said irritably as he pulled off his shirt.

"Want to tell me about it?" Fitz asked, setting aside her book. Tom sighed and began to explain his day as he undressed; the more he talked, the less irritated he seemed.

Fitz tried to stay focused on Tom's words, but it was difficult. She didn't really understand the ins and outs of his job; instead all she could think about was *him*. Standing bare-chested in the bedroom, Tom looked every bit as handsome as he had the day she married him. He was still broad and strong; the muscles of his chest and arms clearly defined. She was still attracted to him, she knew that. So why was it that when she looked at him, instead of the butterfly flutters of love and attraction, did she feel an uneasy buzzing, like there was a hive of wasps living within her chest? *What is wrong with me?*

"Patricia," Tom's sharp tone snapped Fitz out of her thoughts, and she realized she'd been staring at him without hearing a word he'd said. "Are you even listening to me?"

"Yes, I'm sorry, I was but..." she began. *I wasn't though, was I?* "Why do you ask about my day when you can't be bothered to..." Tom put his hands on his hips and let out a *whuff* of air.

"I'm sorry, Tom, I do want to know. I just don't always understand, but I love hearing you talk about it," Fitz said sweetly; she didn't want a fight tonight. He looked at her appraisingly, his gray eyes narrow. She smiled cautiously at him. *Please, let's just have a nice calm night,* she silently prayed. The corner of Tom's mouth turned up and he raised his eyebrows in question.

"What *were* you thinking about, Patricia?" he asked, his voice suddenly soft and low. Fitz knew that voice and she could feel her cheeks burn as Tom crawled onto the bed beside her. The buzzing anxiety inside her grew frenzied.

Tom bent to kiss her, but Fitz turned her head so that his lips found her cheek instead. It wasn't what he wanted, she knew, but she couldn't go from being snapped at to being kissed, just like that. She held her breath as she waited for him to react to her rejection.

"I take it you're not *in the mood* then," he grumbled.

"No, not really..." she began. Tom sighed deeply. *Maybe if we talked some more,* Fitz thought, but she couldn't say it. To say that would be like promising something that she wasn't sure she could deliver.

"I shouldn't be surprised," Tom muttered under his breath. "You never are." He looked at her, his expression daring her to argue, but she didn't have the energy for a fight tonight.

"I'm sorry," she said. Tom shook his head and picked up his phone. Fitz chewed her bottom lip; seeing him give up so quickly somehow stung. She didn't want him to push her into making love, but she didn't like being ignored either. "Come on Tom, put down your phone. I didn't mean for you to stop talking or to go away, I just..."

"You just *what*, Patricia?" Tom snapped, clearly exasperated.

"I just... wanted a little attention, is all—" she began but he cut her off.

"You want attention but you don't want *attention*," he grumbled. "You want me to *talk to you* but you don't want to hear anything I have to say. What is it that you want, *specifically*?" he asked, his eyes burrowing into hers.

"I don't know, I didn't..." Fitz's mind was suddenly blank. She didn't have a clue what to say to her husband. "I wasn't trying to pick a fight, Tom. I'm sorry. Forget about it."

Tom let out another long sigh. "Do you need me to *buy* something else for you? Didn't I *just* give you permission for some new hockey thing?" he asked.

Is that all he thinks I need him for? Money? "No, I don't need anything, I—" Fitz stopped when her phone buzzed. She could see Tom roll his eyes as she picked it up to read the message.

Tessa: Are we still on for tomorrow? I really could use a beer out with you guys right now. This week has been a nightmare.

The tightness in Fitz's chest loosened at the suggestion. It sounded wonderful. *I could use a beer out too*, she thought as her lips twitched in a small smile. Next to her Tom huffed.

"Care to *share*, Patricia?" he asked sarcastically.

"It's just hockey stuff," she said dismissively, tucking the phone closer to her chest as she typed out her response.

"Of course it is," Tom groaned. "I'm going to sleep. I have *work* tomorrow." Tom turned out the light and rolled over to face away from her.

She hated how he did that: said '*I have work*' as if he was the only one who did anything useful. But she was done picking fights for the night; besides which, she had much more exciting things to think about.

Fitz curled onto her side, phone in hand, and continued to text her teammates until long after Tom fell asleep.

Michelle

Friday, April 14th

The restaurant Fitz had chosen for their big 'team meeting' was totally adorable. Michelle immediately approved. It had a sort of retro-casual thing going, with kind of a suburban-hipster-mom vibe. Completely different from the Dart. *Too bad this place isn't across the street from our rink.* The patio was packed. Michelle wove her way through people and tables toward Dawn and Fitz.

"Hey, I thought I was late!" Michelle slid into a seat opposite Fitz. "Woah, Fitz, look at you!" Michelle was used to seeing Fitz in a hoodie and ponytail, all gross and sweaty from hockey, but today she was like a whole different person. *Is this how she does it, out in the 'burbs?* Fitz was wearing a pale-blue sweater that matched her eyes; her long hair was styled in large soft curls, and her make-up was totally on-point. Michelle was impressed. "You're, like, *hot* all cleaned up! Who knew?"

Fitz rolled her eyes and shook her head dismissively at Michelle. *Take the compliment, bitch.*

"So where's Tessa? Is Jess coming?" Michelle looked at Dawn. She looked the same as ever: short tight curls, no makeup, sweatshirt, and mom jeans. Happy and utterly unselfconscious.

"Tessa is on her way, Jess isn't coming," Dawn replied.

"So, this restaurant's pretty sweet," Michelle said, sitting back. "Nice call, Fitz."

"Thank you. I know the owner; our kids are the same age. She's amazing. I can't imagine starting a business while dealing with little kids and all that. But it's fantastic, don't y'all think?" Fitz beamed.

"Yeah, it is awesome," said Dawn. "Although I kinda feel like we're cheating on the Dart."

"I think the Dart will survive if we get a couple of beers elsewhere." Fitz grinned.

"Well, I'm glad to be *anywhere* with beer, honestly," said Michelle. "Work has been fucking *in-sane* this week." Michelle rolled her shoulders, trying to work out some of the tightness there. "I'm so ready for it to be the weekend."

"So say we all," said Dawn, with a nod. "I've had double-shifts twice this week. Lot of babies born in the spring, you know."

"I don't know, y'all. For me, the weekend is more work than the week, I think." Fitz shook her head. "My kids' activity schedule... Heaven help us."

Michelle rolled her eyes; she did not understand parents who let their kids dominate their lives. Of course, Ella was too young for most structured activities, but still, Michelle couldn't imagine running herself ragged to take her daughter to a dozen different sports and clubs and all that shit. *I need time to relax too.*

"How old are your kids again?" asked Dawn.

"Tyler's seven and McKayla's twelve... twelve going on seventeen. She's already got the whole teen attitude." Fitz cocked her head to the side and rolled her eyes. "*Like oh-em-gee, my mom is soooo embarrassing!*"

"Threat of embarrassment is a strong weapon, baby girl," said Dawn with a chuckle. "Trust me, I have three teens, and nothing halts their shenanigans like the threat of Mom doing something embarrassing. Especially the mom who's the gyno nurse." Dawn grinned mischievously. "With teens, it's all about showing them love, setting boundaries, and letting them know you *will* bring out the crocheted vagina when their friends are over. So they might as well put that attitude away before this sleepover turns into health class."

"Ha! That's awesome." Michelle laughed. "Honestly, I can't even imagine. One toddler has already got me like, *ugh.* If Ella's three-nager stage is anything to go by, I am so totally fucked for when she's a teenager. That girl has attitude in spades."

"Sorry I'm late!" Tessa appeared suddenly and dropped heavily into her seat. "Work, oh my God, I need like twelve beers," she huffed.

"So, you seem stressed," Michelle observed. Tessa only snorted in response. She reached up and undid the bun in the back of her head. Her thick unruly hair tumbled down around her shoulders.

"Never work with men," she grumbled. "Work has been a nightmare, and it's so frustrating because they're making everything harder than it has to be."

"What's going on?" asked Fitz.

Tessa took a deep breath and let it out slowly. "So, I'm team lead on this project, and I know we could make our deadline if we just followed my plan. But *every step of the way*, the guys are like, 'Yes, but what about this and what about that.' And I just know they're going to come to the same conclusion I did and act like they came up with it themselves. Which is frustrating enough, but if their bullshit causes us to miss our deadline, I just—" Tessa clenched a fist and pounded it into her open hand. "Guh. I wish I could just punch them."

"Sounds frustrating," said Fitz sympathetically.

"It's ridiculous," Tessa scowled. "I'm trying to lead them, I know what I'm doing, but they're constantly undermining me. I kind of want to talk to my boss about it, so that he understands why things are taking so *fucking* long, but I'm the only female engineer there, and I don't want him to think I can't handle this project because the project is *not* the problem—it's all these stupid *boys* who can't get it through their thick skulls that *little ol' me* might be smarter than them. I'm so over it. I like the work itself, but I'm seriously thinking of looking for another job. The culture at Hill House just *blows*."

Tessa sat back in her chair; she looked worn out, but maybe a little less aggravated than when she'd first arrived. *It must have felt good to get that off her chest.*

"I'm sorry, boo-boo, that really sucks," said Dawn.

"I had been thinking of applying for the next open manager position at the company," Tessa added. "But I don't know. Management could be a chance to change things for the better, or it might just mean even *more* of my time would be spent dealing with dickheads who don't listen."

"Speak up, girl. They should be listening to you. Somebody needs to knock that into their heads. Maybe your boss could help," Michelle counseled.

"Better than knocking their heads myself, huh?" said Tessa, "It feels kind of like tattling, but I'm pretty sure they already all think I'm a bitch anyway."

"If they think you're a bitch, then you're doing *something* right," said Michelle. "Which reminds me, we need to toast. Cheers, bitches!" They clinked glasses.

"Okay, enough about me," Tessa said, setting down her beer. "Let's talk hockey."

"Yes! Our new team!" Fitz exclaimed, sitting up straight and grinning widely. "Dawn, you talked with Connie, right?"

"Yup."

"What did she say when you told her you were quitting the Hot Shots?" Michelle leaned in to ask. She wanted details. Her imagination was running wild, picturing Connie's reaction to having so many players defect at once. *She's got to be pissed.*

"She said something like 'that's interesting.'" Dawn shrugged slightly.

Michelle whistled. "*Interesting?*" She narrowed her eyes. "Isn't 'interesting' midwest-speak for 'fuck you' basically?" Michelle asked.

Dawn shook her head. "No, I mean, yes, sometimes it does mean that, but I don't think so in this case. I think she was just surprised, is all. She knew Jess was leaving, but I don't think she expected all of us..." Dawn shrugged into her hoodie. "I don't know. She really was pretty understanding, all things considered."

"Come *on*," Michelle groaned. "Five of her players are leaving—that's like a third of her team. She *has to* have been upset." Michelle couldn't believe it was all sunshine and rainbows. Sure, maybe Connie was too Minnesotan to say something outright, but still. *Fuck. Five players!*

"Can we just drop it, baby girl?" Dawn implored.

"Yes!" said Fitz, a bit too loudly. If Connie was upset, Dawn apparently didn't want to talk about it, and Fitz certainly didn't want to hear it.

Michelle sat back and sipped her drink as Dawn told them all the distinctly *un*-juicy details of her conversation with Connie, followed by Fitz and her mountain of 'new team' research. Michelle let most of it float in one ear and out the other. *This is so much detail, oh my God.*

"This is a lot. I don't know, guys," Michelle said, shaking her head. She had assumed they had until the fall to get their collective shit together, but now here Fitz was talking about recruiting and summer assessments. *Why did I think this was a good idea before?* "Maybe we should reconsider—"

"There's something else I think we should do this summer," said Fitz, as if she hadn't heard Michelle. "I'm really excited about it."

"Ooh, what?" asked Tessa, looking at Fitz like an eager little puppy.

"There's a tournament the first weekend of June," said Fitz. "We could do that as a sort of test run or recruiting thing. The timing is perfect." Fitz looked at them like she'd just won the lottery; she was that excited.

Oh, for fuck's sake. Michelle wasn't feeling as *enthusiastic.* Planning hockey in the summer was one thing, but *playing*?

"What tournament?" asked Dawn.

"The name is really dumb." Fitz made a sour face. "It's a beer league tournament, so it's called The Kegstanley Cup—get it, like 'keg stand' plus 'Stanley cup'? Har har, right?" They all groaned. *What is with adult hockey and ridiculous puns?*

"I like the idea," said Tessa.

Of fucking course you do. Tessa and Fitz were like two peas in an overly excited pod.

"I always like the chance to play more in the off-season. It's even better if it's with you guys," said Tessa.

"I'd totally be up for it," Dawn nodded, "if we can get enough players."

"Summer hockey?" Michelle scoffed. She still needed convincing. "Summer is for boating, and tanning, and margaritas..." The idea of going into a cold rink when you could be out in the sunshine was counterintuitive.

"I'm sure I can find some players," Tessa said, completely ignoring Michelle once again. "Just send me the tournament info, and I'll start talking to people."

"Alright, it sounds like all y'all are interested," Fitz said happily.

Yeah, 'all y'all'. Uh-huh. Michelle maintained her aloof posture.

"What's up, Michelle?" Dawn asked with a tilt of her head.

Good to know somebody remembers I exist. "Like I said, I don't really *do* hockey in the summer..."

"But it's going to be so much fun!" insisted Fitz.

"Come on, boo-boo," said Dawn. "It does have 'keg' in the name. What's more you than that?"

They were all looking at her now. *I suppose that doesn't sound like the worst thing ever.* Slowly, Michelle sat up and sighed dramatically.

"Alright, fine," she acquiesced. "But there *has to* be a tailgate party or something. It is summer. I'm not sitting in a fucking ice rink a second longer than I have to."

"If you're going to organize it, social captain, then it's a deal," said Fitz.

"Do we have a team name yet?" asked Dawn.

"Oh my God! We didn't even talk about it! Again!" Michelle slapped her palms flat on the table. "Okay, what about, like, the Blueline Bitches."

"I don't think we can put 'bitches' on a jersey," said Dawn, "but nice try."

"How about The Mighty Drunks then?" Michelle raised her glass.

"I like it, but no, I don't think we should put 'drunks' on a jersey either." Fitz shook her head. "Besides, Jess doesn't drink." It was quiet for a few minutes while they all thought. Michelle silently ran through a list of hockey-related words: net, goal, sticks, ice. *Something* had to inspire another idea.

"Hot Tricks? Like Hat Trick but—" Michelle started.

"Hot what, now? No, sorry. Hot Tricks sounds a little prostitute-y for me, thank you," Fitz said.

"Team names do *not* have to be terrible puns, you know," Tessa said, wrinkling her nose. "We could try to do something a little more classic, NHL-style, like an animal or something."

"I like the idea of doing something classic and classy, Tess," agreed Fitz. "Okay, let's see... Animals... Hawks? Tigers?"

"Or *cougars*," Michelle said with a suggestive growl.

Fitz sighed. "I don't know. Nothing sounds quite right."

"It doesn't have to be an animal to be classic—think of, like, the Jets and the Flyers," Tessa added, drumming her fingers on the table. Michelle sighed and drained her glass. Naming a team was not at all as much fun as she had been expecting.

"It would be good if we could come up with something that means something to us," Dawn said. "We should have a reason for picking it as our name."

"Like what?" Michelle asked. "We can't be The Hot Shot Drop-Outs. And you guys already eliminated booze, bitches, and hockey puns. What does that leave us with? Other than that, we have *fuck-all* in common."

Tessa frowned at her, but Michelle just stared right back. *You know I have a point.*

"Hey, y'all, what about the Darts?" said Fitz.

"Name ourselves after the bar?" asked Tessa.

"It does seem appropriate." Michelle instantly liked it.

"It's not just a bar; it's *our* bar. And Darts are fast, like arrows, they fly to a target. I think that makes it work as a team name." Fitz's voice was getting louder as she got more excited. "Oh! And if we did name ourselves after the bar, maybe we could get them to sponsor us or something—maybe that could help pay for our jerseys!"

Jerseys. Fucking hell. Another detail to keep track of.

"I think Darts is a perfect name," said Dawn.

"We'll need our own logo," said Michelle. "Intellectual property aside, I don't think we want to look like we have a fucking bar sign on our jerseys. We're not NASCAR drivers."

"Maybe Dragon can draw something for us," suggested Tessa.

"You mean *man-friend?*" Michelle teased. Tessa rolled her eyes. She was still adamant that despite all the shit he did for her (like maybe a nice *free* team logo), that he was not her boyfriend— hence 'man-friend.' He did have a very manly look to him... somewhat lumberjack-esque. *I'd fuck him if I were her.*

"If he did make something for us, we should pay him a commission, though," Tessa added.

"Of course we would!" Fitz pushed Tessa's shoulder lightly.

So much for free. Michelle rolled her eyes. Commissioning artwork, recruiting players, buying jerseys, *summer hockey?* Michelle's head was starting to spin. She hoped the others were ready to take on all that shit. *I'm just here to sign the checks and start the party.*

Fitz

Saturday, May 6th

Fitz's eyes scanned the sidelines of her son's soccer game, searching for her husband. She spotted him among the cluster of parents; Tom looked completely at ease as he greeted the other mothers and fathers with handshakes and warm smiles. He really could turn on the charm—he was a natural at it. Everybody who met him loved him. Fitz forced a smile and joined him. It wasn't as easy for her; she didn't have his natural confidence, nor his connections. Tom had known some of these people since grade school. Fitz always felt like the odd one out. She was grateful when the game got underway and they all turned their focus to the field.

"Let's go! Tyler! Wake up! Come on, come on!" Tom clapped his hands together as they watched their son play. Tyler was athletic, and he loved to play soccer, but he could use some foot skills training at home.

Practice would help him gain confidence. The thought reminded Fitz of something she'd been meaning to ask her husband.

"Tom?" She linked her arm with his and gave him her winningest smile. "Would it be okay if I bought a hockey net and board for the house? To practice shooting and stickhandling?"

"A hockey net?" he responded absently. He looked across the field and scowled. Fitz followed his gaze. Tyler had been subbed out and was jogging to the sidelines. "Tyler shouldn't have been pulled out so soon," Tom growled under his breath. "There's no way that it was his turn. I should really have a *talk* with that coach. He's such a dumbass—"

"Please don't," Fitz pleaded. She didn't love Tyler's coach any more than Tom did, but arguing with him wouldn't do any good for anyone. "About the hockey net..." she redirected. "It's a little pricey but I was thinking it could be good for the kids... and me... to practice. May I order it?"

Tom stared at her for a moment; he looked like he was going to say no.

I should have just said it was for the kids. She bit her lip and blinked up at him pleadingly. The corner of his mouth turned up.

"Fine." He kissed her cheek. "Anything for my family."

"Aren't you two the sweetest?" said Holly, one of the other mothers. Fitz dropped Tom's arm and turned.

"Oh, good morning, Holly," Fitz stammered, flustered. "How are you doing?"

"I'm good. So you're already thinking about the hockey season? Sorry to overhear, I've been looking into things for Jackson and Aja. Practicing at home sounds so *practical.*" Holly sighed. "Between spring league and morning skates, I feel like I'm always in the car on the way to the rink. And there are so many summer camps to look into yet."

"I wish there were hockey camps for adults, I would love to go..." said Fitz wistfully. Holly stared blankly back at her. Fitz's ears burned. She'd been thinking about her new team so often lately it had just come out. Although she was proud that she played hockey, it wasn't something she usually brought up with other parents. It felt self-centered.

"Oh, yes, I think I'd heard that you play hockey. Good for you!" Holly exclaimed. "Hey, Bob," she called to her husband, "did you know Patricia here *plays hockey*?"

Bob regarded Fitz for a moment. His eyes passed up and down her body. Fitz didn't like the way he looked at her, but she forced herself to smile pleasantly.

"So, do you play *women's* hockey?" he asked. Fitz maintained her smile, but inside she was grumbling. *Why do they always ask that? If a man said he played hockey, nobody would ask, 'Oh, do you play men's hockey?' For heaven's sake.*

"Yes sir, I play in a women's league," Fitz answered politely.

"So, Tom, your wife plays hockey?" Bob called to Tom over Fitz's head. Tom turned sharply; Fitz looked at her feet. Bob laughed. "You're a brave man; you'd better be careful, or she might rough you up!" Bob seemed to think this was hilarious. Fitz kept her eyes on her feet and prayed that she hadn't embarrassed Tom. "Hey, Bob, how's it going, man?" Tom's tone was friendly as he side-stepped the hockey comment. Fitz raised her eyes to the field. She listened as Tom and Bob talked briefly about sports and mutual acquaintances. Fitz did not attempt to join in, and they did not attempt to include her, talking past her as if she weren't there.

Eventually, the conversation drew to a close. Fitz stole a glance at Tom. He was looking at her, his lips pressed tight. *I did embarrass him.*

"Tyler's back in the game," she said, averting her gaze once more.

"About goddamn time," Tom muttered. He turned to watch the rest of the game, alternately yelling at Tyler and grumbling about the coaches. Fitz said a silent prayer. Tom's mood could put electricity into the air; it made her chest tight.

Although the air between them remained electric, when Tyler's team pulled out a narrow win, the stormcloud that had been brewing around Tom seemed to diminish. Fitz gave her son a loving squeeze on the shoulder as they walked back to the car.

"Good game, honey," she said. "Did you have fun?" Tyler nodded, his mouth full of goldfish crackers.

"I'd like to see a little more hustle out there next time." Tom clapped his hands together several times in front of Tyler's face. The small boy nodded seriously at his father. Tom folded his arms. "What your coach lacks in brains, you kids will have to make up for in hard work this season." Fitz shot Tom a warning look. He knew she hated it when he bad-mouthed coaches in front of the kids. Tom saw her look and snorted.

"Well, you boys did alright today." His eyes held hers like he was daring her to stop him. "No thanks to that jackass—"

"Tyler, honey, let's get into the car now," Fitz said quickly, ushering the boy inside the SUV. Tom smiled ever so slightly as he climbed into the driver's seat. *Why does he do that?* Fitz wondered, as she sat beside him. *Talk about something else.*

"Holly talking about summer camps got me thinking about summer vacation," Fitz said as they drove. "I was thinking that maybe this year we could go back to North Carolina. There are places along the outer banks—"

"Patricia," Tom groaned. He glanced sideways at her. "We've talked about this."

"We wouldn't have to spend any time with my family," Fitz reasoned. "There are hours of driving between my parents' house and the outer banks. We could rent a little house, just the four of us."

"We couldn't go to North Carolina without visiting your parents, and you know that," Tom countered.

"We could just pop in, say a quick hello, we wouldn't have to stay—" Fitz began.

"It's not a vacation if I have to deal with my in-laws," Tom cut her off sharply.

"But it's been so long since they've seen the kids."

"Then maybe they should visit *here*," Tom snapped. This was quickly escalating into an argument. Tom tightened his grip on the steering wheel. "I don't see why I should have to waste my hard-earned vacation time on *them*. You don't see me suggesting we vacation with *my* parents, do you?"

"But your parents live *two miles away!*" Fitz countered, letting her voice rise higher than intended; she glanced back at Tyler. The boy was staring at his lap. *Poor Tyler.* Fitz hadn't meant to start a fight. In front of Tyler, no less. *What can I say to turn this back around?*

"I'm sorry, I just..." Fitz stammered, searching for something to say. "We *usually* take a summer vacation and—"

"I didn't say we weren't going on vacation, Patricia," Tom interrupted.

"I didn't *say* you said that—"

"Would you cut it out?" Tom growled. "Why do you always have to pick at every little thing?" Tom let out a long frustrated sigh and ran his fingers through his sandy hair; the way his chest heaved she could tell he was calling for patience. Fitz dropped her eyes to her lap and did the same. *Arguing never solves anything.*

"I'm sorry," Fitz said softly. "I only want to spend time together as a family. *Our* family." She gingerly put her hand on his arm. Under her fingers, she could feel his muscles tense and then relax at her touch. He looked at her, his expression softening.

"Don't worry about it," Tom said. "I'll find something we'll all enjoy. You want a beach? Maybe... California? That sounds better, doesn't it?" Tom looked in the rear-view mirror at his son. "Like the sound of a California beach vacation, champ?"

"Yeah!" Tyler piped up enthusiastically.

"What do you say, Patricia?" Tom asked. "Something new, no family obligations."

"I suppose," Fitz agreed.

"It's a deal then." Tom gave her a small half-smile. "You're lucky I like to spoil my family."

"Thank you, Tom," Fitz said quietly. *If anything is excellent or praiseworthy, think about such things. California isn't so bad. And he did agree to let me buy the hockey net.*

When Fitz got home, after she ordered the net, she poured herself into researching jerseys, ice arenas, league rules— anything she could think of pertaining to her new hockey team. *The Darts. This team will come together; I will make it come together.*

Monday, May 8th

Tessa: I heard from AJ, she's in for the tournament, go ahead and register us!
Fitz: YAY!!!! That totally makes my day!! I'll register today!!!!!

Michelle

Monday, May 8th

Michelle stood outside her apartment door and tried to calm her nerves. It had been a long day. From the icy rain during her morning run, to the traffic jam on her way home, nothing had gone quite right. She felt like an overstretched rubber band, ready to snap. And she didn't want to snap at her family. She took several deep breaths before opening the door.

A pleasant aroma greeted her inside the apartment. Immediately Michelle could feel her stress diminish. Oregano, basil, and thyme. *Tomato sauce.* Ella's nanny must have cooked dinner. Michelle closed her eyes and let her shoulders relax as she took in the scent.

"Oh my God, have I mentioned how much I love having an Italian nanny?" Michelle said as she strode into the kitchen.

"Only two or three *million* times," Ben replied with a laugh. He grabbed her by the hips and pulled her into an embrace. She rested her arms on his shoulders and kissed him. His lips were soft and warm. Heat bloomed in her chest, and she kissed him harder.

"I'm stirsty!" a tiny voice squeaked behind her. Michelle turned. Ella was bouncing on her toes, her chestnut curls bouncing along with her. Reluctantly Michelle and Ben parted to attend to the little girl.

"It's dinner time, so you get in your chair, and I'll get you some juice, okay?" Michelle said. "I could use some 'juice' myself," she added under her breath. Michelle filled Ella's sippy cup before pouring herself a generous glass of red wine.

"How was your day, babe?" Ben asked as they sat down to dinner.

"Not great." Michelle watched as Ella began to eat like a starving animal. She tried not to let the growing mess concern her.

"No? What happened?" Ben asked.

"Just lots of little things, really. I had to deal with the most tedious crap at work, and all day long, my phone just keeps blowing up with *hockey* shit. They will not stop texting. It was like, settle the fuck down—nobody cares what color our jerseys are, Jesus. Only apparently they do care—like, *a lot*. Fitz even left me a voicemail! A *voicemail*! Who the fuck leaves voicemails anymore? What is she like ninety years old, or something?" Michelle realized she was getting herself worked up. *I should probably stop swearing in front of Ella one of these days.* She took a sip of wine. "Anyway, I'm not listening to it until after dinner, at least. Love her to death, but bitch needs to learn that if she wants something from me, she needs to get it to me in text."

"I thought you were getting *too many* texts," Ben ribbed her.

She flipped him off as she took another sip of wine. "Shut up. Don't you know husbands aren't supposed to actually *listen* to what their *hysterical* wives say?" She snorted. "I'd rather have a million texts than have to listen to one goddamn voicemail."

"I've told you before, I could help you set up your voicemail so that it would transcribe it and send you the voicemail in text," he reminded her. She glared at him. He put up his hands. "Sorry, I guess I was listening to you again."

After dinner, Michelle and Ben began to get Ella ready for bed. Michelle didn't know if it was because of her own crabby mood or if Ella truly was being particularly petulant, but the bedtime routine was even more stressful than usual. Ella fought them every step of the way.

"I can't even with three-year-olds right now!" Michelle threw her hands up in frustration as Ella writhed on the floor, screaming like a death metal rocker. "It's been almost *an hour and a half* since we started to get her to bed!"

"It's okay, babe," Ben said calmly. "I've got it from here."

"Thanks." She gave him a small smile of gratitude. Michelle looked down at her distraught progeny.

"Goodnight, Ella. I love you," she said in the sweetest voice she could muster.

"No!" Ella kicked at her. Michelle gritted her teeth and stalked out of the room. *Why did I want to be a mother again?*

"Hey, princess, how would you like Daddy to sing you a night-night song and sit with you while you fall asleep?" Ben said soothingly. He was such a natural at the whole parenting thing; it made Michelle wonder what was wrong with her. She was a smart, capable person. She'd gone to a top-notch college and survived the rigors of law school. But somehow, a toddler had her stymied? Life made no sense.

In the kitchen, Michelle poured herself another glass of wine and tried once more to shake off her frustration. She looked at her phone, then wished she hadn't.

> Fitz: Just wondering if you got me voicemail! LMK! Thanks!

Fuck me sideways. Michelle had almost forgotten about the stupid voicemail. She didn't want to deal with it, but if Fitz was going to keep pestering her, she figured she might as well get it over and done with. After another large gulp of wine, she opened the message.

"Hi, Michelle! This is Fitz from hockey..." *Like I know any other people called 'Fitz,' Jesus.* Fitz's sweet, bubbly voice somehow made Michelle even more annoyed. The message was long and almost physically painful to sit through. Fitz went on and on before getting to her point. *Oh my God, spit it out, woman!* Michelle was about to hang up when the pain finally ended. *How the hell did that require a two-minute-long voicemail?*

Fitz wanted Michelle to register the team for the tournament. *Hockey is not supposed to make me do things*, Michelle grumbled internally as she sat down at her computer. She didn't want to deal

55

with the stupid registration; today had been long enough. All she wanted to do was relax with wine, and Ben, and a good fuck. But for some reason, she had promised to help with this sort of thing. *I need to watch my fucking mouth.*

"Whatcha doin'?" Ben appeared behind her and massaged her shoulders. *Mmmmm.* His touch felt good. "The Kegstanley Cup?"

"Yup. Remember how I said I'd help the team with the 'money stuff?' Well, *apparently,* I have to do the whole damn registration *myself* because Fitz's husband would 'blow a fuse' if she put the tournament fees on her card, even if I gave her the cash like tomorrow. Dick. So, I guess *this* is the motherfuckin' 'money stuff.' Registration plus eight hundred dollars for a goddamn summer tournament."

"Is that how much these things normally cost?" Ben asked.

"Who the fuck knows; I just hope we have more than six skaters to split it with. This is a *loan*, bitches!" She forwarded the confirmation to Fitz. "Okay, babe, I'm done. Now distract me before *I* 'blow a fuse.'"

"I can think of something else you could blow..." Ben said suggestively as he pulled her up out of her chair.

God, he smells so good. "Smooth, babe. Super smooth." She put her arms around Ben's neck and pressed her lips to his. The warm glow she'd felt before began to grow in her once more. "But I have something else in mind." She kissed him again, long and hard. Electricity shot through her, making her toes tingle, and her insides melt.

"Oh yeah?" he asked, pulling away, teasing her. She groaned. She needed him *now*. Walking backward, she pulled Ben by his belt in the direction of the bedroom.

"Ella's asleep, right?" she asked. Ben moaned an affirmation against her lips. They reached the side of the bed with a bump. She unbuckled his belt; he pulled off her shirt. Just as her lips found his again, her phone chirped. She ignored it. It chirped twice more in rapid succession.

"What the fuck do you want!?" she yelled at it. It was Fitz again. *Because of fucking course, it is.* Michelle was getting the sinking feeling that 'being the money and the booze' might not be as simple as it sounded.

"Keep getting naked," she commanded Ben, her voice steely. "This won't take long."

> Fitz: Got the registration, thanks!
> Fitz: I've been researching jerseys. And I even talked to a guy at the store
> Fitz: I think we can get the ordered in time for the tournament without the logo and add that later
> Fitz: ...but it costs money too. Probably about $850.

Michelle quickly scanned the texts until she saw the dollar sign. She growled quietly in frustration. She didn't have unlimited funds to be throwing at this team—a team that may or may not even exist by the fall—and she was more than a little peeved with Fitz's timing. Right now, she just wanted to enjoy her husband's *company.* Not deal with hockey bullshit. She texted back as fast as she could.

> Michelle: I just spent $800, not gonna throw in more already! I'm not a fucking bank! Ask the dart like you said you would. idgaf I'm busy. Figure it out WITHOUT ME.

She switched her phone to silent and tossed it across the room. "That's that, for now," she said darkly. She pulled her focus back to Ben. He was sitting and watching her; he hadn't moved a muscle. With a wicked smile, she pushed him roughly down on the bed. "I thought I told you to get *naked.*"

Tessa

Monday, May 8th

Tessa sat cross-legged on her sofa, typing furiously. A chat from one of her coworkers had drawn her into what was turning into a full-scale online argument—an argument about an issue she thought they'd put to rest three days ago. Tessa had been trying to unwind, watch the Wild game, and enjoy a beer.

But no, we couldn't have that, could we? She tried to think of a polite way to tell her coworkers that they were acting like total asshats. *If Dan says 'well actually' one more time, I'm going to reach through the computer and strangle him.*

Her team was only a couple of days out from the project demo, and they still could not reach a consensus on the remaining details. There was one issue Tessa knew she could fix. But her solution meant making a small change to an element her coworker Dan had taken over as his 'baby,' and he was fighting her hard on it. If they demoed the product without her modification, it wouldn't look good for any of them. But still, Dan wouldn't budge, and for some reason, her idiot coworkers were following his lead. *You're* my team; *you're supposed to follow* my *lead, assholes.* Tessa's chest burned with frustration as she typed. She was close to telling Dan to go fuck himself when her cell buzzed.

Fitz: hey can I ask you a favor?

Tessa smiled, her frustration cooling. The interruption was precisely what she needed. She deleted the angry message she'd been typing to her colleagues. Instead, she offered to revisit the issue in the morning and signed off.

Tessa: of course, what's up?

59

Fitz: kind of a long story but the short version is I need to actually try to get that sponsorship from the dart if we want to get jerseys before the tournament
Fitz: sooooo I was wondering if you had any time to come with me to the dart to ask?

The mere thought of hanging out with Fitz did wonders for Tessa's mood.

Tessa: the *favor* is for me to hang out at a bar with you?
Tessa: lol of course I'll do that! Duh
Fitz: awesome, thanks so much, you totally made my night
Tessa: ditto

Friday, May 12th

Tessa met Fitz on the sidewalk in front of The Dart. Fitz looked tired, run-down, and absolutely *gorgeous*. Her hair flowed in soft golden waves, and she was wearing a sundress that highlighted her long legs and athletic frame. Dressed like this, Fitz reminded Tessa of Keri Walsh all dolled up for an interview. Tessa looked down at her polo and khakis and wished she'd changed since work. *Not that anything I could wear would make me look half as good.*

"Tessa!" Fitz threw her arms around Tessa. "I am so glad to see you. Really, you have no idea."

"Yeah, me too," Tessa replied as she awkwardly hugged her teammate. Fitz pulled open the door, and the pair stepped out of the spring sunshine and into the familiar musty air of the bar. *Home sweet, Dart.* Tessa felt a little odd being here without having played hockey—like she was a different person than the Tessa that normally walked through those doors.

"So, how's it going?" Fitz asked once they'd settled in.

"Oh, it's going..." Tessa thought about work and shook her head. "I want to hear the long version of why we're here. Oh, but first..." Tessa tentatively raised her glass. "Cheers, bitches?" Fitz raised hers to meet it. Clink. Drink.

"So, speaking of *bitches...*" Fitz began. Tessa felt her eyes widen; it was unusual to hear Fitz swear outside of their traditional toast.

"What?"

"No, sorry, bad start—it's not that big of a deal. I'm sure I'm just reading too much into things. I'm all frazzled from the whole week and... please forget I said that. I just think Michelle might be mad at me or something." Fitz shifted uncomfortably in her seat as she told Tessa all about the tournament registration and jerseys. It came out in an emotional jumble that Tessa struggled to follow at first. Then Fitz showed her Michelle's text.

Tessa winced. *Okay, so Michelle might be a little upset.* Tessa looked at Fitz. She was staring into space, her expression filled with concern and disappointment. *She really cares about this.* Tessa bumped her shoulder gently against Fitz's.

"Hey. Ignore Michelle. So she's not going to be as big of a help as we might've liked. That's fine. We kind of dragged her into this. What did we expect? She did pay for the tournament, right?"

Fitz shrugged, her expression unchanged. Tessa bumped her again.

"You know if you left planning a hockey team to Michelle, you'd end up with four skaters, five bottles of Fireball, and nothing to wear, right?"

Fitz let out a small strangled 'hah.' *She isn't going to cry, is she? Oh, please don't, Fitz. I don't know what to do with crying people.*

"Well, I think it's great that you did all that legwork. You're the driving force here, and I'm totally behind you, and so is Dawn. It's all going to be fine." Tessa tried to sound reassuring. After a moment, Fitz turned and gave Tessa a small, warm smile.

"Thank you, Tessa. I appreciate that." Fitz sat up straight. "You're right. It'll work out. I have faith. Now I suppose we should try and get that sponsorship."

Fitz

Tuesday, May 23rd

When Fitz and Tessa had asked the Dart's owner to sponsor their team, she'd responded by asking for a formal sponsorship proposal. For the next few days, Fitz had spent any free time she'd had researching, writing, and texting with Tessa. If Tom had noticed that she'd had something on her mind, he hadn't said anything.

Fitz didn't exactly know what she was doing, but Tessa's constant encouragement gave her confidence. After she'd sent in the proposal, Fitz felt so accomplished that she'd picked up her phone and ordered a full set of team jerseys on impulse. She didn't know if it was faith, intuition, or delusion, but Fitz was sure that everything was going to work out.

But a day went by, then a week, and there was no word from the bar owner. Fitz tried to stay optimistic, but it was harder by the minute. She prayed on it every night. She hadn't told anybody what she'd done, and as time went by, her faith began to waver. She tried calling the Dart. No luck.

When the day came to pick up the jerseys, she went into a full panic. She didn't have the money, but she also didn't have much choice, she had to get the jerseys. She felt faint, almost numb, as she drove to the shop.

Two boxes sat on the counter, waiting for her. At the clerk's insistence, she opened the first box. Fitz sighed. The jerseys were beautiful. She ran her fingers across the dark red and green fabric, touched the laces at the collar. Fitz was in love. Any doubt she had faded to the back of her mind.

"Those look right?" the clerk asked.

"Perfect." Fitz smiled. "They're perfect."

"Alright. Will that be cash or charge?" The man tapped his pen impatiently on the counter.

"Oh, um, well." She rummaged through her purse. "Charge, I guess." *I can probably get the money before Tom sees the credit card statement.* As soon as she'd seen the jerseys, her faith had blossomed again. *It will work out.* Fitz drove home from the store with a song in her heart. She hummed to herself as she parked her car in the garage and opened the trunk. She smiled as she lifted out one of the boxes.

"What are those?"

Fitz whipped around. Tom was standing just inside the garage, arms crossed. Fitz looked between the box in her arms and the one in the trunk and then back at Tom. *He knows something.* Her mind drew a blank. She couldn't think of a thing to say. A little voice in her head kept repeating, '*oh no, oh no, oh no,*' to the rhythm of her hammering heartbeat. When she didn't answer, Tom stepped closer.

"Could they be related to the credit card charge I was called about today?" His voice was like venom. Fitz opened her mouth, but nothing came out. Tom took the box from her hands and opened it. At first, he looked confused, but then something clicked, and he scowled. Fitz somehow found her voice.

"They're for my hockey team—"

"Damnit, Patricia!" Tom threw the box back into the trunk with enough power to knock out half of the contents. Fitz winced. Tom stared at her, nostrils flared. "What the hell? Did you think I wasn't going to find out?"

"We're going to get paid back." Her voice came out in a squeak. "We're getting a sponsorship." It was almost true. They were *trying* to get one. Fitz bit her lip.

"I don't care! You have to tell me *before* you spend money like that, not after!" he yelled. Fitz flinched. Tom turned away from her, clenching and unclenching his fists. Fitz's throat was tight and dry.

"I'm sorry. I just needed—" she began.

Tom's head snapped back around. His face blazed red. "Need? None of this is a *need*! God, you want to talk about needs, Patricia?" He gritted his teeth. "Needs," he repeated darkly. "Taking care of this family, paying the mortgage, those are needs. This is... God, you're such a selfish, spoiled little b—"

"Stop!" Fitz cut him off. "Just stop. Please. I'm sorry."

"Are you?" Tom's voice echoed through the garage. "Do you even give a shit?"

"Yes." She forced herself to look him straight in the eye as she spoke. "Now, do you want the whole neighborhood to hear you? The kids?" Fitz could hear the tremor in her voice. Tom turned his back on her again. He didn't say anything. Fitz took a slow deep breath. "I said, I'm sorry. Okay? I'll get the money. I'll try to get it before the credit card bill comes."

Tom sighed and ran his fingers through his hair.

"It's not about the damn money, and you should know that," he muttered under his breath so quietly she could barely hear him. Fitz took a couple of slow steps toward him. His breathing was slow and measured, his shoulders tense. He turned and regarded her coolly. "You should have told me first." With that, he walked past her and into the house.

With trembling hands, Fitz put the jerseys back in their box. *I should have told him.* Before closing the box, she stopped to stroke the dark red fabric. *No, he wouldn't have understood, and we wouldn't have gotten these.* She folded the box closed. *Maybe I am a spoiled brat. Or bitch. Whatever he was about to say.*

She moved the boxes to an inconspicuous corner of the garage where they wouldn't remind Tom of the fight. The continued troubles between her and Tom weighed heavily on Fitz. She felt angry, guilty, and sad, all at once. *Why does it have to be like this all the time?*

Tessa

Friday, May 26th

> Fitz: I got a call from the Dart! We got the sponsorship!!!
> Meet me there to celebrate when I pick up the check
> tonight?
> Tessa: AWESOME!! I'll be there!!

Tessa rushed out of the office to make it on time to meet Fitz. She didn't even bother with 'polite' wording in her last email to Dan. No 'as per my last email, blah, blah, blah' this time. He got an 'RTFM,' and would have to figure it out himself. It was already more than he deserved. She was functionally doing his work for him anyway. *Asshole.* Tessa's stress must have been evident on her face because Fitz asked her about work right away.

"Well, you remember the project I was leading that I thought could be improved? The one I thought was going to be a disaster because the VP was bound to notice the glaring issue?" Tessa pulled her hair out of its bun. *Oh, that feels better.*

"Yes, of course, how'd it go? Did the guys see reason and do what you said?" Fitz looked at her expectantly.

"No, we presented it without my modification." Tessa rolled her eyes. "But it actually turned out much better than I expected."

"Did the VP overlook the problem?" Fitz asked.

Hardly. Tessa couldn't help but laugh.

"Nope, he noticed it right away! And when he asked the team about it, the guys sat there like a bunch of idiots, but I was totally prepared with the fix in hand. He asked how long it would take to implement—which wasn't long—then he told the team, in no uncertain terms, that they had to follow my lead on it, and we actually, finally were able to put out a prototype I'm proud of; and

I got some really great feedback from my boss, because apparently, the VP was really impressed with me." Tessa was proud of how that whole thing had wrapped up.

"That's awesome, Tess!" Fitz beamed at her. "Is your team falling into line now?"

If only it were all that simple. "Yes, and no, they followed my ideas for the modification, but I don't think they're ever going to stop being little assholes." Tessa recalled Dan's expression when he'd acquiesced to her plan. At that moment, she knew that he would never respect her decisions without the express support of those higher up. "But hopefully, I won't have to put up with that crap if I'm their actual boss." Tessa grinned.

"So, does that mean you applied for the manager promotion?" asked Fiz.

"Yup, I had the interview a couple of days ago, and I'm pretty confident that I'm going to get it. But it's not official yet!" Tessa didn't want to jinx it, but it felt so good to have something to be hopeful for at Hill House. She rapped her knuckles on the wood bar top, just to be safe. Fitz threw her arms around her in a sudden embrace that caught Tessa off-guard, almost knocking her off her seat.

"I'm so proud of you! The world needs more women like you." Fitz looked genuinely impressed.

If only the guys at work would look at me like that. "Thanks." Tessa could feel her face get hot. "So, uh, what's new with you?"

"Not a lot... Oh, but I got the jerseys!"

"What? Our jerseys? Already?" Tessa was shocked; she stared at Fitz.

"I'm sorry, I should have run it by you. It was impulsive. Please don't be mad, Tessa. I would kill myself if I managed to upset you *and* Tom." Now it was Fitz's turn to blush.

"I'm not mad; I'm just confused. How did you get them before we had the money? Is Tom upset about it?" Tessa asked.

Fitz shook her head. "It doesn't matter; we're getting the money now, right?"

"Yeah, I'm just surprised you ordered them before we had it."

"I probably shouldn't have, but I had this gut feeling. Maybe it was divine intuition—or just temporary insanity—but I was so sure. And now, here we are." Fitz smiled at her. "I think it was meant to be."

Looking at Fitz's eager expression, it was hard not to agree, even if it made no sense—even if her actions had been a little reckless. *If she had asked me, I would have told her to wait for the money. But look how happy she is now.* Fitz believed in what she was doing, and Tessa believed in her. She smiled back.

"Thanks, Fitz. I can't wait to see them."

Dawn

Saturday, May 27th

Dawn pushed through the doorway, struggling to maintain a solid grip on the two grocery bags in her arms and the twelve-pack of Mountain Dew dangling from her fingers. As she slid the bags onto the counter, Dawn lost her grip, and the Mountain Dew fell to the ground with a clattering thunk.

"What was that?" Sharon appeared at the edge of the kitchen. Dawn finished situating the bags safely onto the counter with a grunt. She looked down.

"Uh, you might not want to open any of these pop cans any time soon." Dawn nudged the box with her toe.

"I've been trying to cut back anyway." Sharon's voice was as vacant as her expression. There were dark circles under her eyes. *She looks like she could use a little caffeine.* Before Dawn could make the mistake of telling her wife just how tired she looked, her phone binged. *Tessa.* Dawn texted for a bit before realizing that Sharon was watching her with her arms folded and a frown creasing her forehead. Dawn pocketed her phone.

"Sorry, did you say something?" Dawn asked. Sharon unfolded her arms and looked away with a sigh. *Somebody's in a bad mood.*

"You know, if you'd just take multiple trips that wouldn't have happened," Sharon said.

"You know I'm too lazy for that, boo-boo," Dawn said with a laugh. Sharon's expression didn't change. "You okay, sweetness? Something wrong?"

"Not really. I'm feeling a little crabby is all." Sharon's voice was sharp, but her grim expression was more sad than angry. Sharon leaned against the counter. Her shoulders slumped as she jammed her hands into the pocket of her hoodie.

"Would you like a hug, sweetness?" Dawn opened her arms, but Sharon stayed put and shook her head.

"No, thank you, I'm *fine*," Sharon snapped.

She didn't look or sound 'fine.' Dawn let her arms drop. Sharon had been in a dark mood for a few days; Dawn suspected that Sharon's depression had gotten worse again. Dawn considered asking directly about it, but that didn't usually help. *One does not simply fix depression.*

"What was all the texting about?" Sharon asked, obviously trying to take the focus off her sour mood.

"Hockey stuff." Dawn put away the last jar and closed the pantry. "I'm helping Tessa with the roster. Remember that girl I mentioned from work? Emily, the receptionist? She and her girlfriend are going to play with us. Her girlfriend is supposed to be really good. I met her once; she looks like a raven-haired Starbuck. She seems like she'd be a good hockey player, but we'll see. Hopefully, it works out."

"Yeah." Sharon's voice was distant and uninterested.

"Oh, and apparently, Fitz got jerseys for us," Dawn said. Sharon perked up.

"Yeah? What are they like?"

She would be more interested in the uniform than the actual team. "Tessa said they're the same colors as Wild's jerseys."

"Try again," said Sharon, shaking her head. "For those of us who don't do the sportsball thing."

Dawn pulled out her phone and showed Sharon the images Fitz had sent them earlier.

"Oh, nice, I like those. Earthtones. What's the logo look like?" Sharon started towards the family room, Dawn followed close behind.

"I don't know. Tessa said her man-friend is still working on it."

"Man-friend?" Sharon repeated.

"Yeah, you know, Tessa's... uh, man-friend. He wants to be a graphic designer, so we hired him to draw something up for us—"

"Wait. What?" Sharon stopped so suddenly that Dawn almost ran into her.

"We needed a team logo, so we asked Tessa's man-friend—"

"You didn't think to ask me?" Sharon folded her arms, her eyes burrowing into Dawn's. If she'd been crabby before, she was angry now. *Uh-oh.* Dawn felt like a squirrel caught stealing from the birdfeeder.

"Well, no, I, I didn't think—"

"You didn't think of asking your wife, who is a published illustrator before asking some, some 'man-friend'? Whatever that means." Sharon's voice was sharp and bitter.

Dawn's head spun. It had not once crossed her mind to ask Sharon. *Why didn't I think of her?* Dawn opened her mouth and closed it again, searching for something she could say to make Sharon feel better.

"I'm sorry, sweetness, I didn't, I mean, I just," she stammered. Sharon turned, walked the rest of the way to the family room, and sat down hard on the sofa. Dawn followed and sat down beside her. *Okay, how can I fix this? Why didn't I ask her? Ugh, you know nothing, Dawn Johnson.* She racked her brain, looking for an excuse.

"You're so busy, I didn't want to add to your stress, I didn't think—"

"Oh, bologna." Sharon's voice cracked. "You weren't thinking about my stress. You just weren't thinking about me at all." Sharon swallowed. Dawn felt terrible.

"I'm so sorry." She put her hand on Sharon's shoulder, but Sharon brushed it off.

"You don't think of me as a professional artist at all, do you?" Sharon's eyes were shining with unshed tears.

Well, that escalated quickly. Dawn sat back and gave Sharon a stern look.

"Now, you know that's not true, sweets. You know that I believe in you." Dawn studied her wife's face. Sharon averted her eyes, and Dawn sighed. "Come on, love. Of course, I think of you as a professional artist. I'm sorry that I didn't ask you. Tessa just suggested man-friend so quickly, it just… there wasn't time to. I'm sorry, okay? I'm so, so sorry."

Sharon didn't respond, but sniffled and wiped her eyes.

Dawn edged closer to her. "I love you; you know that. I love you like crazy," Dawn said.

Sharon looked at her, then away again. "I know," she squeaked, "I love you too. I just feel like, like sometimes you don't think I'm… like my career is real—that I'm just a stay-at-home mom with a hobby—and it's so frustrating." Sharon began to cry. Her body shook with the sudden intensity of her emotional outburst.

"Oh, my love." Dawn engulfed Sharon in a hug. "I never want you to feel that way." Sharon didn't pull away. Now Dawn knew for sure this wasn't about the logo; this was the depression talking.

When she was going through depressive episodes, Sharon was more prone to self-doubt. It was as if she suddenly couldn't see her own self-worth. It was always hard, Dawn knew, but it was also temporary.

Depression lies, baby girl. Dawn stroked Sharon's head and back as Sharon continued to cry. *What can I say that she will understand and believe right now?*

"First off, there's nothing 'just' about being a stay-at-home mom. You're a kickass mom," Dawn said.

"But I'm—" Sharon began, but was cut off by her own choked sob.

"And you're also a super fantastic writer and illustrator. You know I think what you do is amazing. You're so incredibly talented, Shar. Come on," Dawn said firmly.

Sharon shrugged inside Dawn's embrace, her sobs fading to whimpers. After a while, even the whimpers quieted, and Sharon was able to pull her head up. Dawn kissed her.

"You know I believe in you, right?" Dawn asked. Sharon nodded slightly. "Well, I do, one-hundred percent. And I'm sorry if

I ever did anything to make you doubt that, sweetness." She put a hand on Sharon's pink, tear-streaked cheek. "What can I do to make you feel better?"

"I'm okay now." Sharon gave Dawn a quick soft kiss before burrowing back into her embrace. "I love you," Sharon whispered into Dawn's shoulder.

"I love you too. Would you like to watch something?" Dawn asked, picking up the remote.

Sharon nodded, then stopped and let out an unexpected cry.

"What?" Dawn sat up, startled.

"I have to pick up the twins from robotics in, like, ten minutes." Sharon's voice quivered, threatening to break into another round of tears. Dawn rubbed her thigh.

"I can do that," Dawn assured her. "Don't worry about it. You relax. You deserve a break."

"You sure?" Sharon looked at her. Her eyes were red. She looked so tired.

"Of course, sweetness." Dawn kissed her forehead, and a smile brushed Sharon's lips. Dawn handed her wife the remote, and Sharon began to flip through shows. She stopped on *Battlestar Galactica* and pointed to the screen.

"Wait, earlier, did you describe somebody as a 'raven-haired Starbuck?'" Sharon raised her eyebrows at Dawn.

Dawn laughed. "Yeah, I did."

"You're such a dork." Sharon nudged Dawn. She still sounded down, her eyes clouded with sadness. But Sharon's smile was genuine, and that made Dawn smile too.

"You know it, baby."

Tessa

Friday, June 2nd

Tessa tried to calm her nerves as she walked through the tournament arena toward the locker room. She was excited about the game, but she was anxious about playing with this group of skaters for the first time. They all knew Jess, and both AJ and Andy were at least somewhat familiar, but the last four were complete unknowns. Dawn was bringing in two women she knew through work, and Tessa had recruited two of her former teammates from youth hockey, Nikki Hernandez and Katie Christiansen. She had barely talked to either since they were teens. They were Facebook 'friends,' but in reality, they were barely acquaintances; she'd gone out on a limb by contacting them at all. She had no idea how well they'd play together.

"Hey, Tess!" Dawn greeted Tessa with a smile. Tessa smiled back and looked around. In the middle of the locker room, a tan, lean, and very muscular woman stood wearing only her sports bra, jock shorts and one shin pad. She held her other shin pad in her hand, gesticulating wildly, and grinning ear to ear. Her face was more weather-worn than in Tessa's memories, but it was still familiar: Nikki.

"Tessa!" Nikki exclaimed and ran over to give her a big hug. "Oh my God, how are you? I'm so glad you're here! See?" She said to the room, pointing at Tessa, "I am in the right place, not just crashing your locker room! I'm with Tessa!" The other players smiled. Tessa was sure nobody had accused Nikki of crashing anything. "I had to come early to see if I still remembered how to put this all on." Nikki gestured broadly with the shin pad in her hand. "How are you doing?"

"I'm doing good," said Tessa. "How about you?"

"Oh, you know, getting old, resenting it, the usual." Nikki resumed putting on her gear. "I am so nervous you guys; I bet you guys are all so good—I haven't been on a real team in ages! I'll probably fall flat on my face!" Nikki had a crazy bubbly type of energy to her, just as Tessa had remembered.

"You'll be fine; it'll be great. Have you met everybody? That's Fitz, just coming in," Tessa said, pointing.

"Hi, Fitz!" Nikki shouted. Fitz waved. Nikki pointed to each of the other women in succession. "And that's Dawn, Jess, and oh, oh, I know this one, it's initials, DJ?"

"AJ," Tessa corrected. "You're so good with names."

"No, I'm terrible! That's why I have to practice." Nikki finished tying her skates and looked down. "Shit, you guys! I forgot to put on my pants!" she squealed. "Oh wait, I'm back in Minnesota I should call them breezers! Shit, you guys! I forgot to put on my breezers!"

"Don't worry, you have time to take off your skates." Tessa laughed, she'd forgotten just how loud Nikki was. Nikki shook her head and sighed theatrically.

"Or just be really careful when you put your breezers on?" Tessa amended.

The door opened, and two unfamiliar women walked in. *Those must be the players Dawn got.* They sort of looked alike, in a way. They were about the same height, with similar builds, and pierced noses. Only one's hair was jet-black, the other white-blonde. Both were very cute.

Right away, pantsless-Nikki dropped the conversation to run over and greet them. They introduced themselves as Tiffany and Emily. Nikki filled them in on her skates-before-breezers predicament.

"I'm such a ditz, guys! This is so embarrassing! Now you're all going to think I'm so dumb!" Nikki was still grinning her wide, crooked grin; she didn't look embarrassed at all.

When Katie Christiansen slowly stepped into the room a few minutes later, Tessa waved her over.

"Katie! Come sit by me. How're you doing?"

"Good," Katie said quietly as she sat down beside Tessa. Katie looked nervous.

"Don't worry if you haven't played in a while, we're pretty low key," Tessa tried to reassure her. "Some of the people here didn't play until they were adults."

Katie blinked at Tessa, an odd expression on her face, before silently starting to dress. *I guess that didn't reassure her.* Tessa looked around the room. Everybody had arrived except Michelle, but Michelle was almost always late. *It might be a good time to start figuring out positions anyway.* Tessa stood up and cleared her throat.

"Guys, guys!" Tessa called. The room was a cacophony of conversations. Tessa could barely hear her own voice over the din. "Hello?!"

Dawn looked up. Noticing Tessa's feeble attempt to get everyone's attention, Dawn put her fingers in her mouth and whistled. Loudly.

"Listen up, Tessa has something to say!" The locker room went quiet. "Go ahead, baby girl."

"Thanks, Dawn. I want to figure out lines before we go out. What position does everybody like?"

"Oh, oh! I like reverse cowgirl!" Nikki exclaimed. Tessa put her hand over her face and shook her head. The room erupted with laughter.

"Hockey positions!" several people said at once.

"Oh, I know what you meant! I just thought I'd share!" Nikki winked.

"Ignoring that unnecessary bit of information..." Tessa continued, "who plays defense?" Andy raised their hand, as did Katie, and the dark-haired one, Tiffany.

"Okay, wow, perfect. The rest are forwards then. I'm thinking Fitz centering Michelle—" The door burst open and in walked Michelle.

"Speak of the devil," said Fitz under her breath. Tessa scrutinized Fitz's expression. *Has she talked to Michelle since that text?* Fitz lowered her head as she tied her skates, but her eyes kept flicking up to Michelle and then back down again. *I'm guessing not.*

"Sorry I'm late, everyone!" Michelle walked through the middle of the room. All eyes were on her in her tank top, short shorts, and heels that made her legs seem almost impossibly long.

"Like I was saying, Fitz will center Michelle and Nikki—" Tessa continued.

"Who's Nikki?" interrupted Michelle. She dropped her bag and looked around the room at all the new faces.

"I am!" Nikki waved at Michelle enthusiastically.

Michelle grinned. "Awesome! I'm Michelle. Nice to meet you—"

"And the other line—" Tessa cut Michelle off before she lost the room's attention again, "is Jess centering Dawn and..." Tessa paused. *Crap.* She'd already forgotten her name. She gestured to the young woman who was pulling her blond hair back under a rainbow bandana. "I'm sorry, what was your name again?"

"Emily."

"Emily," Tessa repeated, trying again to commit the name to memory. "Okay, Fitz, Michelle, and Nikki are one line, and Jess, Dawn, and Emily are the other. On defense, Katie, you'll play with Tiffany. And that just leaves Andy and me." Andy grinned at Tessa.

"And I'm the goalie!" shouted AJ. Somebody whooped, and the room descended back into a chaos of conversations.

I hope that works for everybody. Let me know if you want to change anything. Or don't, since I'm not actually saying this out loud. Tessa rubbed her face with her hands. *Man, I hope this works out.*

Tessa's thoughts were interrupted when a pair of jerseys hit her square in the face.

"Earth to Tessa." Fitz was standing above her grinning. "These are the jerseys that caused all the trouble. What'd you think?"

"They look awesome." Tessa held one up in front of herself. "Ordering them early was a great idea, Fitz."

Fitz grinned, face flushed with pride as she turned to face the room at large. "Okay, y'all!" Fitz yelled over the din. "These are our jerseys, but they're not done. I need to get them back after Sunday's game! So y'all better bleed on them!"

"Are they all the same size?" Michelle asked, waving her arms. The jersey hung large on her thin frame, and the sleeves flapped like wings.

Fitz ducked her head. "Yeah, other than the goalie, all y'all's are the same. I erred on the side of getting them a little big. I hope that's okay."

"They're great, Fitz, thank you!" Tessa said loudly. She wanted everybody to appreciate the work Fitz had put into getting them, even if they were a little big. Michelle shrugged and slipped on her gloves.

"Ice is ready!" Fitz shouted. "Let's go, Darts!"

Once on the ice, it quickly became apparent that their opponent, the Hawks, were much better than the newly formed Darts. Tessa watched the Hawks warm up their goalie with a series of bullet-like slapshots. *We are going to get murdered.* She'd been so tied up in team logistics that Tessa hadn't considered what would happen if the games themselves went terribly.

Although summer tournaments were infamous for having uneven match-ups, that didn't make Tessa feel any better when the Hawks scored a goal ten seconds into the game. By the end of the first period, the score was five to nothing.

"Jesus mother fuck, who is this team?" Michelle huffed between periods.

"I have no idea," said Tessa. "But, I'm sure they wouldn't be in our division normally."

"I should hope not! Shit!" AJ said. She was dripping with sweat.

"You're doing amazing, goalie." Nikki patted AJ on the back. "You're a baller."

"Thanks," AJ squirted water into her mouth. "Hopefully, they'll let up a little since they're clearly going to win."

The Hawks did not let up.

"At least they're not cheap," Andy muttered from their place beside Tessa on the bench. It was true. The Hawks weren't playing rough or physical with the Darts.

Hell, they're barely touching us. Probably because we never have control of the puck long enough to be worth it. Tessa had given up any hope of scoring, when a bounce in the Darts' favor, coupled with some impressive speed and shooting by Katie, put their team on the scoreboard. But as exciting as it was, one goal didn't change much.

"I hope this isn't what all the games are like," Emily whispered to Tiffany. Tiffany gave her a sympathetic look. Emily was so out-paced, she wasn't even really participating anymore. She kept getting on the ice but she was more of a pylon than a player when she was out there. Tiffany, on the other hand, was playing well, all things considered. On top of which, she seemed to be enjoying herself. Tessa was enjoying herself too—her legs were burning, her heart pumping; it was exhausting and exhilarating at the same time.

"I'm sorry guys, but I'm not going one hundred percent this last period. I just don't want to get hurt, it's not worth it." AJ shook her head.

"Don't worry about it, boo-boo," said Dawn, putting her arm around the goalie. "Forget the score. I'm just having fun messing with them a little; they're so serious! Like when that one lady had me against the boards, I was like, 'oh, sorry baby, I see what you want, I just don't feel that way about you,' and she actually took a step back!" Dawn laughed.

"Just try to have some fun out there, y'all," said Fitz. "We're going to lose, but at least we're getting a good workout. We're earning our beer, that's for sure!"

"Cheers to that, lady!" Michelle reached into her bag. "I was going to save this for after the game, but we could use some now." She pulled out a bottle of *Fireball* whiskey; that got the team to perk up. They passed the bottle around; Tessa took a large gulp of the fiery liquid. It felt good.

Now, this is beer-league hockey. "Woo! Hell yeah! Let's go, Darts!"

Michelle

Saturday, June 3rd

The Darts' second game was almost a full one-eighty from the first: a six-to-nothing blow-out against the Ice Savers. After their decisive win, the locker room filled with happy, boisterous celebration. Michelle's blood coursed with post-game adrenaline, as well as pre-party excitement. She barely heard the conversations around her because her thoughts were already on the tailgate. *I'm gonna need some help.*

"Hattrick lady," Michelle called to the new player who had scored half the team's goals. "You're dressed; come set up the party with me." The woman looked at Michelle then passed her to the door.

"I have to go." She hurriedly picked up her bag and walked out of the room. *Rude.*

"What the fuck's up with whats-her-name?" Michelle said aloud to nobody in particular. Dawn shrugged. *Whatever.* Michelle needed another set of hands, but most of the team was still only half-dressed and too busy talking to be of any use. Andy was the only other person available. *Great, the quiet, awkward one.*

"Andy, are *you* going to help me set up the party?" Michelle put her hand on her hip and gave Andy her best do-what-I-want stare.

"Sure." They shrugged.

Love the enthusiasm. Andy seemed like they'd be an interesting person to hang with. They were a great player, and looked cool, with their half-shaved head, funky piercings, and cuffed jeans. But they were just so damn quiet, and Michelle didn't know what to do with quiet people. She'd never been quite a day in her life.

"The rest of you had better get your asses out there soon!" Michelle shouted. "It's time to celebrate, bitches!"

Outside, the sun was shining, and the sky was clear and blue. Michelle couldn't have asked for anything better. *It seems I'm not alone.* All across the lot, the hockey community was tailgating. More than a dozen groups had set up with lawn games, grills, and coolers full of beer.

A faint breeze brushed against Michelle's flushed skin, and she closed her eyes. The air smelled of grilled meat, and more faintly of hockey gear, as scores of players had laid their equipment out to dry under the warm summer sun. Michelle could have done without that *special touch.* She opened her eyes and noted a yellowing jockstrap dangling from the mirror of a pickup truck. Michelle wrinkled her nose.

"Well, that's fucking nasty!" Michelle shuddered. "Team rule: no nasty-ass equipment in the immediate tailgating area!"

"Noted," said Andy with a smirk. They followed Michelle through the lot to her car. She'd parked across two spots to be sure that they would have enough space. Maybe that made her a bit of an asshole, but she didn't really give a shit.

"Alright, let's get this bitch set up!" Michelle and Andy went to work; Andy did as instructed, but was otherwise quiet. Silences drove Michelle crazy, so she tried to keep up the friendly chatter, although she felt like she was talking to herself most of the time.

"I fucking love tailgating, don't you?" she asked.

"I guess," Andy replied with a shrug.

"What do you mean, you guess?"

"I haven't really tailgated much." Andy shrugged again.

"Well, you just *have to* on a day like this. The weather is so fucking perfect. And we even won our game! It's like a sign from the party gods that we deserve a little fun, don't you think?"

"Yeah, it was a good game."

"I know, right?" Michelle grinned.

Jess and the goalie, AJ, arrived shortly after they'd gotten the tables set up. AJ handed Michelle a heavy grocery bag and Michelle peered inside.

"Oh my God, AJ! This is so much!" Michelle exclaimed. The bag contained at least two-dozen hamburger patties. "I guess we know the answer to 'where's the beef'!" She laughed but AJ only stared blankly back at her. *She's too young to get it. Damn.*

"Does that joke date me?" Michelle asked Andy.

"Yup," said Andy, grinning.

Michelle laughed. "Well, shit. If I've already outed myself as old, I guess I might as well throw on some nineties music." Michelle took out her speaker. "Parties need music, and this is starting to look like a party."

Players began to filter in. When Fitz arrived, Michelle immediately reached into her cooler and pulled out a Coors Light. She'd been getting the sense that Fitz was avoiding her, and she wasn't about to let that stand.

"Now, you can't ever say that I don't love you when I was willing to be seen in public buying this crap for you." Michelle grinned, the beer in her outstretched hand.

Fitz blinked at her. "Oh, thank you," she said quietly, and took the beer. Michelle scrutinized her teammate's face.

What's making her act so weird? Michelle watched as Fitz turned and cheerfully began to chat with Tessa. *Is it just me? What the hell did I do to her?*

Michelle didn't have much time to speculate, as Tiffany and Emily wandered up, arm-in-arm. They were a perfect pair: complementary like a yin-yang. *Tiffany looks like a hockey player, but Emily looks more like a milkmaid.* Michelle smirked to herself. *Too bad she's such a shitty player, she's fucking adorable. I wonder if we'll get to keep her.*

"Hey, newbies! Welcome to soiree de Michelle!" she greeted them. "Anybody want jello-shots?"

"Oh, I'll have one of those!" said milkmaid-girl. "So will Tiff."

"Thanks for skating with us," Fitz said to the pair, after declining Michelle's offer. "Who do y'all play for in the regular season?"

"Rampaging Moose," said Emily as she slurped her jello.

"Both of you?" Tessa asked, clearly surprised. Rampaging Moose played at the Hot Shots' level.

"Yup," answered Tiffany.

"No way!" said Michelle. "How the fuck did you place into that division, Tiffany? You're way too good—no offense to anybody else here. But you know you could kick pretty much all of our asses, right?"

"I wanted to play with Em, so I went to assessments with dull skates and a righty stick," Tiffany said with a shrug. "I shoot left, so I looked pretty terrible."

"You tanked it on purpose?" Fitz was aghast, but Michelle found it highly amusing.

"That's fucking amazing! And now, when you play with us, in a division that you're probably still too good for, nobody will be able to say shit!" Michelle grinned until she saw Fitz and Tessa exchange a look. *Oops.* Tessa might have mentioned that she didn't want to promise the new folks spots on the team without discussing it as a group. *Oh well. Too late.*

Over Tessa's shoulder, Michelle noticed Nikki was walking towards them with a bottle of Fireball and an old hockey stick with four plastic shot glasses attached along its shaft.

"Oh my God, Nikki, is that a 'slap shot?'" Michelle clapped her hands together in delight as Nikki proudly held up the stick. "Fuck yeah, it is! Nikki, you're my new favorite!"

"What is it?" asked Tessa, inspecting the stick as Nikki and Michelle filled each shot glass with *Fireball.*

"Come on, Tess, I'll *enlighten you.*" Michelle hooked her arm through Tessa's. Tessa looked apprehensive, but she let Michelle lead her into place. Emily thrust her plate into Tiffany's hands and rushed to join them as well.

"I love these new people! They are totally my kind of bitches!" Michelle shouted just before they tilted the stick back, dumping the shots into their mouths simultaneously. *Fuck, that's good.*

Michelle was starting to feel the effect of the alcohol. Her face glowed with warmth and happiness.

The tailgate got rowdier by the minute. The Darts ate burgers, played games, made jokes, and consumed a *significant* amount of alcohol. Nikki flirted hard with a group of young guys from a neighboring tailgate.

Ah, to be single, Michelle thought—then she took a second look at the drunk hockey boys, and thought of Ben. *Nevermind, being single sucks.* Michelle took out her phone and sent Ben a short but *very dirty* text. *I wonder if a mid-tournament booty-call would be asking too much? He might need to pick me up anyway. I am most certainly getting close to maybe being quite drunk.*

"This has been so much fun!" Michelle gushed as Tessa and Fitz helped her pack everything away at the end of the party. "I love the new girls, especially Nikki, we totally click. We just *have to* keep her for the season."

"Yes, I'm glad you reached out to her, Tessa. Thank you." Fitz nodded. "I think we could really use her." Tessa beamed back at Fitz, lapping up her approval.

"Yeah, and she says she wants to play with us, so that's awesome." Tessa picked at her nails. "But um, I meant to tell you guys, Katie's not going to be playing," she said, her voice slurring almost imperceptibly.

Fitz shrugged. "Oh well, there's no way she'd be allowed to play in our division anyway, even now that we're moving up. She's much too good," said Fitz.

Tessa scratched at the back of her neck. "No, I mean, she's not going to play with us anymore this weekend."

"What?" Michelle was confused. *Did I miss something?* Michelle's head swam with Fireball and beer. Fitz's eyes were wide with shock. *No, see, she's confused too. Ha.*

"She just messaged me; she's not coming back."

"Do you know what happened?" asked Fitz.

Tessa shrugged and stood with her hands in her pockets. *She looks embarrassed.* She may have been blushing, but it could have just been the red-tan of her skin after an afternoon of drinking beer in the sun.

"Not really. She isn't really my friend, and apparently playing with us just isn't... isn't what she was looking for." Tessa frowned. "I guess she wasn't enjoying it."

"So what? She thought she was too good for us, so she decided to bail in the middle of the tournament?" Michelle snorted in derision. "What the fuck, dude? That's such a douche move."

"Did she give you back the jerseys at least?" asked Fitz.

"Crap. No." Tessa's frown deepened. "Ugh, sorry, Fitz. I'll get them from her somehow. That's my fault, I didn't even think about that."

Fitz winced. She and Tessa both looked so deeply unhappy when they had been laughing and having fun just minutes before. Michelle put her arms around the two of them.

"Hey, screw her anyway, we don't need her," said Michelle. "We have that good new one, what's-her-face... Tiffany! Plus Emily."

"We're going to have to talk about that," said Tessa. *She looks like an unhappy little pug dog when she frowns.*

"Maybe we should have a team-founders meeting," Fitz suggested. The way she said it sounded so serious. Too serious.

"Yuck, meetings suck." Michelle stuck out her tongue. "I have meetings at work. I don't want meetings at hockey. That's not fun." Parties were fun. Skating was fun. Meetings sucked.

"Fitz is right, we need to talk about a few things," Tessa sounded too serious as well. Michelle threw her head back and groaned dramatically but Tessa ignored her. "How about before the final game tomorrow?"

"That sounds good; I'll let Dawn know," Fitz said and turned to Michelle. "Michelle, you're going to be there, right?" Michelle stuck out her tongue again. Fitz narrowed her eyes. "We really could use your help," she said sternly.

"Fuck, okay, fine! I'll be there, but can we drop it? Can we just enjoy a little buzzed hockey now?"

"I think you're a little more than 'buzzed,'" Fitz commented.

But she didn't mention the meeting or other team business again.

Fitz

Saturday, June 3rd

Fitz was glad when the time came to shut down the tailgate party and get back to the rink. The cold air of the arena was refreshing, invigorating. Now that she was out of the sun, she felt more alert. She felt ready to play hockey but she worried about the others—they looked pretty drunk.

Fitz had managed to dodge all the invitations to do shots. She wanted to be fully prepared for the upcoming game against Bad News. It would be their first game against a team from their new division. *This game is the real test.* Fitz opened the locker room door just in time to hear the punchline to a joke.

"See you next month!" AJ shouted, and the room erupted into a mix of groans and giggles.

"What was that about?" Fitz asked.

"You don't want to know," Tessa said, shaking her head. She looked past Fitz and lifted her chin. "I think you're going to have your hands full with those two, by the way."

Fitz turned around. Her linemates were both wasted. *Michelle and her damn party. What am I going to do with them?* She looked around the room. AJ was tipsy as well, and Emily seemed half asleep. *What am I going to do with all of them?* Fitz chewed her lip.

"Don't worry too much," said Tessa. "I bet the other team has drunk players too. It'll balance out."

Fitz couldn't help but notice that even Tessa was swaying slightly. But she was right. It didn't take long to see that Bad News wasn't at their best either. The game was sloppy on both ends of the ice.

"I think we're doing okay, all things considered," Fitz said to the team after the first period. "But we need to get more shots."

"Shots!" cheered Michelle and Nikki. Michelle waved the almost-empty Fireball bottle. Fitz rolled her eyes.

"On net." *I should take that bottle away from them.*

"Why not both?" Nikki grinned.

Fitz was doing her best to ignore Nikki and Michelle. They were playing alright, considering how drunk they were, but their constant giggling chatter was starting to wear on her nerves. *If they would just take it a little more seriously, we could win this thing.*

"Keep your eyes on number twenty," Tessa jumped in. "She's their best player, although it looks like she might be even drunker than you two."

In the second period, the Darts had better luck getting the puck to the offensive zone, but they still struggled to score. With only a couple of minutes left in the period, Fitz had a clear shot on the net. She shot. The puck hit the post, disappeared *behind* the goalie then popped out the other side. Fitz looked to the official, who waved her arms. No goal. Fitz groaned.

"That went in!" Michelle yelled at the ref. "It totally crossed the goal line before it bounced out!" Fitz steered her boozy teammate back to the bench.

"Shut up, Michelle," Fitz grumbled. She thought it had gone in too. *There's no video review in beer league, so why piss off the ref by arguing?*

"Well, that was fucking ridiculous." Michelle sat down hard on the bench. "This game is stupid—where's the Fireball?"

Fitz shook her head. *Getting drunk before playing is what's stupid.*

"They didn't score that period," said Emily cheerfully.

"But neither did we," grumbled Tiffany. Tiffany looked frustrated.

Fitz was frustrated, too, but she tried not to show it. "Hey, y'all, I know that was a tiring period, but just keep working hard. We can do this!" Fitz put as much enthusiasm into her voice as she could muster. *Fake it 'till you make it. This was my idea; it's my job to step up and lead.*

The whole team was exhausted and starting to get lazy. Towards the end of the third period, Nikki reached out with her stick rather than skating to catch the player. It tangled in the Bad News skater's feet, sending her flying forward onto the ice.

"Two minutes for tripping," the ref pointed at Nikki. Fitz groaned. It was a stupid penalty to get.

"I was going for the puck," Nikki protested without conviction. Fitz gave her a stern look, and Nikki skated over to the box. Bad News scored their second goal while the Darts were short-handed.

"I'm so sorry, that was totally my bad," said Nikki when she got back to the bench. Michelle punched her in the arm.

"Don't apologize, bitch!" Michelle grinned. "It's hockey. Shit happens."

Fitz bristled. *This was our test for games in our new division— doesn't Michelle get that?* Fitz felt like they'd failed the test. Now that Bad News had a two-goal lead, the Darts had lost any hope of winning. *Maybe this wasn't a good idea. Maybe we need to play in our old division.* Fitz didn't want to play there, where they'd be forced to face-off against the Hot Shots, but she didn't want to lose every game either. *Maybe I made a mistake trying to start a team.* Fitz felt sick about it. She was so wrapped up in her thoughts that she didn't notice Dawn beside her until she spoke.

"Thanks for organizing this tournament, Fitz." Dawn nudged her. The game ended, and the team filed off the ice. "Seriously. Thanks for organizing this, boo-boo," Dawn repeated, smiling broadly. "It's been perfect."

"Really?" Fitz stopped just outside the locker room door.

"Yeah, this is exactly what we needed."

"But we lost," Fitz pointed out. "That's the type of team we'll be facing, that was our test, and we *lost.*"

"Don't take it so hard," Dawn laughed. "We'll get there, baby girl." She patted Fitz on the shoulder and walked past her into the locker room. "Good game."

It was so simple, what Dawn had said, but it had been honest and heartfelt, and it made Fitz feel a lot better.

"Tough game," Fitz said, sitting down next to Tessa.

"We'll get them next time," Tessa said. She looked past Fitz. "You just gotta stop being such a thug, Nikki!"

"Oh yeah, one tripping penalty, I'm such a goon," Nikki said sarcastically. She giggled. "Broad Street Bullies here I come."

"Hey." Tessa nudged Fitz. "It really wasn't a bad game, all things considered. Once we get our shit sorted out, I think we'll have a good shot at beating them during the regular season." *During the regular season.* Fitz liked the sound of that.

Fitz left the rink feeling not entirely happy—she was still annoyed with Michelle for getting the team drunk, and at herself for letting it happen—but she was hopeful. *If there is anything praiseworthy, think about these things.* Her teammates had fun today, and that was important too.

Fitz's house was as silent as a tomb when she arrived home. Most of the lights were off. Fitz put away her gear and crept through the noiseless kitchen.

"Hello?" she called out. She knew her kids were out of the house—she'd arranged it that way herself—but where was Tom? She listened. Nothing. She checked her phone. No messages. *Where the heck is he?* She went to his den to sneak a peek at his calendar. *Maybe he was going out with his friends, and I forgot.*

"Hello there."

"Oh my God! Tom, you almost gave me a heart attack!" Fitz put her hand over her thumping heart. Tom was sitting in the lounge chair. She hadn't seen him there. "Didn't you hear me when I came in? Why didn't you answer when I called?"

He shrugged. "So, is your little tournament over then?" Tom swirled his drink, his expression unreadable.

"For today; we have one more game tomorrow."

"Ah." Tom stared at her. The dim light from the desk lamp created shadows on his face that highlighted his gold-blonde hair and sharp features and made his eyes seem to glow. He was striking.

I must look such a mess, all sunburned and sweaty. "I'm, uh, I should go shower," Fitz pointed back behind herself.

"Need help?" Tom smiled coyly. Fitz could feel her already red face burn hotter.

"No... I... What? No..." she stammered.

His smile faded. "Relax, Patricia; it was just a joke." He turned his eyes away from hers. "You're so uptight."

Am I uptight? Fitz asked herself as she walked upstairs. Maybe she had been a little uptight today. Michelle probably would have said so. But the team had such great potential, and with a bit more work, they could be a real team. She thought about the game and about what Tessa had said.

'*When we get our shit sorted out...*' There was still so much to sort out, but Fitz was determined to see them succeed. *If that means I have to be a little uptight sometimes, so be it.*

Dawn

Sunday, June 4th

Dawn paused a moment outside of the locker room. She was feeling some trepidation regarding this whole 'team founders meeting' thing. She worried that Fitz and Tessa wanted to talk about 'cutting' Emily. And Dawn didn't want that. No matter what happened at the rink, Dawn would continue to see Emily at work. That could be majorly awkward if they rejected her. The thought made Dawn's insides twist. *It'll be fine. This is going to be the no drama team, remember?* Dawn took a deep breath and opened the door.

Inside, Fitz and Michelle were engaged in a heated discussion. Tessa stood next to them, face pinched, shifting uneasily from one foot to the other. *No drama, no drama, no drama.* Dawn crossed her fingers.

"There's just no way, I couldn't do it." Michelle shook her head violently.

Dawn dropped her bag with a thud. "Do what? Did you start the team meeting without me?"

"Oh, no," Michelle turned back to Fitz. "Fitz was just trying to initiate us into her hippy vagina cult again." Michelle rolled her eyes and Dawn breathed a sigh of relief.

"It is not a 'vagina cult'!" Fitz insisted, crossing her arms. "Menstrual cups are better for the environment, and so much more convenient. You should at least give it a try; you would never have to carry around tampons again!"

"But, you have to..." Michelle pantomimed the act of removing and emptying a menstrual cup but with an expression like she was handling roadkill. Michelle shook her head violently. "Ugh, no, ew, to even consider... Just no. I'll *stick* with my tampons, so to speak."

"So to speak." Dawn chuckled.

"This is so disgusting," Tessa groaned. She had closed her eyes and was shaking her head.

You'd think she'd be used to this by now; you can't get a group of women together for long without period talk.

"No, baby girl, you want to hear something disgusting?" Dawn leaned in. "I met some women at my college reunion who were doing *shots* out of theirs."

"What? Oh my God, that is so gross!" Michelle shouted recoiling.

Tessa kept shaking her head, mouthing *'nope, nope, nope'* over and over.

"Whatever, y'all are so dramatic. I'm sure they washed them." Fitz rolled her eyes. "You can't tell me you've never put something in your mouth that's been inside a—"

"That's not the same thing!" Michelle squealed. Fitz and Michelle began to talk at once, but before they could get into a playground-style exchange of 'is too' versus 'is not,' Dawn waved them quiet.

"Okay, okay, I think this has gone far enough," she said. Fitz and Michelle both folded their arms and shut their mouths. *What am I going to do with these two?* They seemed to skirt the line between real friends and *frenemies* some days.

"Thank you, Dawn." Tessa let out an exasperated sigh. "Let's get to what we came here to talk about: the new players. Right?"

"Yes. I think it would be ideal if we could talk to everybody today about who's playing in the regular season. But the four of us should be on the same page first. We did this tournament partly to figure out if we really could put together a team, and I don't know about y'all, but I think this group has worked out pretty well."

Dawn was glad to see that Fitz was more positive about it than she had been yesterday.

"Yeah, for the most part," Tessa nodded. "I know Katie didn't work out; I'm so sorry about that, by the way."

"That's okay," Fitz assured her. "I don't think we need players like her to be successful, not if we have players like Nikki. Drunken penalties aside, she's a decent player. I assume we want her on the team, right?"

"Obviously! She's the fucking best!" Michelle grinned. Fitz glanced briefly at Michelle. It was subtle, but Dawn thought she could see a hint of real animosity there.

"Tessa, you said she wants to be on the team, right?" Fitz asked.

"Yup, Nikki is totally on board. And Andy is too now. Andy said they've had a great time this weekend," said Tessa. Michelle lifted a single eyebrow.

"They were having fun? Oh, yeah, I could totally tell." Her voice dripped with sarcasm. Tessa scowled.

"Fantastic!" Fitz continued, side-stepping Michelle's comment. "The next question is, what about Tiffany and Emily? Do they want to play with us?"

"Do we want them? If it means taking both of them?" Tessa asked bluntly. "Could we just ask Tiffany?"

"They want to play together, so they come as a package deal," said Dawn. She rubbed at her belly, where the tension was squeezing her insides.

"I adore Emily; she's so much fun!" Michelle cooed. "I'd say we should take both—"

"Could Tiffany maybe sub up with us?" Fitz acted as if she hadn't heard Michelle, her eyes steadily trained on Dawn. "Could she maybe stay on her normal team with Emily but also play with us?"

Dawn rolled that one over in her head. *If Tiffany had just wanted to sub up, she probably would have said so.* "I don't know. Maybe but... I don't know." Dawn imagined it from Emily's perspective. *It's sort of like, how would it feel if Rich stopped inviting me to game night just because Sharon is a bigger gamer?* Dawn knew she'd feel terrible.

"Well, I think we should ask them both," Michelle interjected sharply. "Emily is a sweet girl, and she's not so God-awful that she's going to drag us down. We aren't in the NHL or the Olympics or something. This isn't *Miracle on Ice*; it's more like retarded *Mighty Ducks*."

"Don't say that!" Fitz snapped.

"What?"

"The R-word. It's not funny, it doesn't make you clever, and it's hurtful!"

"Sorry!" Michelle didn't look particularly sorry, her lips were tight and her arms crossed. If anything, she looked angry. "I'm just saying it's not like we're some big deal team."

Fitz put her fingers to her temples and closed her eyes. The room was silent for a moment. The tightness in Dawn's stomach had found its way to her chest.

"I know what you're saying, just say it another way next time," Fitz said through gritted teeth. She took another deep breath and opened her eyes. "In any case, I actually agree, I think we should ask them both to join us."

"Me too." Dawn smiled, relieved. The three women looked at Tessa. She pulled off her cap and ran her fingers through her hair. She didn't look convinced, but she also didn't look like she had the energy to argue.

"Okay, I guess we'll invite both of them then." Tessa nodded.

At least that ended up ok.

"So if they play full-time we have nine. We need one more— somebody solid," said Fitz.

"My contacts are tapped out." Tessa frowned. "Sorry."

"Don't worry about it. Assessments start in a month or two. We'll scout a little, it could be fun. And in the meantime, let's make sure Tiffany and Emily are willing to join us. Do you want to ask them, Dawn?"

"My pleasure." Dawn stretched. "Now, if that concludes our team meeting, I have to take a trip to the wiz palace."

By the time Dawn returned from the bathroom, Emily and Tiffany had arrived. *Gods save us, but these two are babies. Was I ever this young? Were Sharon and I ever this stinking cute? Well, Sharon was.*

"Hey, baby girls!" Dawn said. "Or is it babies girl, like attorneys general?" Dawn's greeting was met with confused looks. *Stop being such a nerd, Dawn.* "I was sent over to ask if you two would like to join the Darts for the regular season."

Emily and Tiffany cheerfully accepted, and Dawn went into the final game bouncing with happiness. The Darts were starting to feel like a team.

They were starting to play like one too. *Good thing... this game is going to be close.* The Darts were playing a team called No Pucks Given, but as Tessa put it, they seemed to give plenty of *pucks* about a fifth-place game in a beer league tournament.

No Pucks Given played a hard, dirty game. But their cheap tricks worked to the Darts advantage, and Nikki scored the game-winning goal while on a power-play. The Darts finished the last game of the Kegstanley Cup in fifth place.

"Damn, Fitz! You're going to be seeing *that* bruise for a while," Tessa commented as they peeled off their equipment post-game. Fitz looked down at her inner thigh. Dawn whistled. The dark purple mark stood out starkly on Fitz's pale skin.

"Yeah, that's going to be a pretty one!" said Dawn.

"Y'all say that like it's a good thing." Fitz furrowed her brow and poked at the mark. "I hope it doesn't get any darker." Tessa looked at Fitz as if she were crazy.

"Why not?" Tessa asked, rubbing at her forearms where Dawn could just make out a yellow-brown bruise on her tan skin. "Bruises are like a badge of honor: shows the world you're a badass hockey player."

"Yeah? Because I'm afraid my doctor is going to think that my husband beats me." Fitz scowled.

"I know, right? I think it's *hilarious!*" Michelle smirked. "It's like a total running gag between Ben and I. Tell your husband to be extra nice to you, or you'll 'report him.'"

"No! I don't think Tom would find that joke funny at all!" Fitz gasped, the color draining from her face. "If Tom ever thought... Oh, I'd rather cancel my appointment! I can't imagine what he would do."

A tickle of concern nagged at the back of Dawn's mind. *Too close to home?* There was an awkward silence. Fitz must have realized what they were thinking, and she suddenly put her hands up.

"Oh no, Tom has never done anything like that!" Color returned to Fitz's face in a sudden flush of red. "It's just that he would be so upset if he thought anybody could ever *think* such a thing of him!" Fitz shook her head, as if shaking off the notion, and cleared her throat. "Don't y'all forget to give me back the jerseys before you leave. I'm going to send them in to get the numbers and logos put on."

When the rest of the team had cleared out, Fitz was still there, carefully folding jerseys and packing them neatly into their box. Was it Dawn's imagination, or did she look a little misty-eyed? Dawn sat down beside Fitz. *She's crying.*

"You okay, boo-boo?" Dawn asked.

Fitz wiped her eyes and laughed a short embarrassed little laugh. "Oh, I'm fine," she sniffed. "These jerseys... it's silly but they just mean *so much* to me. What they represent..." Fitz wiped her cheeks. "Oh, I don't know why I'm crying. I feel so blessed by how well this tournament went. Every time another piece falls into place for this team, I feel so... so much *emotion*. It's like watching my kids when they learn something new." She laughed. "Oh my gosh, that sounds so stupid. I know it's just hockey, but..."

Fitz softly touched the jersey in her lap. Dawn felt a warm glow of affection for her teammate. She put a hand on her shoulder and squeezed. Fitz started, almost like she'd forgotten Dawn was there. Fitz hastily folded the jersey and put it in the box.

"Clearly, I'm a little too emotionally invested."

"Nothing great in this world ever happens without somebody getting 'a little too emotionally invested.'"

Tessa

Friday, August 11th

Tessa dropped into the seat of her car with a grunt. She leaned her head back and took a deep breath—or tried to. The air in the car was stifling hot from sitting all day under the August sun. She turned the key in the ignition and cranked the AC up to max. Tessa put the car into drive, then after a second, threw it back into park. She didn't have the energy to drive home just yet. Tessa sat motionless, eyes closed, trying to find the will to move.

Work had been killing her since her promotion a couple of months ago. *What the hell made me think being a manager would be easier?* Some crazy optimistic part of her had actually believed that the power of the 'manager' title would help alleviate *something*. It did not. Oh boy, did it not. Her authority was higher, but so were her responsibilities. And the pushback from the sexist little shits working under her just made everything ten times harder than it had to be.

Most days, Tessa worked until she crashed. She could feel that crash coming, and unless she wanted to crash her *car*, Tessa needed to find a way to perk up before the drive home. Tessa pulled out her phone. She didn't check her texts or personal emails while at work, but her notification light had been blinking all day. *Maybe Dragon finally texted me back.* There weren't any texts from Dragon, but there were a couple from her teammates.

> Fitz: I just heard back from the league, there are some
> conditions but the good new is that we're in!!
> Fitz: They're adding our team to the division!
> Michelle: nice!
> Dawn: woohoo!

> Fitz: I had to list a captain and I put myself... I hope that's ok
>
> Dawn: It should be you boo-boo!

Tessa heaved a long sigh of relief. When Fitz had first contacted the league to register the Darts, the board denied her request. Fitz had been in fight mode ever since, refusing to give up on her dream of building this new team. She sent emails to every member of the board, stating their case and begging them to reconsider. Fitz had gone so far as to call those members whose phone numbers she could dig up. She was relentless. But apparently, it paid off.

> Tessa: That's great news!
>
> Tessa: I was starting to get worried although it didn't make any sense for them NOT to let us in

The rumor Tessa heard at summer hockey was that the league rejected the Darts because so many of them were from the Hot Shots. Tessa didn't know if the board had something against the Hot Shots, or if the Hot Shots had told the board something about them. Maybe neither. Tessa hadn't told Fitz about the rumors. She would have taken it too personally, and Fitz was agitated enough already. *I guess it doesn't matter now.*

> Tessa: Thanks for all your work, Fitz. Dawn is right, you should be the captain

Tessa put down her phone and wiped the sweat from her palms. She tried to imagine what it would be like with Fitz as their captain. It felt right. *Fitz is so passionate about the team; she's going to be a perfect captain.*

Outside her car window the sun was low in the sky, a burning orange orb hovering just above the horizon. *I should go home.* The moment her tires hit the open road Tessa's phone rang. It was Fitz.

Tessa usually really hated phone calls, but this was *Fitz*. She couldn't ignore her new *captain*.

"Hey, Fitz."

"Hi, Tessa! I hope it's okay that I called, I just didn't think I could get this all out over text." Fitz's familiar voice was bright and energetic.

"That's okay, what's up?" Tessa asked.

"I wanted to fill you in on the specifics of the league's decision about the Darts," said Fitz.

"You said it was a yes, right?"

"More like a 'yes but.'"

"Yes, but what?" Tessa asked. Fitz let out an exasperated sigh. Tessa could practically hear her rolling her eyes.

"But we'll be 'on probation' because they have 'concerns' about our ability to put together a team that can be competitive at this level, so they think we need an 'evaluative season' to be sure." Fitz scoffed. "So that kind of sucks."

"What does that even mean?" Tessa asked.

As Tessa drove home, Fitz explained the details of their 'probation.' If the Darts placed last in the division, they would automatically be sent down a level without opportunity for argument, although the league board reserved the right to keep any high-performing individual players from moving down with them. If they placed within the bottom three, they would remain on probation for the next season as well.

"So let me see if I've got this straight," said Tessa, pulling into the driveway. "If we come in last, they can tear apart our team; if we aren't quite the worst, we stay under the microscope; but if we do better than *three* other teams, that will get them off our backs entirely?"

"Yes, ma'am—and the way they put it, I don't believe they think we can do it."

"Well, shit," Tessa said, "I guess we'd better not suck then."

"We won't. This team is meant to be," Fitz said firmly. Tessa could picture Fitz's bright-eyed, eager expression on the other end of the call.

"You're really okay going to the assessments?" Fitz asked.

"Of course!" Tessa let herself into her apartment. "You've already done so much; I wish I had time to do more to help. You're the best, Fitz," Tessa said as she grabbed a beer and sank onto the sofa, relaxing into its familiar squeaky sag. "Really, thanks for all your work, *captain*."

"Oh, it's all my pleasure, really!" Fitz paused. "I hope people are really okay having me listed as captain."

"Of course!" said Tessa. "Why wouldn't we be? You're doing pretty much all the work! You're totally the captain here. It was your idea, after all."

"Yeah, I suppose. Thank you, Tess. I'm so glad you're doing this with me."

Tessa felt her cheeks get hot. "Me too," she mumbled.

"I am just so excited to see it coming together!" Fitz gushed. "Honestly, it really doesn't feel like work at all. It's nice to have something to distract myself from life... You know. How are you doing, Tessa? How's your job treating you these days?"

"I'm fine." Tessa felt her smile fade. "I mean, I'm pretty much living in the fifth circle of hell, but otherwise... I'm fine." She glowered across the room at her work bag and the many challenges it represented.

"Anything I can do to help?" Fitz asked, sounding genuinely concerned.

Tessa wiped a hand across her face. *I shouldn't have said anything.* She didn't want to make Fitz worry. "No, thanks, it's just work stuff. I'll feel better once hockey starts again." Tessa forced a laugh. "I think I just need to hit something. Get out my frustration on the ice."

"I thought you were playing in a summer league," said Fitz.

"Yeah, it's not the same." Tessa didn't know why, but it was true.

"Well, you're always welcome to come over and hit some pucks at my place."

"I might take you up on that," Tessa warned. It sounded wonderful.

Tuesday, August 22nd

Fitz: I'm going to call to officially book the ice
Fitz: Michelle I'm putting you down for the billing for the ice. That's still ok right???
Michelle: for the millionth time yes ffs
Fitz: sorry, I'm just so excited do get another thing DONE!!
Fitz: remember I can't go to the assessments this week, I'm in CA until the 25th :(
Fitz: Dawn, Tessa, are you still ok to go??
Dawn: Sure thing
Tessa: Yup!
Fitz: thank you!!! I'm soooooo sad I can't be there
Fitz: Text me right away! Tell me EVERYTHING!
Tessa: Ok but I doubt it's going to be all that exciting

Thursday, Aug 24th

Tessa sat in the arena lobby, waiting for Dawn to arrive and assessments to begin. She found a seat on the far end of the large glass window that overlooked the ice and sat down. Tessa glanced around the lobby. From across the room, she caught sight of a familiar face and froze. *Oh shit.* It wasn't Dawn. It was Jackie.

Tessa quickly turned away, hoping Jackie hadn't seen her. *Don't come over here, don't come over here, don't come over here.* Running into Jackie was the last thing she'd expected or wanted.

She could hear footsteps approaching her. Slowly Tessa glanced over her shoulder and almost cried with relief when she saw Dawn.

"Sorry I'm running late—" Dawn began but stopped and examined Tessa's face, "Now what is going on with you, boo-boo? You look like you've seen a ghost!" Tessa tilted her head slightly in the direction of Jackie. Dawn looked around and back at Tessa and mouthed '*ohhhh*.'

"What should we do?" Tessa whispered. Her throat felt dry. Out of the corner of her eye, she could see Jackie sitting down at the other end of the viewing area. "Should we say hi or...?"

"Naw, don't worry about her, baby girl. Let's just focus on what we're here to do." Dawn patted Tessa's knee. Dawn was right. They were here for a reason.

As assessments began, Tessa and Dawn made notes and began to zero in on the players who might fit in with their team. *This is a lot more fun than I thought it would be.* Tessa and Dawn eventually narrowed their list down to five players.

The results were posted outside the locker room a few minutes after the players cleared the ice. Dawn and Tessa started in that direction, but before they'd gone five feet, Jackie stepped into their path.

"You have a lot of nerve," Jackie hissed.

"Excuse me?" said Tessa.

"You heard me." Jackie glared down at Tessa. She had a good four inches on her, but Tessa wasn't about to shrink back.

"Get out of my face, *Jackie*," Tessa growled.

Dawn pulled her back. "Hey now, let's calm down, boo-boo," she said softly. She turned to Jackie. "How are you doing, Jackie?"

"How am I doing? How do you *think* I'm doing?" Jackie asked, challenge in her tone. "Why do you think I'm *here*?" Jackie didn't wait for them to respond. "I'm here, at this rink, at this moment, because some *assholes* I know decided that they were too good for us, and now the Hot Shots—you remember us *surely*—have to find five more fucking players."

"I'm sorry, we didn't—" Dawn began.

"You should be sorry," Jackie cut her off. "Not that all of you will be missed," she added, looking pointedly at Tessa.

Right back at you, bitch. If Jackie was trying to hurt her, it wasn't going to work; she didn't give one solitary fuck what Jackie thought of her.

Seeing that she wasn't going to get a rise out of Tessa, Jackie shifted her gaze to Dawn, looking at her with an expression of pure contempt. "But Connie expected a little more *loyalty* out of you, Dawn. How could you do this to her? She thought you were her friend. But I guess not. Bitch."

Dawn swayed as if struck; she looked absolutely gutted. Jackie smirked, her words apparently having their intended effect. With considerable effort, Tessa resisted the urge to punch Jackie in her smug face.

"Back off, asshole," Tessa growled. "We don't owe you shit, so just leave us alone."

Jackie lifted her chin and took a step back. "Whatever," she let out a short, harsh laugh, "but don't expect it to be easy to pick up new players. Once they find out what kind of *teammates* you are, they won't want to touch your team with a ten-foot pole."

"Go. The. *Fuck*. Away." Tessa spoke slowly and sharply, letting all the anger she'd ever felt for Jackie soak into her words. After a beat, Jackie turned and sauntered over to the assessment results—and after a quick satisfied glance back at them, disappeared through the door to the locker rooms.

"What an absolute *twatwaffle*," Tessa muttered. As the adrenaline of the confrontation wore off, her hands began to shake. She shoved them in her pockets. Tessa could see tears welling in Dawn's eyes. *Come on, don't cry.* Tessa nudged Dawn with her elbow.

"Hey, you didn't deserve that," she said. Dawn sniffed and wiped at her face with the sleeve of her jacket. It was hard to see Dawn looking so hurt. Tessa shot another dirty look at the door behind which Jackie had disappeared. *Goddamnit, Jackie. What the hell is wrong with you?*

"I really thought Connie had been understanding and that there were no hard feelings," Dawn said softly.

"Don't beat yourself up. We didn't do it to hurt them. What Jackie said was intended to hurt." Tessa mentally kicked Jackie in the shin. "You shouldn't let her make you feel bad. You don't deserve it."

"Thanks, boo-boo." Dawn didn't sound convinced.

Tessa gritted her teeth. *If I think about this too much, I'm going to punch a hole in something.*

"Hey, let's look at the results and see if any of the people we picked out are going to be worth contacting," Tessa said. Dawn nodded. In the end, only three of the players they'd noticed ended up in the right division for the Darts.

"Man, we suck at assessing people, apparently!" Tessa grinned.

"No NHL recruiter careers in our futures," Dawn snorted. Tessa promised to put all the information about the players in an email and send it to Fitz first thing tomorrow. She wouldn't mention Jackie.

Fitz

Thursday, August 24th

Fitz checked her phone again. No new messages. She'd been hoping to hear from Tessa today. The sun was still high in the California sky, but back in Minnesota, it was getting late. Fitz looked out at the surf where Tyler and McKayla bobbed in the water. *Getting the kids back on central time is going to be a nightmare.* Fitz wished for the millionth time that she could have talked Tom into going to North Carolina instead. The beaches of the Outer Banks were just as nice, and the time change was easier. And she would have been *home*.

Fitz hated how infrequently she got to visit her childhood home and all her friends and family there. She glanced at Tom, sitting in the beach chair next to hers, engrossed in his phone. *'You can't have a real vacation around in-laws.'* Fitz rolled her eyes. *Some vacation.*

Fitz shifted uncomfortably in the small 'sexy' bikini she'd bought just for this trip. She thought it would catch Tom's attention; it would be nice to have his attention during *daylight* hours for once. But all it seemed to do was ride up her butt and make her feel self-conscious. *What was I thinking, buying this thing?* Fitz pulled at the too-little fabric. It was the skimpiest thing she'd worn in since having kids. She took out her phone and checked her selfie angles. *Maybe I'm just too old for bikinis.*

She looked at Tom again. He had promised her that this vacation would be romantic. He'd booked an executive suite in the hotel and had it prepared with flowers and wine when they arrived. That first night was so lovely. It was the first time they'd made love in a while, and it had given Fitz such hope for the trip.

But the next day, Tom barely spoke to her. He hardly even looked at her despite all the effort she put into her appearance every day. No matter how cheerful she tried to be, his demeanor with her was always cool. They may as well have been back home. There was no romance. No connection. Only stupid wedgie bathing suits and mounting frustration.

Fitz checked her messages again. Nothing. With a sigh, she tossed her phone toward her bag. It landed in the sand.

"You should be more careful," Tom tisked, not looking up. It was the first thing he'd said to her in hours. She swallowed a snide retort and walked off to retrieve the children. As she walked toward the water, she paused and glanced over her shoulder at Tom. He wasn't watching her walk away. *He used to always watch me walk away.* She sighed, turning back to the water.

"Tyler! McKayla! Time to go!" she called.

"No!" they both cried back. Fitz put her hands on her hips and gave them a stern look.

"You know that I already gave y'all an extra hour, so no complaining. Do you have any idea what time it is back home?" The kids rolled their eyes, but they did as they were told.

"Dad, Dad! Did you see that big wave I got?" Tyler called as he climbed up the slope of the beach. Tom put down his phone and smiled at his son.

"Sure did! Nice job, buddy!" he lied. He hadn't seen anything, and Fitz knew it. But Tyler was beaming with pride, so again she bit her tongue.

"I rode it for like a minute longer than McKayla!"

"It was not a whole minute, booger-brain!" McKayla snapped. "You fell like two seconds after I did. And I had more longer rides than you today anyway."

"Nuh-uh! I totally kicked your butt, buttface." Tyler stuck his tongue out at his sister.

"Did not!" McKayla yelled. She looked ready to fight; her steely eyes narrowed on her brother.

"No arguing," Fitz admonished. She rubbed her temples. "You both caught a lot of waves. And you had fun. Be grateful for that." The kids muttered apologies as they began to dry off.

"Can we get ice cream?" Tyler asked. Fitz sighed. The deal had been that if she let them surf longer, it was with the explicit understanding that they would be giving up their trip to the ice cream shop.

"No, remember what we—"

"Sure thing, buddy!" Tom cut her off. Fitz whipped her head around to glare at Tom. He was smiling broadly at his son.

"We said they couldn't have ice cream if we stayed," Fitz said through gritted teeth.

"Oh loosen up, Patricia, it's vacation," Tom said without looking at her. He picked up Tyler and swung him around as the boy squealed with delight.

"Yes, but we're going home tomorrow, and their sleep schedule is so messed up as it is," Fitz insisted. Tom put Tyler down and stood up straight. Now he did look at her; he was still smiling, but the warmth was gone.

"Don't worry about it; they'll sleep on the plane." He spoke calmly but with an edge to his voice.

Fitz stood her ground. "No, they won't. They never do." Her jaw was starting to hurt from clenching. Tom frowned, his eyes narrowing. He stepped closer to her until his face was inches from hers. Fitz's heart skipped a beat.

"I said, don't worry about it," he hissed. Then he stood back, and his smile returned. "Now, let's enjoy our vacation! Ice cream time!" The kids clapped and happily skipped away from the beach. Fitz picked up their beach bag and followed unhappily behind.

"Why do you always do that?" Fitz asked Tom once the kids were asleep, and they were back in their own bedroom within the hotel suite.

"Do *what*, Patricia?" Tom asked blandly.

"Undercut me with the kids, like you did tonight with the ice cream." Fitz was still frustrated about the whole interaction, just one in a long line of unhappy vacation moments.

"All I wanted to do was to make my children happy. What's wrong with that? I thought you wanted me to 'connect' with them more," said Tom.

"But not at my expense! Not by making me the mean parent who has to say 'no' all the time!" Fitz replied. She sat down on the bed with a huff. "You promised *me* a good time on this vacation too, remember?" she said as she lay down and pulled up the covers to her chin.

"Well, I'm sorry it hasn't lived up to your *expectations.*" Tom rolled his eyes. "What *did* you expect? Wine and flowers every night? Candlelit dinners? It's just a family vacation, Patricia."

"I know," Fitz said quietly, rolling away from him. "But at least you could pay *some* attention to me." The mattress moved as Tom climbed in. He slid up behind her.

"I'm sorry you feel ignored," he whispered in her ear, not sounding the least bit sorry. He ran his hand along her waist and hip. "I can give you attention now."

"No, thank you," she said firmly. Her heartbeat thundered in her chest, fueled by frustration and the sensation of his touch. She stiffened as he continued to caress her body.

"Come on, Patricia. I thought you wanted a romantic vacation." He kissed the back of her neck.

"I'm tired, Tom," she said. Still, he didn't move back. "Really, I just want to go to sleep. We were in the sun all day; the kids were up late. I'm exhausted."

"Fine." Tom turned away.

While Tom fell quickly asleep, Fitz remained wide awake. She was too aggravated to sleep. She crept out of bed. Channeling her frustrated energy, she quietly tiptoed around their hotel suite packing and tidying up. By the time she returned to bed, the suite was spotless.

Friday, August 25th

The next morning, Fitz was tired but ready to give the children one last happy memory before they finally went home.

"Hey kids, how would you like to go for one more dip in the pool before we head to the airport?" Her suggestion was met with squeals of delight.

"Do we have time for that?" Tom asked.

Fitz smiled sweetly. "Yes sir, I've gotten everything else packed up! We're all set—plenty of time for one last swim!"

"Alright, if you say so." He bent over and kissed her cheek. "Thanks, *Belle*."

Fitz stared at him. She couldn't remember the last time Tom had called her 'Belle,' the old pet name he'd given her back in college. It made her heart flutter. Fitz smiled to herself as she changed for the pool. It was nice to have Tom notice her during daylight for once. *At least we're ending this trip on a positive note.*

"What happened to the bikini?" Tom asked when they arrived at the pool. Fitz looked down at herself. She was wearing a plain black one-piece today. Her 'mom suit.' It wasn't sexy, but it also didn't ride up her butt.

"I already packed it."

"Too bad," Tom smiled at her, "I liked that bikini."

Fitz's face flushed. She didn't know whether she was flattered or annoyed. *If he liked it, why didn't he say so when I was wearing it?*

Tom pulled off his shirt and jumped into the pool with the kids. Fitz stared after him, watching him play with the children for a long while until she noticed the notification light blinking on her phone. She had a message from Tessa. Opening it, Fitz began to grin. Tessa and Dawn had gotten information on three potential new teammates. She immediately messaged them back.

"Now look who's on their phone." Tom stood next to her, dripping wet. "Always nagging me and now... Tisk, tisk." He shook his head.

"I have not been on my phone hardly at all, I just..." she stammered defensively.

"Calm down, it was just a joke." Tom's smile was small and teasing.

"I suppose we'd better start heading back to the room soon," Fitz said, averting her eyes. "We still have to check out."

"I'm going to go take a quick shower." Tom sharply smacked her backside. It made a loud *slap* sound. "I'll meet you up there. *Belle.*"

He gave her one more small smile before turning and sauntering off. Fitz stood frozen, too shocked to react or to ask him to stay and help get the kids out of the pool. She rubbed the spot where his hand had hit her. *It's the attention I was asking for, isn't it? So why does it make me feel worse?*

Tessa

Monday, September 18th

Tessa sat in the stairwell at work, eating her tuna fish sandwich alone. She wanted to be alone. She was hiding from her coworkers after a particularly frustrating design meeting. Tessa knew she had to go back in there in a mere twenty minutes, but she needed every second of that time to decompress and recenter herself. She opened her phone and texted a few friends. Fitz was the only one to respond.

> Fitz: Hey girl! It's good to hear from you!
> Fitz: Start of school has me so stressed! How are you?
> Tessa: I'm hanging in there
> Fitz: Do you have time to come over and shoot pucks this week? I miss hanging out with you!

Tessa desperately wished that she had the time to hang out with Fitz. But she had so much to do. Work was absolutely killing her. *Find time,* she told herself. Something had to give one of these days. She couldn't keep up her current pace indefinitely. *I'm hiding in a fucking stairwell. Obviously, I need a break.*

> Tessa: I miss hanging out with you too. Maybe next week?
> Tessa: Hey, did you hear back from any of the players we emailed yet?
> Fitz: OMG yes, can I call you?
> Tessa: ok

Tessa's phone immediately began to vibrate. She hunched down in the corner, hoping her voice wouldn't echo too loudly in the empty stairwell.

"Hey, Fitz. What's up?" she asked quietly.

"Oh, where to start? I am so frustrated." Fitz sounded frazzled.

"Why?"

"A million things, honestly. But I called to tell you about the hockey emails."

"From the players?" Tessa asked through a mouthful of tuna.

"Yes. I've gotten two replies, *both* turning us down," said Fitz with a sigh.

"That sucks."

"Well, at least the first one was polite. This second email, well, I suppose it's technically polite, but this Chloe person basically accused us of having a bad team culture. She said she wouldn't 'fit' with what she's heard of us."

"Team culture? We don't even have a team yet really." Tessa huffed.

"I know, right? I thought it was ridiculous at first," said Fitz.

"At first?"

"Well, I was thinking," Fitz began. "When is the one time our team has ever played together?"

"The tournament," Tessa said slowly.

"Right! And what happened at the tournament?"

"Uh, we got fifth place?"

"The party!" Fitz exclaimed. "Doesn't it make sense, Tessa? The party was so rowdy—"

"A lot of parties were rowdy..."

"But Michelle and Nikki got so drunk. You could tell by the way they were playing. Nikki got that penalty, and Michelle yelled at the ref!"

"Fitz, I think you may be overreacting," Tessa said. *She is definitely overreacting.*

"But how else would anybody have heard rumors about our team?" Fitz asked.

Tessa swallowed the last remaining bits of her sandwich and let out a long breath. "Well, I might have some idea," she said. She told Fitz all about the confrontation with Jackie at assessments and her own theories about the rumors surrounding their team. When she finished talking, Fitz was so quiet Tessa thought the call had been dropped. "Fitz? Are you still there?"

"Yes. Oh my Lord, Tessa, you are so right. It has to be Jackie." Fitz groaned. "Wow. I don't know why I was so quick to blame Michelle. I feel so foolish."

"Don't feel bad. I should have told you sooner." Tessa kicked herself for that.

"It's okay. I'm just so glad I called you today." Fitz's voice had lost its frantic, panicked energy. Tessa felt like she could almost hear her smile over the phone.

"Yeah, me too," Tessa smiled. Her watch vibrated, indicating the imminent start of her next meeting. "Sorry, but I have to get back to work."

"I should go too," Fitz said. "But seriously, thank you for talking me down. I know if I'd stayed so worked up, I would have picked a stupid fight when Tom got home. And we've had enough of those as it is."

"Oh, yeah, no problem," said Tessa; she always felt uneasy when Fitz talked about her husband like that. "Talk to you later?"

"Okay, yeah. Bye, Tess."

"Bye."

Dawn

Thursday, September 21st

> Fitz: We got a new teammate! Brooke is joining the Darts!
> Dawn: huzzah!
> Michelle: Who tf is Brooke?
> Michelle: Nmnd don't care, yay new people!
> Fitz: I'm soooooooo relieved! See you at the scheduling meeting, Dawn!

Saturday, September 23rd

Dawn came home from the league scheduling meeting and immediately collapsed on the sofa, exasperated and exhausted. She threw a pillow over her face.

"I hate drama so much," she groaned.

"So the scheduling meeting, not big happy fun times?" Sharon asked. Dawn lifted the pillow just long enough to give her wife a dirty look before letting it fall back down.

"Yeah, real fun," she mumbled sarcastically. She felt dark and hollow like there was a black hole in her chest.

"Do you want to talk about it?" Sharon sat beside Dawn and held her hand.

"No," Dawn grunted. *Come on, Dawn, are you a pouting child today?* She felt a little like a child; she felt small. She took the pillow off her face and rolled her head towards Sharon.

"The donuts didn't even have sprinkles." She made her most pitiful face. Sharon leaned forward and kissed her protruding lips.

"My poor baby." Her tone was both teasing and caring at once. "What will make it better?" Sharon traced the outline of Dawn's cheek with her index finger. The black hole in her chest didn't seem quite so dark when Sharon touched her. Dawn looked gratefully into her wife's face.

"Pizza, booze, telly?" Sharon suggested, affecting a slight British accent. Dawn smiled; she could never resist a good *Dr. Who* reference in a bad British accent. She nodded, and Sharon began to rise, but Dawn tightened her grip on her wife's hand, keeping her seated.

"In a minute," Dawn snuggled closer to Sharon, nuzzling her face into her wife's chest. She closed her eyes and let Sharon's warmth and presence soothe her. If she stayed cuddled up here with Sharon, then maybe she could face the things that had left her feeling hollow. Or at least talk about them.

"The meeting was just rough. We saw Connie there and I don't know, sweets, somehow today I left feeling like the villain of the story." Dawn sighed and looked up at Sharon. "Are the Darts the bad guys?"

"Who says there have to be good guys and bad guys?" Sharon twirled her fingers through Dawn's short curls, massaging her scalp. Dawn sighed and relaxed further into Sharon's arms. "It's just old lady hockey, remember?" Sharon added.

Old lady hockey. Dawn would normally have made a crack about Sharon calling her an 'old lady,' but she didn't have the energy. Sharon stopped twirling her hair.

"Come on, let's forget about it. Pizza, booze, telly, right? I'll go preheat the oven." Sharon tried to get up again, but Dawn didn't let go.

"Can we order delivery?" Dawn knew she sounded like a child again, but she didn't care. She was still feeling small; she might as well lean into the part.

"Woah there, big spender!" They were on a pretty tight budget, but at that moment, Dawn didn't give a hoot. She wanted warm, soft breadsticks to go with her warm, soft woman.

"Pretty please?" Dawn nuzzled Sharon.

"Okay, fine. Now, can I get up to get the booze?" Sharon squirmed; Dawn reluctantly relinquished her grip. Sharon stretched as she stood. Dawn watched as she pulled her shoulders back, pushing her chest forward. *Someone's not wearing a bra.* Sharon caught her gaze, and her mouth twisted in a knowing smirk.

"Are you looking at my chesticles, woman?" Sharon wagged a finger at Dawn. "It's pizza, booze, telly. Not pizza, booze, titties."

"But what if I want titties?" Dawn pouted. *The kids are out of the house.* Sharon let out a single bark of laughter as she walked off toward the kitchen.

"Do you want a cider?"

"With bourbon?" *More strong equals more happy, right?*

"Anything for you, baby!" Sharon was the best wife ever when she was feeling well. Dawn was glad she was feeling well today, Dawn really appreciated being taken care of. Sharon was so empathetic and caring; Dawn didn't know how she'd gotten so lucky. Dawn's phone binged. She pulled it out and looked at the screen, then wished she hadn't. *Fitz.*

Dawn didn't want to think about the scheduling meeting. She didn't want to think about the hurt she'd seen in Connie's face. Sharon came back holding two pint glasses filled almost to the brim. Dawn gulped down a large mouthful of 'burbonated' cider and tried not to look as disquieted as she felt. Sharon leaned over to look at the phone screen. It binged two more times.

"What happened at that meeting? Really." Sharon tilted her head, giving Dawn her come-on-and-spill-it-already face.

"Well, apparently Tessa told Fitz all about the little episode we had with Jackie, and somehow Fitz got it in her head that she needed to sort it out. She wanted to talk to Connie in person at the meeting. I tried to talk her out of it, but Fitz gets so stubborn. She wanted to smooth it all out, or at least call a truce." Dawn pinched the bridge of her nose. *I should have stopped her.*

"What happened?"

"You know, love, I hardly even know. Connie was nice enough, but then Jackie and Cindy showed up. They accused us of starting drama, and it all went downhill from there. Fitz got in a few words. I don't think I've ever seen her so mad. Unsurprisingly, nothing got *smoothed over*. We basically just walked away. Cindy and Jackie were so angry, but Connie just looked... sad." Dawn sighed. "Later, Fitz said something about leaving Connie to deal with all that drama. And that made me feel so bad for her. Instead of helping her fix the team, we just left. Makes us seem like a bunch of jerks, doesn't it?"

"No way," Sharon said firmly. Dawn shrugged. Sharon looked at her earnestly. "Really, hun, you are good people."

"You have a biased perspective. You married me; you're contractually obligated to like me." She didn't feel like good people. She felt like *poodoo*.

"But sweetness," Sharon rubbed her back. "It's not your problem to fix. It's Connie's team and Jackie's drama. Connie clearly enables her. She might be 'nice', but did she ever do anything to make it better?" Sharon asked. Dawn shrugged. "What you guys did when you left wasn't about being a bunch of selfish jerks; it was about creating a safe place to enjoy hockey without that nonsense. It was like a form of self-care. I don't know two things about hockey, but I think I go to enough therapy to know self-care when I see it. You shouldn't feel guilty. I think this team is a good thing for you. You were so happy during that tournament. You were glowing, baby."

"Yeah, I guess." Dawn rubbed at her gut. "I just wish thinking about Connie didn't make me feel like a big jerk-butt."

"Hey now, my wife is a good woman, and I don't want to hear you call her a 'jerk-butt' again, you got it?" Sharon put an arm around her and squeezed.

"Yes, dear." Dawn snuggled up to Sharon and rested her head on her shoulder. She felt better for having talked it over. Her phone binged two more times, but Dawn didn't reach for it. Instead, she reached for her wife and kissed her. Hockey could wait. The season was more than a month away. Sharon was here right now.

Michelle

Saturday, October 28th

Michelle sat in her home office, looking back and forth between the Darts' schedule and her calendar. Through the wall, she could vaguely hear the TV in the other room. *Fucking Dora. That stupid map song is going to be in my head all day.*

She counted out the weeks and games. *I can probably play twelve—a dozen is a pretty good number.* She smiled and resisted the urge to touch her abdomen. It was way too soon for that sort of thing. *I'd better get my ass moving.* Today the Darts had their first regular-season game, and she didn't want to be late.

"Ben! I'm leaving!" she called from the hall.

"Wait, wait, wait!" Ben appeared from around the corner, still in his flannel pajama pants and old t-shirt, his hair disheveled. He looked like a frat boy who'd just woken up after a long night—a frat boy holding a sippy cup. He hopped briskly over to her and gave her a deep kiss, his free hand cupping the back of her head. Michelle started to melt into the embrace—her chest blooming with warmth. She pulled away.

"Jesus, it's only a hockey game, I'll be back in a couple of hours." She swatted at his chest with her hat.

"What? Can't a man say goodbye to his wife?" Ben grinned, his eyes alight with laughter.

God, he looks sexy today. Michelle's chest burned. He looked so kissable, his bottom lip so biteable. She couldn't resist. She grabbed him by the shirt and kissed him hard before abruptly pushing him away.

"You're going to make me late, asshole." She gave him another whack with her hat.

"Sorry, babe."

"No, you're not."

"No... but I love you."

"I love you too, asshole. Now, go watch *Dora* and leave me alone."

Michelle finally made it out of the apartment, arriving at the arena just in time to see Tessa jogging across the parking lot in her sweatshirt—no jacket, not even a hat. Michelle shivered. It was biting cold. *She is old enough to dress herself for the weather. For fuck's sake.*

"Are you insane? You are going to freeze to death!" Michelle shouted over the wind.

"Why do you think I'm running?" Tessa called back.

Michelle shivered again and followed Tessa inside. The heat and smell of the locker room hit Michelle like a wall, and she stopped dead. It was like she'd walked into a third-world back-alley sauna. It stank of sweat, piss, and rotting trash.

"Oh, my sweet Jesus fuck this room reeks!" She wrinkled her nose. Although the heat of the room was a relief on her freezing limbs, it also served to intensify the stink. "Seriously, where is that smell coming from? Satan's asshole?"

"I think it's the shower," said AJ.

Michelle took a few steps towards the shower and almost gagged. It smelled like a gas station men's room, right down to the stench of cheap urinal cakes. But there weren't any urinals.

Oh my God, did the rink owners just give up and put urinal cakes in the shower? Michelle backed away, pinching her nose, and fanning the air in front of her.

"You're being a tad dramatic, don't you think?" Fitz said from her seat near the piss shower.

"Oh my God, how can you even sit there?" Michelle settled for a spot on the far side of the room. "Is it too late to find a new home rink?"

"Yes." Fitz scowled.

"At least it's warm." Nikki sat next to Michelle.

"True." Michelle unbuckled her belt and shimmied out of her jeans.

"I would much prefer to be cold than what's going to feel like actual, literal hell when the game is over," Tessa said, shaking her head.

"Hell no, if I'm taking off my pants in the middle of the fucking winter, I'd better be doing it in a warm room," Michelle said. Warm or not, the smell was making her sick. She rushed to dress so she could get the fuck out of there.

As they dressed, Fitz walked around the room, handing out jerseys. She looked very business-like. *Captain-like.* Fitz was taking the captain title to heart, that was for damn sure. Michelle was still getting used to the idea. *Oh, captain, my captain.* She wasn't entirely sure how she felt about it. She wondered what Fitz's husband thought. *All the shit she's been doing has to be time-consuming.*

Michelle watched as Fitz consulted with Tessa and Dawn over the scoresheet. An unexpected pinprick of emotion pierced Michelle's chest. Something about watching the three of them bothered her. *Why do I care? I'm just the team bankroll to her.* Michelle's stomach turned again. *I need to get out of this stank.*

Once the game got started, Michelle forgot about her stomach completely. The Highlanders hit the ice hard in their God-awful tartan jerseys, and scored one on the Darts right away.

Jesus Christ, these bitches have legs. Michelle hadn't skated since June, and she could feel it. It took some time for the Darts to find their feet, but by the end of the first period, they were holding their own, making it a tight match.

It may have been their first game in a new division, but the most remarkable thing was how unremarkable it was. The Highlanders were good, but the Darts made them work for their win. Three periods flew by, and before they knew it, the first game of the season was over, and it was time to head to the bar.

"Hey, Jess! I haven't heard from you in a while! How's it going?" Michelle asked as she slid into a chair next to Jess.

"Good. Mostly the same," Jess smiled faintly and fidgeted with the end of her long ponytail. Michelle raised an eyebrow.

"*Mostly*? Ohh, do you have a new boyfriend?" Michelle asked.

"How did you know?" Jess asked, surprised.

"I've got like, sex-dar or something. And girl, you look like you just got laid." Michelle laughed. Jess grinned sheepishly. Michelle laughed again. "Yeah, thought so. So, what's he like?" She pumped Jess for details as the rest of the team arrived.

When everyone had settled, and they began to place orders, Michelle held her breath. *Let's see how this goes. Coors Light* for Fitz and Tessa, cider for Dawn, *Diet Coke* for Jess. Nikki ordered a vodka tonic. *Nice.* The waitress turned to Michelle. She let out her breath.

"Just water for me, thanks," she said.

"You? Order water?" Nikki snorted. "Come on! Are you pregnant or something?"

Michelle allowed herself a coy smile.

"No way." Fitz stared at her in transparent shock. Michelle gave her a little shrug. Fitz sat back, looking dumbfounded and not particularly pleased. "You are actually pregnant?"

"I am," Michelle leaned back, mirroring Fitz's posture. She smirked; Fitz's unmasked astonishment was somewhat entertaining. *Believe it, bitch. I am pregnant.* Michelle was still getting used to it herself.

"Oh, my goodness! Congratulations!" Dawn gushed as she hugged her.

"This is good news, then?" Nikki laughed.

"Yes, *obviously.*" Michelle whacked Nikki in the arm. "I do know how that shit works, you know."

"Congratulations, what wonderful news," Fitz said sweetly, recovering from her initial shock. She smiled at Michelle.

That is the fakest fucking smile. "Thanks, *captain*. But keep it between us, okay?" Michelle pointed around the table at each of them. "No *Facebook* posts or *Snap* stories or anything. It's super early. Nobody knows aside from my husband and I at this point."

"The team is always the first to find out." Dawn laughed.

Isn't that the truth. Teammates have a weirdly personal connection: different than friendship, more like sisterhood.

"Yeah, well, and who knows if it'll even stick," Michelle shrugged. "I had two miscarriages before I had Ella, so I don't want to get too, you know, invested or whatever."

Across the table, Fitz's fake smile faded. "Oh, yes, I understand that," she said. Fitz fiddled with her wedding ring. "I had a miscarriage too before I had Tyler. I didn't tell a soul, but I wish I had. Back then, I didn't realize how common it was. I felt so alone."

"Tom had to know, though, right?" asked Michelle.

"Oh, yes, of course. But he's a *man*," Fitz said dismissively. She sighed. "I really could have used a friend."

Michelle stared at Fitz. She remembered the pain and grief of her past experiences; it was one of the hardest things she'd ever gone through. It had made her feel sad, empty, and hopeless, but she'd never felt alone—Ben had shared all that pain with her. *Poor Fitz.* Michelle shook her head.

"Yeah, well, if something happened, who would understand better than my hockey bitches, right?" Michelle said, clearing her throat. *This is getting sappy AF.* She flipped back her hair. "I mean, what was I going to do, fake drink?"

"That's what I did!" Nikki said, raising her hand. "When I was knocked up with my kid, I'd order drinks and then sneak back to the bar and to tell them to make them virgin. I had people fooled for months. I wouldn't be surprised if there are people out there who still think I was drinking all pregnancy long."

"That's hilarious, although I don't think I could be that sneaky, I'm much too big of a loudmouth." Michelle laughed. "Hell, I didn't get past the first game."

"How far along *are* you?" asked Fitz.

"Only like five weeks."

"Oh my God, so you really just found out!" Nikki gasped. "I don't think I even knew I was pregnant at five weeks. Were you trying?"

"Not trying per se, but not preventing either, and since I usually have a really consistent cycle, and we do fuck on the regular..." Michelle smirked as Tessa covered her ears. "I figured I might as well take a test."

She and Ben had tried very hard to get Ella. It was so stressful. This time, when they decided to forego contraception and just let whatever happened happen—trying without *trying*—it had been much more relaxing. And much, much sexier. After two years without birth control, Michelle was convinced that it was never going to happen. She'd put it completely out of her mind. Well, almost anyway.

"I never have understood that concept, not trying but not preventing." Fitz shook her head, "I'm much too much of a control freak for something like that. Either I am trying, or I am *not*."

Michelle could easily believe that. *I wonder if Fitz even has sex when she's not 'trying.'*

"You haven't answered the most important question yet," said Tessa. "Are you going to keep playing?" Tessa didn't want to hear about sex and miscarriages, but she did want to know how they affected the hockey team.

"Yeah, I'm going to keep playing," Michelle confirmed. Fitz looked expectantly at her. Michelle sighed. "...for the first trimester, which is about December twenty-first. Or at least that's my plan, so I should be good for the first twelve games."

"What's the due date?" asked Dawn.

"Fourth of July. Technically maybe like the second, but due dates are mostly bullshit, so I'm rounding up. My baby'll be patriotic as shit." Michelle caught a look that passed between Fitz and Tessa. "But like I said, I haven't even been to the doctor yet;

there's always the chance you'll be stuck with me for the whole season. So you two bitches had better not be thinking about replacing me yet."

"No one could replace you, boo-boo," Dawn assured her, but Fitz bit her lip and said nothing.

Michelle wasn't an idiot; she knew that the team would have to find a substitute for her if and when she left. And she knew that was just what Tessa and Fitz were thinking. The idea of being replaced stung more than Michelle would have admitted. *Fuck, why does that even bother me? Pregnancy hormones can seriously go suck a dick.*

Fitz

Sunday, November 12th

Fitz went home from the Darts' first win feeling more anxious than celebratory. She hadn't yet found a new player to replace Michelle, and she was getting worried. The Darts had lost their first two games, tied the third, but then lost again in the fourth. Fitz was concerned that convincing someone to join the team would be harder if they had a lousy record. Their win tonight felt like a sign. It was time to find a new player.

As soon as she got home, she sat down at the kitchen table with her laptop, determined to make some progress tonight. Time was ticking, and their prospects were probably declining rapidly now that the season had started. She was apprehensive about bringing in a new player sight-unseen, but she had to start somewhere.

Fitz began to write a 'player wanted' ad for the league's message board. Tom wandered through the kitchen. He might have said something, but she didn't process it; she was focused on the task at hand. Her cursor hovered over the *post* button. She drummed her fingers on her laptop. Slowly, as she sat there, hesitant to post, she became aware that Tom was standing on the other side of the counter island, watching her.

"Tom, would you read this and tell me if it sounds alright?" she asked. "We need another player for the Darts and—"

Tom slammed the cupboard door shut with a loud bang. Fitz jumped.

"No!" he snapped. "No, I will not read your stupid hockey shit!"

Fitz was taken completely aback. She looked at her husband. He was leaning forward across the counter, jaw clenched, his eyes fixed on her.

"What are you yelling for?" She crossed her arms. She was not in the mood for this. She had things to do, things her teammates

139

were counting on her to do. He didn't move; he continued to glare at her. She pressed her lips together and waited.

"Just trying to get your attention," he said. "Did you even notice that I was here?"

"Yes, of course, I—"

"Do you know what I said when I first came in?" Tom demanded.

Fitz opened her mouth to speak. She didn't know what he had said. She hadn't been paying attention. She closed her mouth again.

"No, of course, you don't because you don't give a shit," Tom growled. He stood, hands on his hips, scowling at her. "All you can think about is your little team, and to hell with me, right?"

"Tom, please. I hardly think it's worth—" Fitz began.

"Damnit, Patricia, you didn't even say hello when you got home!"

"You do the same thing all the time!" She jumped up, furious at the hypocrisy of his statement. "When you get home from work, you're immediately off to your den or back on your phone! You do it every day! I ignore you once—"

"Once?!" he barked, his face flushing crimson. "Once? Are you kidding me? You've been obsessing over that hockey bullshit for *months!*"

"And what about all the *years* I've spent sitting here, ignored, while you're buried in your work?" Fitz balled her hands into fists to keep them from shaking.

"I am because I *need* to be. It's my *job!* It's *important!*" He was practically screaming now.

"Well, hockey is important to me!"

"Yeah? Important to *you.* You and only you. You're so goddamn selfish!" Tom threw his hands up in a sudden sweeping motion that made Fitz take a step back. A tingle ran up her spine. *Selfish.* He'd said it before.

"I work hard for this family every day," Tom growled. "But when I come home, when I come to *you*..." Each of his words burned with fierce heat. "I come to you, and I can't say anything. Because I don't matter. You act like you don't even want to be here half the time."

"That's not true," Fitz whispered. She bit down hard on her bottom lip to keep it from trembling.

"You're right; it's not! You *never* want to be here," Tom said darkly.

"That's not true," Fitz repeated, clenching her jaw.

"You don't care about any of this!" Tom gestured broadly, and Fitz felt her throat burn.

"How dare you say that," Fitz growled, trying to ignore the tears welling up behind her eyes. "How dare you say I don't care! I do everything around here! I do all the housework; I make the meals! And the kids! Who makes sure they do their homework every day—that they get to all their activities? Me! I do everything for this family. Don't tell me that I don't care!"

"For Christ's sake, Patricia, I'm not talking about cleaning the goddamn house!" Tom shouted. "I'm talking about you and me! I'm talking about the fact that I thought I had a *wife*, not a live-in nanny who leaves every chance she gets!"

That stung. Fitz didn't say anything because she knew if she opened her mouth again, she would cry, and she didn't want Tom to see her cry.

"Jesus, it's like we're not even a couple anymore!" Tom continued to fume. "We don't do anything together, aside from the kids' games and shit." He pointed an angry finger at her. "And you'd better not suggest I go to your goddamn games; I'm not your father, I'm your fucking *husband*!"

What he was saying hurt, but Fitz couldn't deny the truth in his words. She wanted him to understand how abandoned and ignored he made her feel, but she couldn't find the words to tell him without sounding ungrateful for all that he did.

She sat back down in the chair and lowered her eyes. The silence stretched out between them. Fitz could feel his eyes trained on her. *He's waiting for me to say something.* She swiped at a tear that had escaped and rolled down her cheek.

"I... I know," she started slowly, "I know things haven't been great lately. And I know you work hard. I just feel... I feel like you don't appreciate what I do—"

"I do appreciate it!" Tom snapped. Fitz gritted her teeth.

"Well, I don't *feel* appreciated!" she snapped back. "I don't feel like you even see what I do, let alone think it's important." She took a deep breath. "Everything I do just seems invisible to you, and it hurts. Being invisible all the time hurts, but when I go to hockey—" As soon as the word '*hockey*' came out of her mouth, Fitz regretted saying it. Tom's whole body tensed.

"Hockey!?" he shouted. "Are you kidding me? Don't you think that maybe you could *deal* with our shit rather than running away to hockey?"

"I'm not running away!" *I'm not, am I?*

"Aren't *we* supposed to be partners? Isn't there a priority here? When's the last time you put half the *effort* that you put into that damn team into our relationship?" He made it sound so one-sided, like all the problems in their marriage were her fault.

"Effort?" she hissed indignantly. "And what effort are you making, Tom? Starting this fight? Is this your effort?"

He stared at her, mouth slack, as if she'd just asked the world's stupidest question. "What effort? Are you kidding me?" he asked, his voice incredulous. "I try, almost every night, I try to initiate things, and you just reject—"

"Wait, is this about *sex*?!" Fitz was back on her feet again, knocking over her chair. Hot angry tears spilled onto her cheeks. "How am I supposed to... to...? When we barely even talk... but then you... and I'm just going to..." She shook her head; she felt sick.

Tom let out a frustrated sigh. "I'm just saying that you could try."

Fitz was shaking all over. "I thought you cared about our relationship," she said bitterly. "But if all you care about is *sex*—"

"That is *not* what I said!"

"Well, it sure *sounded* like that's what you said!" Fitz choked back a sob.

Tom closed his eyes; his chest heaved as he took slow deep breaths. When he opened his eyes and looked at her again, she could see anger, frustration, and pain in his dark expression. *He looks hurt.* Tom never looked hurt.

"I'm trying to... Jesus, Patricia." He put his hands on his hips and looked down. "I'm trying to express how it feels as a husband to be rejected by my *wife*. By the person I *love*. How it feels when it seems like all I am to you is a convenient roommate."

"And you need sex not to feel like a roommate?" Fitz growled, trying to cover her pain with anger, although she was running out of energy for either.

"Yes!" He said it like it was obvious. Fitz's insides twisted; she couldn't believe what she was hearing. Tom's gray eyes burrowed into hers. "Come on, Patricia. Isn't *making love* an important part of being husband and wife? Without that, what are we?"

"I don't know," she whispered. She couldn't agree with him, but she couldn't argue anymore, either.

Tom stiffened. "I guess you'd have to love me to want to make love." He had regained his composure; his voice was cold. "Maybe I'm wrong. Maybe the lack of sex isn't the problem after all."

Fitz put her hands over her face and wiped away her tears. *I can't do this anymore.* She felt hollow and weary; the roller coaster of emotions she'd just been through had taken its toll. She had nothing left. She stood up and began to walk out of the room.

"I'm going to bed." She paused at the edge of the room and looked back at him. "I do love you."

Tom turned away and Fitz went to bed, wondering if he believed her at all.

Monday, November 13th

In the morning, Fitz affected a cheerful disposition as she got the kids ready for school, but underneath she was all tension and nerves. Tom didn't say a word as he got ready for work, just stared at her darkly while he poured his morning coffee. When he left the house without so much as a goodbye, Fitz felt both relieved and incredibly sad.

McKayla looked at her with concern, unasked questions in her eyes. *She looks so much like him.* Fitz wondered how much the children had heard last night.

"Don't you look pretty today! You all ready for school, honey?" Fitz squeezed her daughter's arm and forced herself to smile. She pushed herself to keep her emotions in check until the kids were gone and the errands were done. The effort was taxing. Eventually, she couldn't keep it bottled up one minute longer.

Alone in the car, hidden in the garage, Fitz let herself cry. *Why does marriage have to be so hard? How are we ever going to get back to good? Were we ever even good to begin with?* Fitz rested her forehead on the steering wheel and cried until she couldn't cry anymore.

When the tears had abated, she took a deep breath. *Be thankful in all circumstances, for this is God's will for you who belong to Christ Jesus.* She dried her tears and prayed again for her marriage. It made her feel calmer, more centered.

Fitz wasn't *happy*, but crying and praying had been cathartic, and she was able to smile genuinely at her children as they came crashing into the house from school. She cooked supper as the kids did their homework. Tom wasn't home yet, and the house was quiet. Fitz leaned on the counter, mindlessly scrolling through

Facebook. As she scrolled, an email notification popped up. *HOCKEY TEAM??* She clicked it open.

Dear Dart Team,

I am very interested in playing with your team for the remainder of this season. I have been playing hockey for many years but there was an issue with the team I had planned to play with this season and I was so excited to see another team in the same division post that they have an opening. I played pond hockey with the local boys growing up (my mother wouldn't let me play organized hockey because she thought it was too dangerous but for some reason thought that playing on a frozen lake outside in -20 windchill was totally fine, I will never understand her logic but at least I got to play) There wasn't a women's team for me in high school and college (I know that dates me). I started playing adult hockey once I was out of college and established in a career. And although I am getting older I am still in great shape (I do crossfit) and work hard on the ice. I saw that you needed a wing which is perfect. I prefer left wing but I'll take either (my old team had me at defense a lot and it isn't my strongest role, although I'll roll with whatever you need (get it?))I just hope that you will take me aboard. You can call text or email, my info is attached. I can pay up front. I looked on the website but your team doesn't have a picture. What colors do you wear? Are there specific socks I should buy? I assume you have a jersey for me. I normally play under number 14 but honestly it doesn't really matter. Anyhow, I hope to hear from you soon. If I don't I might give you a call, I hope that alright since you did post both a phone number and email address. Talk to you soon.

xxxChristinexxxx

It was long, but it was precisely the type of news Fitz needed today. *This lady is a little intense. But at least she wants to play with us.* Fitz scanned the email again. *She's asking about numbers already? And specific socks?* Fitz chuckled as she forward the email to the other team founders.

"What's so funny?" Tom's voice made her jump. She hadn't heard him come in. In her excitement about the new player, she'd finally stopped thinking about Tom and their fight, but now it all came crashing back.

"Oh, hi, uh, it was just a—." She almost said *'just a hockey thing,'* but she stopped herself. "It's nothing. Supper will be done in fifteen minutes."

Tom looked at her a moment, his expression blank, before he turned on his heel and walked off to his den. The quiet in the kitchen suddenly felt oppressive. Fitz nearly jumped out of her skin when her cell buzzed.

> Michelle: OMG that email! TL;DR!! I have LITERALLY read shorter statutes! this bitch is crazy
> Michelle: sign her up ;D
> Fitz: Does she seem too intense??
> Michelle: Bitch YOU seem too intense. LOL. Honestly idgaf she is my REPLACEMENT
> Tessa: I didn't have time to do more than skim it but she seems fine. A wing even! you should respond
> Fitz: Should I tell her she's on the team?
> Tessa: that's what I was thinking
> Fitz: Ok I will!
> Michelle: Perfect! Nothing to worry about now!

Yeah, nothing to worry about at all. No need to worry about whether she's any good, or if she'll fit in, or if we will be able to win enough games to get off probation. Fitz glanced in the direction of Tom's den. *Or if this whole thing is going to cost me my marriage.*

146

Tessa

Saturday, November 18th

> Tessa: I'm interviewing for a new job on Monday! I'm so
> excited!
> Dragon: Congrats! That's awesome!
> Tessa: I know right?! I can not wait to get away from the
> douche-bros at Hill House!

Dragon didn't text back. No surprise. He'd been so butthurt lately over her comments about men being assholes. She meant the men at work usually, but still, Dragon took any general complaint about men annoyingly personally. *Maybe if I get this new job, I won't work with so many assholes, and he'll stop being so fucking sensitive.*

Tessa was excited about the job opportunity: a manager position at a medical engineering firm called HCAF. HCAF had a stellar reputation for their workplace culture, and Tessa was so done with the culture at Hill House. She had submitted her resume on Monday and was shocked to get called for a video interview by Wednesday. Now she had an in-person interview scheduled for next week. The process had been fast and intense, but so exciting.

Tessa's mind was running through interview questions as she drove to the rink. She was totally thrown for a loop when she found the Darts' new player waiting in the locker room when she arrived. Christine was dressed in jeans and flannel, but Tessa couldn't help but notice the hockey bag at her feet.

"Uh, I'm sorry, didn't Fitz tell you?" Tessa stammered awkwardly. "We don't really need a player until December. Michelle's pregnant but—"

147

"Oh, of course, no, I understood," Christine interrupted brightly. "I figured it wouldn't hurt to come anyway. The schedule's on the website, so I looked it up, and here I am! I can just watch if you have enough skaters. I don't want to put anybody out. I know some people really hate it when there's an odd number of players. There was a lady on my old team that would go absolutely batshit if we had eleven skaters, so I am totally used to that. I'm just here to meet the team! I'm happy to open doors on the bench or—"

"That's okay," Tessa cut her off. *Damn, she talks just like she writes!* "You're here, you should play."

Christine thanked her exuberantly. As the other players arrived, Christine continued to talk non-stop, introducing herself to each person one by one. Eventually, she settled down next to Michelle and started getting dressed.

"So, Michelle, you're the pregnant one, right?" Christine grinned effusively at Michelle.

"That's what pee-stick says." Michelle's tone said, *'why are you talking to me?'* but apparently Christine didn't speak 'Michelle.'

"You are so skinny, I can't believe you're pregnant! How far along are you?"

"About eight weeks," Michelle responded tersely.

"Well, that explains why you're so skinny, and how you're still playing hockey. It's great to get exercise during pregnancy, although you'll probably want to stop soon, I would guess— protect that little one. Women's hockey is non-check, but there are some women in this league who are incredibly physical. It would be such a shame if anything happened, I can't imagine how you'd feel." Christine, dressing as she spoke, was paying no attention at all to Michelle, who was staring at her, looking both shocked and incredibly pissed off.

"Now look, lady—"

"Not that anything will probably happen, of course. Tons of women play pregnant. There was this woman I played with back several years ago who played until her belly didn't fit in her pants anymore. But she might not have even known she was pregnant. It seems like you're more on top of things than that." Christine laughed to herself.

Michelle caught Tessa's eye and mouthed, '*what the fuck?*' Tessa shrugged deeply, burying her head inside her shoulder pads.

'*Sorry,*' she mouthed back. Michelle scowled darkly. Christine was still going. There seemed to be no end to her wealth of pregnancy tips and stories. *I hope she knows half as much about hockey as she seems to know about babies.*

During warm-ups, Michelle pulled Fitz aside. It looked confrontational. Tessa skated to join them.

"Yeah, she talks a bit much, doesn't she?" said Fitz.

"A bit?!" Michelle yell-whispered. She grabbed Fitz's jersey aggressively and pulled her closer. "Bitch just grilled me on what hospital I was going to deliver in then told me stories about every person she's ever known to set foot there! And oh, apparently the doctors are great because they're *Jewish*. Oh my God. I have never heard somebody talk that much. And I'm a lawyer! But hey, I'm probably a good one because I'm *Jewish!*"

"What's going on? Are you talking about Christine?" Tessa asked, even though she knew the answer. Fitz nodded grimly.

"Don't worry, she's just meeting the team today, if she doesn't work out—" Fitz began.

"'*If*?" Michelle tightened her grip on Fitz's jersey. Tessa hoped she was being dramatic and wasn't actually as upset as she seemed. Fitz yanked her jersey from Michelle's hand.

"If she does play with us again, it won't be until after you're gone, okay?" she snapped.

"You'd better be right," Michelle said. "Because I can not drink alcohol right now, and that lady is driving me to the bottle."

"We'll handle it," Tessa promised. Satisfied for the moment, Michelle skated off the ice.

"Are you alright?" Tessa asked Fitz. "You look stressed out."

"It's fine, Michelle's just being Michelle, and she has a point." Fitz sighed. "Really, I'm fine, I've got other stuff on my mind is all. Don't worry about it. Let's play hockey."

Tessa kept an extra eye on Christine during the game. She was good. Astonishingly good. She was smart, quick, and her shot was fierce. *She's better than Michelle.* Christine was reading the ice and making passes so clean it was like she knew the team intuitively. This time the Darts held the Highlanders to a tie.

After the game, Fitz slid into the seat next to Tessa at the Dart and let out a long, contented sigh.

"Ah, home, sweet Dart. Have I ever mentioned that this is my favorite place on earth?" she asked.

Tessa laughed. "Only about every time we come out." Tessa grinned at Fitz. "Good game today, by the way. You played really hard."

Fitz stretched her shoulders. "Thanks. It felt good. Even if we didn't win."

"I'll take a tie. It was a good game," said Tessa.

Across the table, Michelle dropped into her seat with a huff. "Okay, now that we're all here, cheers, bitches!" she said immediately. "And speaking of bitches—"

"We don't even have our drinks yet," Tessa pointed out.

"I really just wanted to say 'and speaking of bitches.'" Michelle dismissed Tessa with a wave. "I need to talk about this Christine chick. Because she certainly can talk. She actually told me I shouldn't use pain meds during labor, and that I wouldn't need them anyway if I 'just had a doula!' Like, who the actual fuck asked you? I don't know about having her play with us. I just can't even with that one."

Tessa grimaced. She and Fitz had already given Christine the spot on the team. Christine was too good to turn away. *Michelle won't even be around, why should she care?* Tessa and Fitz had agreed and acted without talking to the others. *Maybe we should have. Nothing to be done about it now.*

Listening to Michelle complain wasn't going to do anyone any good. And it was clearly stressing Fitz out. This was exactly the type of thing Fitz had been trying to avoid with the new team. Tessa knew she could swing the conversation in another direction, but she hadn't planned to bring it up. *It's worth risking a jinx to help Fitz have a good time.*

"Did I tell you guys I might be getting a new job?" Tessa announced loudly, completely interrupting the discussion.

"What? No!" Michelle exclaimed. And like that, Christine was forgotten as Michelle grilled Tessa for details. Tessa was optimistic about her chances of getting the job offer, but she knocked on the wooden surface of the table when she said so.

Fitz nudged Tessa's shoulder. "It's so cool to see you working hard to get what you need to be happy. You're amazing, I'm totally in awe of you." Fitz put her hand on Tessa's shoulder and Tessa felt her face warm. She shook her head.

"Seriously!" Fitz insisted. "You're a super career woman, strong, smart. Totally amazing. I wish I were half as amazing as you. I'm jealous."

"Jealous? What are you talking about? You've got the whole American dream thing going: a husband, two kids, an insanely gorgeous house. That's the whole package, right?" said Tessa. Fitz shrugged; she looked almost ashamed. "I mean, it's not for everyone," Tessa continued, "but it suits you. You're an amazing mom. You've always got so much going on, I don't know how you do all that you do."

"It's just that until recently, I hadn't given much thought to what I would do if..." Fitz paused a long moment and just stared at her drink before shaking her head. "I mean, now that the kids are in school all day, I'm starting to think about what's next. I guess I didn't expect that, at my age, I'd be asking myself, 'what do I want to be when I grow up?' and coming up blank. I just feel so pathetic."

Tessa cocked her head to the side, looking at Fitz thoughtfully. She couldn't understand how such an incredible woman could have such a low opinion of herself. But at the same time, Tessa couldn't imagine being personally fulfilled without her career, and her sense of self-reliance and accomplishment. For all its frustrations, at least her job gave her that.

"Do you want to start a career? Or just look for a job or something?" Tessa asked.

"I don't know. I'm not sure what I would even do. I don't have experience with much of anything."

"Would you want to go back to school?" Tessa finally got the attention of the waitress and ordered a beer. She needed it; this much emotional discussion was hella draining.

"No, I don't think so. I don't think that would be the right thing for me. I don't have the time. I mean, objectively I guess my life is good. I just, I wish it felt more, I don't know... Satisfying. Like I'm a real adult contributing to society or something."

Tessa got her beer and took a long drink. She felt the edges dull and sighed. She looked hard at her friend. "You contributed this team to society," Tessa said.

Fitz stared at her blankly.

Tessa tried again. "You said you wanted to contribute to society. You started this team, we might be a small part of society, but it makes a difference to us." Tessa gestured around the table. Dawn, Michelle, Nikki, Tiffany, Emily. They all looked happy as they sat, chatting and drinking. Tessa grinned at Fitz. "See? We're a team."

"Yeah, I suppose," Fitz agreed reluctantly. "For now."

"What do you mean 'for now'?" Tessa squinted at her. Fitz ducked her head.

"It's just one thing after another, you know? We had a hard enough time finding players, the league has us on probation, and then we lose Michelle..."

"We haven't lost her yet, and we already have a new skater lined up," said Tessa.

"A player that nobody can stand," Fitz pointed out stubbornly.

Tessa groaned. *I thought we were done bitching about Christine tonight.*

"It's been one game—give her time. She's a good hockey player." *What is up with Fitz today?* Fitz could be intense, but Tessa wasn't used to her being this negative. "So there was a little unexpected drama, who cares? The next game will be better."

Sunday, November 26th

Tessa never should have said the next game would be better. She'd jinxed it, there was no doubt in her mind. *I am such a moron.* For Tessa, it started early in the first period with a simple trip. Tessa barely had time to register the player standing behind her before her feet were pulled out from under her. Tessa hit the ice hard on her ass.

"What the hell was that for!?" Tessa yelled indignantly as the offending player skated away. No refs had seen it. Tessa grumbled as she picked herself back up and got off the ice.

"What the hell is wrong with this team?" Tessa said as she sat down on the bench, "That was blatant and pointless! The puck wasn't anywhere near us!" She took a swig of water. "And it fucking hurt."

"Just be glad you're not pregnant. Falls like that knock the piss out of me, literally," said Michelle. "And I don't need piss-pants, thank you very little."

"For me, the peeing thing didn't end with pregnancy." Fitz chuckled.

"Okay, stop. For the millionth time, you guys, I don't need to hear that stuff." Tessa shook her head.

"You okay?" asked Andy. Andy had warned Tessa that the Ice Queens were dangerous.

I should have taken them more seriously. Andy had played with the Ice Queens for a couple of years prior; they'd left the team because it was 'not their type of people' and didn't make them 'feel safe.'

Andy hadn't said much more than that, but Tessa had made her own assumptions. She had read into Andy's few words that the team hadn't been open and accepting of them. But now that she saw the Ice Queens up close and personal, Tessa had to reevaluate those assumptions. This game wasn't 'safe' for *anybody*. The Ice Queens were playing like they had a personal vendetta against each and every one of the Darts. *Somebody's going to get hurt out here today.* This wasn't fun beer league hockey, this was bedlam and violence and a puck.

"I can't believe you played with these guys," said Tessa. "This team *sucks.* Seriously, are they even playing hockey, or did they just come here to practice their golf swings on our calves?"

"This is about *par for the course* with them." Andy snorted and shook their head. "They do it on purpose. They think it's a strategy. Be glad if it's just a trip, or hey, a hook. Look, they've got Jess right across the belly."

Andy pointed out to the ice. Jess was fighting her way to the net as the Ice Queens tried to pull her down from behind. *Aren't the refs going to call anything?*

Between periods they gathered at the bench. The Darts were getting increasingly irritated by the Ice Queens. Each of them had been hit, tripped, held, or otherwise roughed up by one or more of their players.

"What is up with this team?" Jess grumbled.

"They are a bit dirty," said Fitz.

"A *bit* dirty? They've got more cheap tricks than a ninety-year-old hooker! What the fuck kind of game do they think this is?" Michelle roared. Nikki nodded and giggled. Emboldened, Michelle turned her head towards the other team's bench. "*It's just old lady hockey! Calm your tits!*" she shouted.

She probably wasn't loud enough for the Ice Queens to hear. But all the same, it made Tessa uncomfortable. Fitz didn't look happy about it either.

"Hey, let's not get an unsportsmanlike penalty here." Tessa gave Michelle a pleading look. "We don't want to get on the ref's bad side."

"Whatever," Michelle muttered. "It's not like the refs are *calling anything!*" she shouted again.

"Hey, shut it," snapped Fitz, "Okay, so they're playing really dirty, but we have to keep cool. Don't retaliate, turn the other cheek."

Michelle groaned loudly and rolled her eyes.

Fitz ignored her. "The refs have to call something one of these times, and we don't want it to be on us. We can win this one y'all. We're controlling the puck, we're out-shooting them."

"I agree," interjected Dawn. "They're just trying to get a rise out of us. We have to keep working at it and not let them get to us."

Tessa nodded; Dawn was right—the Ice Queens were being purposely provocative, and they couldn't let themselves rise to the bait.

The second period continued much like the first. If anything, the Ice Queens were even more aggressive, but the Darts were playing well, keeping the Ice Queens on the defensive most of the time. A few minutes in, one of the Ice Queens put a hard shoulder into Nikki that sent her sprawling onto the ice. Everybody on the bench jumped up.

"What was that?" yelled Tessa. The ref put his arm up and blew the whistle.

"Number fifteen, white, two minutes for roughing."

Fifteen glided over to the box to cheers from her teammates.

"About fucking time!" shouted Michelle as she took Nikki's place on the ice.

"Hey, okay, settle down." Fitz hopped onto the ice with her. "Now let's take our time, make good passes."

As the Darts controlled the play, the Ice Queens got visibly more and more frustrated. There was a scuffle in front of the net. Michelle went in after a rebound, the goalie covered it, and the ref blew his whistle. After the play should have been over, the Ice Queen's defender cross-checked Michelle from behind, knocking her down. When she jumped back up, she was fuming. She looked ready for a fight.

"Are you fucking kidding me?" Michelle roared. Fitz jumped in and quickly pulled Michelle away.

"Bitch." Michelle spat as she let herself be led off. Once back at the bench, Michelle turned on Fitz. "How are you staying so *fucking* calm? That cockwagon punched me in the back! *After the play!*"

"Sit down," said Fitz through gritted teeth, her voice stone cold. Tessa tensed. Fitz took a breath. "I am staying calm because I think I'd rather win this game than spend the rest of it in the box. And I think you would too, so *cool off.*"

During the period break, Fitz tried talking to the refs, but from what Tessa could see, the conversation didn't go well. The officials in their league didn't have the best reputation for taking player input well.

"Were the refs upset that you complained?" Tessa asked when Fitz returned. Fitz shrugged and shook her head.

"They didn't really respond, so let's just assume it'll keep being called the way it has been."

"Which is not at all. Fucking hell. If they don't call something, I'm going to seriously lose my shit," Michelle growled as the third period got underway.

The Darts got a second goal, extending their lead, but their celebration was short-lived. During the next shift, one of the Ice Queens brutally slammed Emily into the boards. Tessa froze—time seemed to stand still as she waited to see if Emily would get back up. After a few gut-wrenching seconds, Emily slowly rolled to her back.

The ref knelt beside Emily and, after a short exchange, helped Emily to her feet. Tessa barely had time to register her relief because the next thing she knew, Michelle was up in the face of the player who'd hit Emily.

"Are you an *actual* psychopath?" she screamed. "This is *recreational* hockey! We have jobs and lives to go back to, asshole!"

"She got the penalty," called a woman from the Ice Queens' bench. "Why don't you calm *your* tits, lady!"

Michelle turned on her in a flash. Tessa had never seen Michelle so angry. Her face glowed red with rage as she skated toward the Ice Queens.

"Excuse me?! Who the *fuck* are you to tell me to calm down!" Michelle looked like she was going to take the woman's head off. In a flash Fitz was off the bench and at Michelle's side, pulling her away from the opposing team.

Michelle turned away from the Ice Queens' bench only to turn on the referee. Tessa stood shocked, watching the altercation. Michelle stood toe to toe with the ref, as Fitz tugged uselessly at her arm.

"She should be ejected!" she shouted in his face. "That was boarding! There are rules about boarding for a reason! Because it's fucking dangerous!"

"Ma'am, please sit down before I—"

"Before you what?" Michelle glared, red-faced at the ref. He stared back blandly. Fitz tried again to move her, but Michelle shook her off. "Before you get your head out of your ass and actually do your fucking job?!"

The ref scowled; he'd had enough. "That's it, you need to get in the box, five-minute major."

"Are you fucking kidding me?!" Michelle didn't make a move toward the box, she just stared at the ref, seething. Fitz took Michelle by the shoulders and dragged her along the ice.

"Come on, Michelle, just get in the box," Fitz said. Michelle pushed her off roughly.

"Fuck off! Don't tell me what to do! You don't get to tell me what to fucking do, Fitz! You might be the goddamn *self-appointed* captain, but you know that doesn't mean shit!"

"I *am* the captain, and you're on *my team*, so get in the damn box!" Fitz shouted back, no longer able to maintain her cool.

"*Your* team, huh? Well then do something for *your* team and stand up to those mother*fuckers* over there before they hurt one of us! Did you see what they did to Emily? To me? I'm pregnant, for God's sake!"

"I didn't ask you to get *pregnant!*" Fitz snapped. Tessa couldn't believe this was happening; she looked back and forth between the two. Michelle's face had gone rigid. She stepped back, nodding slowly.

"Well, fuck you too." Michelle's voice was low and cold.

"Michelle, I—"

"Shut up, Fitz!" Michelle threw her stick over the bench with a scream. It sailed over the heads of her stunned teammates and clattered against the wall. "I'm sorry you feel *pathetic* and that your husband's a giant *dick*, but you can't make me feel bad for having a good goddamn life outside of this fucking rink! Fuck your precious team! Fuck the whole damn sport, for all I care! I don't need any of this!" Angrily Michelle pulled off each of her gloves and threw them as well. She clapped her hands together. "I am out!"

Michelle took one more second to flip off the Ice Queens and refs before she ripped off her helmet and stormed off the ice. The whole team stood dumbfounded as she disappeared into the locker room with a bang. Tessa had never seen anybody lose it like that.

"Holy shit," whispered Nikki under her breath. Nobody else on the bench moved or spoke until the ref skated over.

He tapped the top of the boards with his palm and snapped them out their shocked silence. He looked completely nonplussed. Like it was just business as usual to him. *If that doesn't get a rise out of him, he must have seen some really intense shit in his time.*

"Somebody from your team will have to serve her penalty," he said matter-of-factly. There was a chorus of '*what*,' '*why*,' and '*are you kidding*,' but Fitz waved off the team's complaints, silently stepped into the penalty box, and sat down. Her eyes were fixed ahead of her, she didn't look back at the team. Dawn pulled at Tessa's elbow.

"Come on, let's just get this over with."

Michelle

Sunday, November 26th

"I didn't ask you to get *pregnant!*"

Michelle felt like she'd been slapped. On some level, she'd always known that Fitz was pissed that she'd gotten pregnant, but to hear her say it stung more than she would ever have anticipated.

"Well, fuck you too." Rage burned inside her.

"Michelle, I—" Fitz began, but Michelle didn't want to hear another *syllable* from that self-righteous *bitch*.

"Shut up, Fitz!" she yelled. Then she screamed—a primal, angry, scream—and tossed her stick. It bounced with an unsatisfactory clank against the wall. The heat of her fury was too much to contain. "I'm sorry you feel *pathetic* and that your husband's a giant *dick*, but you can't make me feel bad for having a good goddamn life outside of this fucking rink! Fuck your precious team! Fuck the whole damn sport, for all I care! I don't need any of this!" Michelle threw down her gloves. Good riddance. She was wiping her hands of this whole goddamn shitshow. "I am out!"

She flipped off the Ice Queens, and the ref for good measure. *Jackass motherfuckers.* The rage burned in her chest and throat. She hadn't even registered that she'd taken off her helmet until she heard the cracking sound it made as it hit the boards.

Michelle pushed her way into the locker room and slammed the door shut. She ripped off her jersey, balled it up, and threw it across the room with another guttural scream. Michelle was breathing hard, seething with fury. She tore off the rest of her gear and tossed it into her bag. She struggled to untie her skates, her hands shaking too hard.

"Goddamnit," she growled as she fumbled with the laces. She had to keep moving. She knew if she stopped moving, her anger would break, and the lump in her throat would turn into tears, and the last thing she wanted right now was to cry.

Fuck Fitz, goddamn motherfucking bitch. Finally, she got her skates off. *And fuck those motherfucking cunt wenches on the fucking Ice Queens. What the actual fuck is wrong with them?* She stuffed the rest of her equipment away and pulled on her clothes. *And what the fuck is wrong with me? Jesus mother fuck, get your shit together.*

Michelle hurried out of the arena without so much as a glance at the ice where the game had resumed. She could hear the clatter of sticks, the bang of the puck against the boards. Tears welled in her eyes and she walked faster.

Outside it was cold and dark. Soft snowflakes fluttered in the icy breeze. Michelle's eyes stung with the tears she could no longer contain. She screamed once more in frustration and then began to sob. Michelle hated crying. She threw her gear violently into her car. *Did I really just quit?* She didn't want to think about it. She *refused* to think about it. She took a few long deep breaths and gritted her teeth. *Get yourself under control. Jesus.*

Michelle turned on NPR and tried to put hockey out of her mind. By the time she got home, her eyes were dry, and her hands were no longer shaking. Inside she was still frustrated, hurt, and pissed as hell, but for the moment, she'd regained control.

Michelle tried to look back on the game with analytical detachment. There was a reason she'd gotten pissed off: the Ice Queens played like assholes. They made the game dangerous. And the reffing had been such utter *bullshit*. But the way she had reacted might have been over the top.

That was some fit I threw back there. Shit. Michelle could blame some of it on the pregnancy hormones. *'I didn't ask you to get pregnant.'* Michelle didn't want to think about that part. *I know I had already lost my shit, but she didn't have to go there.* Fitz was being somewhat of a high-strung bitch lately, but still, Michelle almost felt bad for yelling at her—almost sorry for what she'd said. Almost, but not quite.

Back at home, she gave Ben only the most basic recount of the game.

"There's more to it, but I don't want to get too worked up about it again." She touched his arm. Ben didn't argue or pry.

"Here then, let me distract you." He pulled her close and kissed her. She kissed him back.

Maybe a good hard fuck will make me feel better. "Give it to me rough," she demanded, pulling him onto the bed.

Ben smiled wickedly. He ran his fingers into her hair and, gripping tight, yanked her head back as his other hand grabbed at her. "Is this what you want?" he asked in a low growl.

"Yes," she breathed. *God, I love this man.* She let herself get lost in the physical sensations of the violent and fiercely primal way he took her. Several orgasms later, Michelle felt lighter, relaxed, centered. *That was exactly what I needed.*

"You have a good time?" Ben asked, kissing her bare shoulder. He was covered in a thin sheen of sweat. He looked tired. He had done all the work, after all.

Michelle smiled. "Mmmmmm... yes, I did." She stretched out on the bed and picked up her phone. She had a text from Dawn. "You go shower, babe. You're all sweaty."

"You're not going to join me?" Ben pushed off the bed. Michelle shook her head.

"Not this time, but hey, that was really good stuff, babe. Just what the doctor ordered." She grinned at him. "Thanks for doing all the fucking work."

"All the *fucking* work..." Ben laughed as he closed the bathroom door. Michelle looked back at her phone; she thought about the hockey game. About her team. About Fitz. Michelle sighed and shook her head. *I told her you couldn't get a group of women together without drama.*

Dawn

Sunday, November 26th

Michelle's outburst and subsequent fight with Fitz threw the Darts off their axis. Even so, there was only so much damage they could do in half a period. The Darts held on to their lead and came out with a two to one win. But it didn't feel like a win. There was no joy in it. Dawn picked up Michelle's gloves and stick on her way back to the locker room after the game. Michelle was gone, along with the rest of her gear.

Dawn undressed slowly, her mind both jumbled and blank. *What just happened? Is Michelle ever coming back?* Michelle had been so upset. Michelle had always had a flair for the dramatic, but had this gone too far? *She is pregnant.* Maybe that would be enough of an excuse for Fitz to let it blow over. Dawn hoped so. She looked at Fitz. From the look on her face, Dawn could see it wasn't going to be easy. Her insides twisted.

"Are you coming out to the Dart?" Tessa asked. Dawn shook her head. She wished she could. Dawn would have liked the chance to talk to Fitz and make sure their captain was okay. But Dawn had an early shift tomorrow, and she owed Sharon some cuddle time yet tonight.

"Sorry," Dawn rubbed her head. "I'll see you next week, though?"

Tessa nodded. Dawn watched her friends file out of the locker room. She gathered up her things, as well as Michelle's, and headed for home.

> Dawn: Hey, I have your gloves and stick fyi
> Dawn: and jersey
> Michelle: Thanks. Sorry. I'll get them from you later.
> Dawn: Are you really done?

Dawn: Playing, I mean
Michelle: IDK
Michelle: Fitz probably wouldn't want me there anyway
Michelle: She must be so pissed lol
Dawn: I don't know. I didn't go out after the game...
Dawn: I hope you do come back
Michelle: We'll see

Saturday, December 2nd

Dawn: Hey, Michelle! Are you coming to the next game?
Dawn: I think Tessa's going to call Christine in early
unless we hear from you
Dawn: Hope things are ok!

Saturday, December 9th

Dawn: Hey baby girl, we missed you today, hope you're
doing ok!

Tuesday, December 11th

Dawn: Were you still going to plan the holiday party?
LMK Miss you!

Saturday, December 16th

Dawn: Hey, Michelle, sorry to keep bugging you but we
miss you, baby girl! We keep losing. :P
Dawn: Let me know about the party, because if you're out
I said I'd host it

Friday, December 22nd

> Dawn: Did you get the evite I sent? Hope you can come!
> Are you showing yet? Miss you, boo-boo!

Dawn texted Michelle every game day, and sometimes non-game days, but Michelle never responded. Time marched on; games came and went. The Darts lost one after another after another. The match-ups were competitive; the Darts could keep up with the other teams for the most part, but they just couldn't find their flow. They would out-shoot a team and still lose. It was like the puck didn't want to bounce their way. Fitz was getting increasingly anxious with each loss.

Fitz's agitation was immediately evident in her posture when Dawn greeted her before the next game. She stood outside the locker room, rubbing her temples, her shoulders hunched.

"You okay, boo-boo?" Dawn stepped up next to her captain.

Fitz rolled her head from side to side. "I'm just thinking about the game today. I'm trying to figure out why we can't seem to win lately. It's so *frustrating*. And now there are only two games left before the holiday break! We really need a win. If we don't start winning more games, we're not going to make it off probation.

"Forget probation!" Fitz's voice grew louder and more frantic as she spoke. "If we keep up like this, we could seriously end up in last place! If we get kicked out of this division, then what? Move down? We'd need to apply to get into our old division, and you know Jackie would fight that. Oh my God, and that would be a whole thing. And even if we did get moved down, you know they wouldn't let Brooke or Nikki come with us. They *just assessed*! And Andy too! Who knows who else wouldn't be able to come down with us!" Fitz was close to hyperventilating. "If they tear our team in half, I don't know what I could even do! I might as well give up the whole thing."

"Hey, hey now, you're spiraling." Dawn put her hands on Fitz's shoulders, forcing Fitz to face her. Dawn looked up into her friend's harried face. There was a crease between her brows, and she was chewing her bottom lip raw. *Come on, baby girl, we play hockey for fun. Remember that. Don't overthink it.* Somehow Dawn didn't think that telling Fitz to stop overthinking would help. "Take a breath. Let's try to focus on today. Who are we playing today, boo-boo?"

"The Sally Cats."

"That sounds familiar... Have we played them?" It didn't make much difference to Dawn, but Fitz was the type to keep track—it mattered to her.

Fitz turned and leaned against the glass. "Yeah, our third game. We tied."

"Well, that's good! That means we have a reasonable shot here!" Dawn grinned up at her. Fitz's mouth moved in what might have been the hint of a smile. "Come on, baby girl." Dawn squeezed Fitz's shoulder again. "Let's start getting ready."

Dawn had been right to be optimistic. The teams were evenly matched, but after their string of losses the Darts were hungrier, and for once lady luck was on their side. By the time they ended the second period they were up three to one, and Fitz seemed to have put aside her doom-and-gloom predictions of the team's untimely demise.

"Lord, it's good to be winning for once," Fitz said with a sigh.

"Jesus, Fitz, when will you learn never to say the W-word mid-game!" Tessa admonished. "If we didn't have that safety goal, I would legit punch you."

"Forget about the safety goal," Christine began. "Just because we're up by two—"

"Yes, I know, *Christine*," Fitz cut her off. She'd taken to doing that a lot lately. Most of the team was sick to death of Christine's commentary, and Fitz was just trying to keep everything running smoothly. "We can't get lazy. A two-goal lead is the most dangerous lead in hockey, especially going into the third period. We need to keep up the hustle. Now let's get out there and do it!"

Halfway through the third period, Tiffany tripped over her own feet; she hit the ice and slid into the boards hard. The Darts momentarily froze in concern, but Tiffany got up quickly and they breathed a collective sigh of relief as she made her way to the bench. Taking advantage of the distraction, the Sally Cats passed to their open player in front of the net who one-timed it, right past AJ, narrowing their lead to three-two.

"Sorry, guys, that was totally my fault." Brooke sat down next to her D partner. "Tiffany, are you okay?"

Tiffany was cradling her right hand, silent tears streaming down her face. *Uh-oh.* Dawn's nursing senses started to tingle. Dawn slid down the bench to her teammate. She helped Tiffany ease off her glove. Tiffany inhaled sharply. Slowly and gently, Dawn walked her fingers along Tiffany's hand. Tiffany winced. *Crap.*

"Okay, it looks like you have a broken finger, sweetie." Dawn put Tiffany's hand down gently. Dawn looked at Fitz.

"I'm going to take care of Tiffany." *Can't skate and nurse at the same time.*

"Don't worry, y'all, we got this." Fitz turned back to the game, and Dawn focused on helping Tiffany.

"You'll be okay, boo-boo," Dawn assured her. "It's only a finger, you know, 'just a flesh wound.'"

"Thank you," Tiffany said gratefully.

"Of course, baby girl," Dawn rubbed Tiffany's back. "You just remember this when I blow it on the ice, and you wonder why I'm even on this team."

After the game, Dawn lingered in the locker room with her teammates. They were at the Sally Cats' home rink, too far from the Dart for a post-game outing. But Tessa had brought a case of beer and Fitz had convinced them to hang out for a while.

"Here's to a big win," Nikki said, raising her beer can. "Cheers, bitches!"

It's so weird to do that toast without Michelle, Dawn thought.

"And to our resident nurse," Nikki added after a gulp, "for taking care of our fallen comrade."

Dawn nodded. "I'm always ready to take care of my girls. Although I'd rather not have to."

"It really sucks that Tiffany got hurt," said Jess.

"Yeah, the Darts really can't catch a break, can we?" Fitz groaned.

"Catch a *break*?" Tessa side-eyed Fitz.

"Pun *not* intended!" Fitz rolled her eyes. "I just mean we finally win a game but at the same time lose another player? It's ridiculous!"

"How long do you think she'll be out?" Tessa asked, looking at Dawn. Dawn shrugged.

"A month or two, I'd guess. It depends on the severity and all that." It was hard to know without x-rays. Fitz put her head in her hands. They'd just won, and their captain was immediately back to looking stressed and despondent.

"We were already shorthanded for tomorrow," Tessa said with a sigh. "That game is going to be rough."

"Sorry, guys. I'm letting you down tomorrow." Dawn hung her head and pushed out her bottom lip into a pout. "I wish I could be there."

Instead of playing hockey, Dawn would be trapped in a crowded auditorium listening to her twins play in the middle school band concert. Her ears were ringing just thinking about it. Dawn would rather be playing hockey, but she loved her kids. Besides, she couldn't leave Sharon to face the cacophony alone.

"Don't even worry about it," said Tessa. "We'll figure it out."

"We have a break in our games because of the holidays coming up. If Tiff's finger does only take a month or so to heal then she shouldn't miss *that* many games," said Nikki.

"Speaking of the holidays!" said Dawn louder than she had intended. They all stared at her. She cleared her throat and continued. "Don't forget to remember to be thinking about your white elephant!" *Smooth, Dawn, good talking. Very English. Wow.* Dawn grinned awkwardly.

"I can't wait!" Christine piped back. Dawn kept smiling, but she knew there were several people on the team who had been hoping Christine wouldn't be able to make the party.

Nothing to be done about it. If Christine noticed the subtle wave of disappointment around her, she didn't show it. *Hopefully, that won't stop Michelle from attending. I miss her.*

Fitz

Saturday, December 23rd

Fitz sat in her car, crying. Again. It seemed to happen a lot these days. She didn't know what else to do. Hockey had once been her happy place, but that was all falling apart. The Darts were a *mess*. Nobody had even bothered to go out after tonight's game. It was the last game of the year, the last game before the holidays, and it had been awful.

It was no wonder they'd lost. The Darts never really had a shot against the Riverside Ringers—one of the best teams in the league—not with only seven skaters. Tiffany's finger was broken, just like Dawn had said, which was probably why Emily had bowed out. Dawn couldn't make it for family reasons; none of their subs were available. And nobody had seen or heard from Michelle since November. *Michelle.* Today would have been her last game.

'*I didn't ask you to get pregnant.*' Fitz had regretted it the moment she'd said it. She didn't blame Michelle for lashing out at her, but her words had stung. '*I'm sorry you feel pathetic and that your husband's a giant dick.*' Fitz couldn't really argue, but it still hurt. Fitz's emotions swung between guilt and frustration. There was nothing she could do but take each day as it came, and pray.

I can't keep wallowing in the car, that is pathetic. Fitz pushed down her feelings, shoved them hard into the deep corners of her mind. She took long, deep breaths until her tears stopped and didn't threaten to come again. With robot-like motions, she stepped out of the car.

"You're back early." Tom was in the kitchen when Fitz stepped through from the mudroom. She felt like she was walking in a fog—pushing away her feelings about her teammates made everything else hazy.

"Yeah, I didn't feel like going out." Her own voice sounded far away.

"I think hell just froze over," Tom muttered.

"Did y'all already eat?"

"The kids are both at sleepovers, remember?" he asked. Fitz hadn't remembered.

"Oh, yeah." She paused and forced herself to focus on Tom. "Have you eaten?"

"I was just about to." He gestured vaguely at the fridge. Left alone, Tom would probably have just eaten cold-cuts straight out of the package, washed them down with a beer and called it supper.

"Sit down, I'll make something." Fitz sighed. "How was your day?"

Tom began to talk about meetings, clients, and coworkers. Fitz had a hard time focusing on his words. Try as she might, she could not stop thinking about her teammates and all the emotions she'd rather not have.

She didn't want to be mad at Michelle for leaving them early, or at Emily for not coming to the game after Tiffany had gotten hurt, or at their subs for not being available to play half the time they were needed. Fitz tried not to be irritated that she was always working to keep Christine under control so as not to upset the rest of the team. Above all else, she struggled not to be bitter over all the time and effort she'd poured into the Darts only to see them lose game after game.

"Are you okay, Patricia?" Tom asked, snapping Fitz out of her thoughts. She blinked at him. It was unusually perceptive of him to notice that she wasn't herself.

"Yeah, I'm fine," she stammered, caught off-guard. "I'm just... mad we lost. And that people didn't show up." She frowned and looked down at her dinner plate. *Tom doesn't want to hear about this.* To her surprise, Tom began to laugh. Fitz looked up, startled. "What's so funny?"

"It's just nice not to be the one you're mad at, for once." Tom stood up, shaking his head and chuckling softly to himself.

He is a dick.

"Why don't you go shower; I'll take care of these, Belle." He picked the plates up off the table.

Fitz hesitated a moment. *But maybe not all the time?* Slowly she nodded and turned for the door. If he was going to offer to do the dishes, something he almost never did, Fitz wasn't about to argue.

"Thanks." She turned and walked slowly up the stairs.

When she stepped out of the bathroom in her nightdress, Tom was in the bedroom, waiting for her. He'd been sitting on the bed but stood when she entered the room. He had an expectant look on his face. He stepped closer to her. His stormy eyes locked on hers, and Fitz's chest tightened. She took an involuntary step back and bumped into the bathroom door.

"Ow," she said reflexively, although it hadn't actually hurt. He drew closer and put a hand around her waist.

"Be careful, Belle," he said, his voice low and husky. Her breath caught in her throat as he leaned forward and began to kiss her. For a moment, Fitz didn't move; she stood perfectly still and let him kiss her. Then his hands began to move along the curves of her body, and an unwelcome shiver crawled up her spine. She put her hands up to push him away.

"Tom, stop." She turned her head, but he continued to kiss her neck, his hands tightening around her waist and pushing his hips hard against hers. "Tom, please, I'm tired."

She wriggled free and stepped past him to her side of the bed. Her hands shook slightly as she put on lotion and slid under the covers. She didn't look back over at Tom, but she could hear him undressing, and she could feel his eyes on her.

"Come on, Belle, relax." Tom's voice was soft and controlled, but Fitz could sense the threat of anger underneath. "The kids are gone, and we had a nice evening alone. Right?"

Fitz nodded reluctantly. She pulled the blankets up around herself and glanced at Tom. He was standing across the bed from her. His mouth turned up in a small carnal smile.

"You look so pretty tonight."

"Thanks," she whispered. His eyes were so intent, his gaze seemed to consume her.

"I love you," he said.

"I love you too, I just..." Fitz turned her head. She couldn't look at him, knowing what he was thinking about. It was written all over his face. Not love. *Lust.* "I'm tired." She rolled to her side, putting her back to him.

"Come on, *Belle.*" Tom switched off the light. Fitz felt the sheets slide across her skin as he crept into bed behind her. The warm pressure of his hand on her hip made her freeze. She didn't move, didn't breathe as he slid up against her, his breath hot on her neck. Her insides twisted uncomfortably.

"I'm sorry," she began, but he hushed her softly and pressed closer to her. She could feel his arousal. At that moment, the sensation of his body on hers was abhorrent to her. This man, whom she supposedly loved, no longer felt like a man, but a beast. Her nerves were set on edge. Fitz's whole body seemed to vibrate with anxious energy; it made her want to run. But she couldn't. She could barely raise her chest to breathe.

She lay motionless while his hands moved around her, touching her, squeezing her, caressing her, as he kissed and nipped at her neck. Fitz felt the instinct for flight, the urge to run from him. The feeling was palpable. Inescapable. But also impossible to act on. She was frozen.

"Tom." She moved only her lips as she spoke, her voice barely audible. "Don't..."

Tom rolled her to her back and put his mouth over hers. Her chest tingled like she could feel each crystal as an icy cage formed around her heart, separating her, protecting her from his touch.

She didn't move. She let him kiss her. He rolled on top of her, his hands sliding under her nightdress. She didn't fight him; she didn't push him off or tell him to stop again. She lay still, motionless as a corpse. If he noticed her detachment, he didn't show it. He made love to her body as she sat entombed within it. When he was done, he kissed her again, told her he loved her, and fell soundly asleep.

Fitz didn't move, not so much as a toe, until she could hear Tom snoring softly beside her. Then she let herself breathe, but she wouldn't allow herself to cry. She had cried so much, and what had it gotten her? She could feel her heart pounding against her ribcage. How long could she go on like this? How many of these nighttime interactions would she have to endure before... *Before what?* She didn't even know. *It can't be like this forever.*

Michelle

Friday, December 29th

"What are you looking at there?" Ben leaned over Michelle's shoulder and peered at her phone. She pulled away, pressing the phone protectively to her chest.

"None of your damn business, asshole." She really hated when people read over her shoulder, and Ben knew that. He also knew how irritable she got when she was pregnant. He wrapped his arms around her from behind and embraced her tightly. His face lowered to nuzzle at her neck.

"Sorry, babe," he whispered into her hair.

She closed her eyes and breathed in the smell of him, her irritation fading as quickly as it had appeared. She noticed scents so much more during pregnancy. Usually, that was a bad thing, but not when it came to Ben. She'd always loved the smell of Ben, but now it was as if she could pick out every soap, shampoo, aftershave, and deodorant he used, all things that mixed with his own sweat, made a scent that was uniquely Ben. It was the scent of home and sex and love.

"It's okay." Michelle turned to face him. She rested her forearms on his shoulders and, with her free hand, stroked his hair. She glanced at the phone clutched in her other hand. Michelle hadn't wanted Ben to know that she'd been checking the league website to see how the Darts were doing. She didn't want to admit that she missed them as much as she did. And she certainly didn't want to confess that seeing that they were losing gave her just the tiniest bit of satisfaction. *Maybe I'm not so replaceable, after all.*

"I'm sure they miss you like crazy," Ben said as if he'd read her mind. He kissed her nose. "Maybe even as much as you miss them."

"Oh, fuck you." She pushed him away. He really did know her too well. Ella came running in and crashed into her legs, breaking through her thoughts like the Kool-Aid man through a wall.

"Mama, are we's goin' skiing?" She looked up at Michelle, her big brown eyes bright with excitement. Michelle bent down until she was face-to-face with her daughter.

"Yes, we are, but we have to wait until Bubbe gets here." She looked the little girl over. "Also, I told you, you needed to wear pants for skiing. Your legs will freeze off in this silly little skirt." Michelle rubbed her daughter's bare legs. Ella immediately went into defiance mode. She folded her chubby little arms and scrunched up her face into a scowl.

"No! I want my ballet dress!" She stomped her foot to emphasize her point. Michelle closed her eyes and called for patience.

"What if we put pants under the skirt, princess?" Ben reasoned. Ella nodded but continued to scowl as Michelle took her to her room to pick out something acceptable. When they returned from Ella's room, Michelle's mom was standing in the entryway. She greeted her mother as she dressed Ella for the snow.

"How's hockey going?" Michelle's mom asked, apropos of nothing. *What did Ben say?*

"Oh, didn't you hear?" Ben sang innocently as if he hadn't started the whole thing. "I thought she told you. Michelle *quit.*"

Treacherous bastard. He knew she hated it when her mother got involved in the details of her life. As they walked out of the apartment and down the hall, Michelle shot Ben her best death glare and mouthed, '*I am going to kill you.*'

"Well, that's too bad. I just know how much you love that team." Her mom shook her head. "Although I have to say I'm relieved. I never liked that you played such a rough sport in your condition."

Michelle groaned. "Ma, it is not that rough. You're going *skiing* with me in my 'condition,' aren't you?"

"Cross-country skiing doesn't count. So tell me Ms. It's-Not-So-Rough, how come you quit, then? Hmm?"

I walked right into that one, didn't I? Michelle's mom had a unique talent for finding the two sides of any debate and somehow arguing for both. It always made Michelle feel fifteen again.

"Look, Ella, the elevator's here," Michelle said through gritted teeth. "Do you want to push the button?"

"Well, excuse me for asking. I just thought you liked this new team of yours, is all."

Michelle knew if she just resisted the urge to respond, her mother would let it go. *Just shut your mouth and ride the elevator.*

Outside it was a beautiful sunny day. The sky was bright blue, and the sun gleamed off the white snow. It was a brisk 10 degrees with no wind. Perfect skiing weather. They let Ella ski as far as she could by her own propulsion, which wasn't very far, and when she tired of that, Ben skied with her between his knees until they reached a trail-side coffee shop.

Ella and her Bubbe stopped to sit and sip hot cocoa while Michelle and Ben continued on their own. Without Ella, they were able to pick up their pace, and soon Michelle was panting as she struggled to keep up with Ben. She relished the sensation of blood pumping hard through her body. It reminded her of hockey, she realized with a bittersweet pang.

When they finally came to a stop, Michelle was completely out of breath. Ben pulled off his hat, and his head steamed visibly in the crisp, dry air. Michelle pulled off her own hat, needles of refreshing cold pricking at her scalp as she tossed her hair.

"Damn, I have a hot wife," Ben said. He was watching her, a small, almost lecherous smile on his lips.

"Oh, shut up." She gave her hair another toss, purely for effect, and grinned at him. He walked over and tried to embrace her. She dodged.

"Ew! Stay away! You're all sweaty!" He grabbed her wrist and pulled her in.

"I just can't help it, when I see you I just have to kiss you." He pulled her closer.

"No!" She laughed as she struggled half-heartedly until he planted a kiss on her cheek. She shoved him back and wiped it off with the back of her jacket sleeve.

"Ugh, so gross! You need a fucking shower!" She could taste salty sweat where his kiss had touched the corner of her mouth. Again she felt a glow of affection for this man who she called her husband.

"Maybe you can join me in the shower. Wash my back?" Ben waggled his eyebrows suggestively. Michelle pressed her lips into a thin smile. She wasn't going to admit how good that sounded. A hot shower with Ben was exactly what she wanted at the moment, but she didn't want to promise anything. Michelle knew her mood could turn on a dime. She lived, breathed, and fucked at the whim of her crazy pregnancy hormones.

After they arrived home and got Ella to go down for a nap, Michelle was happy to discover that she still wanted that shower. She looked at her body in the mirror as Ben turned on the water.

"Will you be joining me?" Ben called as he stepped into the shower. She rubbed her belly. Was that the start of a bump? She turned sideways. No, it was too early still—only about thirteen weeks. *Most women wouldn't have even told people yet.* She pushed out her gut as far as she could, trying to remember how it had felt when she was pregnant with Ella. *Pregnancy is so fucking weird.*

"Seriously, am I doing this alone or what?" Ben called again.

"Calm your shit, I'm coming."

"You will be, oh yes, you *will be*." Ben reached out and pulled her in.

The 'shower' ended with Michelle laying sideways across her bed, eyes closed, every muscle in her body limp with sweet exhaustion. She heard Ben roll off the end of the bed and stand up. Michelle opened one eye just in time to see his naked ass disappear into the closet.

Michelle rolled over and picked up her phone; she flipped through her unread email. Michelle stopped and stared at one of them.

'Evite: You have an invitation from Dawn Johnson!' She tapped it open, read through it again, then marked it as unread—not for the first time.

"Stop torturing yourself and just respond yes." Ben was back, his prior nakedness now covered with jeans and a *BikeMN* t-shirt. He sat next to her on the bed and gently squeezed her bare ass. She opened and closed the email one more time before tossing her phone onto the pillows.

"I should be the one hosting that fucking party, you know," she said. "I am the 'social captain.' Supposedly."

"Babe, you were the one that—"

"Yeah, shut up." She knew what she had done. She had rage-quit mid-game. She had walked away. She had let their texts and emails sit unanswered. But what she hadn't done was anticipate that the party would be planned without her—not consciously. "I'm pissed off anyway."

At first, Michelle hadn't been ready to accept responsibility for any of it. She'd set her feelings about the team aside. *I was going to come back to it all eventually.* But time ticked on. One day, the Evite appeared in her inbox, and it was too late. *You're being a dramatic bitch,* she told herself. She wiped tears from her eyes. Ben put his arm around her shoulders.

"Ugh, stupid hormones!" She sniffed. "It's just fucking hockey."

"Babe, you love fucking hockey."

Michelle curled up to Ben. His jeans were rough against her bare skin. "I love fucking *you*," she said.

He stroked her wet hair. "I love fucking you too. But I think you know what I meant."

"Yeah, maybe. It's not like I'm actually *playing* hockey, though. Even if I hadn't quit so goddamn dramatically, I still would have to stop playing by about now anyway. So why bother with any of it?"

"Who are you trying to convince?" He was so frustrating when he did this: when he forced her to make sense of her own bullshit.

"It's just, what's the point? They're all going to be drinking, and I can't drink, then after they bond or whatever, they get to go play hockey together, and I can't fucking play hockey." *Shit.* More tears. *I have got to remember not to get pregnant again. This sucks so hard.*

"They're your friends," he said with aggravating tenderness. "Wouldn't it still be fun to see them? Talk to them at the party. Clear the air. Then maybe you could even go watch some of the games."

Michelle looked at him, thinking. *What would it feel like to watch the team play without me?* "You'd be okay taking care of Ella alone so that I can go *watch* old lady hockey?" she asked, eyebrow raised.

"If it would make you happy." Ben rubbed her back and looked into her eyes. "Would it make you happy?"

Michelle buried her head in his chest. "I honestly have no fucking clue. But thanks. You're the best."

> Michelle: Hey, Dawn! Sorry for the late reply! I'll be there tomorrow!

Dawn

Saturday, December 30th

The day of the Darts' holiday party, Dawn felt like she was running around like a chicken with her head cut off: always moving, but accomplishing very little. Their house tended to be cluttered—a fact of which she'd been well aware—but she hadn't realized just how long it was going to take to clean up the clutter until she started doing it. After a few hours of work without notable progress, she decided on a scorched earth method, and just started piling junk into laundry baskets and hiding them in her bedroom.

"How are you doing, baby girl?" Dawn put down her last load of miscellany and sat down on the bed where Sharon was curled in a nest of blankets. Sharon looked blankly at Dawn for a moment before shrugging and burrowing deeper into the covers. "You gonna be able to come out and say 'hi' tonight?" Dawn asked.

Sharon shook her head.

"Is it still okay that my team is coming over?"

Sharon nodded.

Okay, so I guess we're non-verbal at the moment. Dawn sighed. Poor Sharon was in day four of one of the worst depressive episodes Dawn had seen in a long time. Dawn leaned over and kissed her on the forehead. "I love you, sweetness."

"I love you too," Sharon managed in a whisper.

"Anything I can get for you?"

Sharon shook her head. What Sharon needed was for Dawn to stay strong. And to maybe find something that would pull her out of the darkness and into the real world, even for a moment.

Dawn looked around the room. It really was a mess. *I guess you really never know how many plushies you have until you try to pack them all away at once.* "This room looks like a hoarder's wet

185

dream," Dawn grinned encouragingly at Sharon. "The sad thing is how we can't even blame the kids for so much of it! How many sonic screwdrivers, lightsabers, and magic wands do two fully grown women need anyway? And don't get me started on the four-foot long dragon—"

"You leave Falkor out of this!" Sharon snatched up the luck dragon from atop the nearest pile. *Bingo.* To anybody looking in from the outside, it might not look like much. But to Dawn, it was a momentary flash of the real Sharon, hidden beneath the depression. Sharon was eyeing the piles of geeky trinkets. "God, we are such cliché fangirls." She burrowed back into her covers. Dawn pulled the blanket away from Sharon's face and kissed her on the nose.

"Mmmm, I have a weakness for cute fangirls." She stroked her wife's unkempt hair. Sharon rolled her eyes, but she also smiled. Just a little.

"Think you could come out for a bit? Maybe help me pick out some music for the party?" Dawn asked. Sharon shook her head. "But, darling, sweetness, love of my life, you know I can't be trusted to pick party music." She tucked a strand of hair behind Sharon's ear. "Don't you remember how poorly my selection went over at our last gathering?"

Sharon squinted up at her. "Oh yeah, your *Outlander* phase. Four hours of bagpipe music. How did you think that was going to go over?" Sharon side-eyed her.

Dawn laughed. "Hey, now, *Outlander* is not a *phase*; it's a way of life. And I could listen to bagpipe music all day. That's just the kind of girl I am. So come on, save me from myself?" Dawn pleaded. She got another small smile out of Sharon, but her wife still would not get out of bed. "Okay, you do you, boo-boo. I'll check back in with you later, okay?"

Dawn went to the front window and looked out. It was so dark that it seemed much later than it really was. *Winter is coming... no, winter is here. Fitz is coming.* Fitz was making her way up the walkway. She had promised to come early to help set-up for the party. She had shopping bags hanging off her arms and a large tray of cupcakes in each hand. Dawn quickly opened the door and took the cupcakes; each one had been meticulously decorated with little crossed hockey sticks.

"Fitz, you are too much, baby girl. These look amazing." Dawn led Fitz into the kitchen, where Fitz pulled out several bottles of wine from one of her shopping bags, along with an exquisitely wrapped gift. Fitz had dressed herself up for the party, too. From clothes to cosmetics, she looked polished and perfect. But only on the surface. Dawn could see that something was amiss right away. There was a deep crease between her brows, and her eyes were glassy and unfocused. She looked worn down and deeply unhappy.

"You alright, boo-boo? You look..." *Don't say terrible.* "...stressed."

Fitz shook her head adamantly and plastered on a bright smile. It wasn't very convincing. "No! Sorry, I'm just a little tired from the drive. Where should I put the white elephant present?"

Dawn directed her to the living room where Dawn's own—less attractively wrapped—gift was sitting on the coffee table. Fitz was certainly an expert at outward appearances. She helped Dawn set everything up, so it looked fun and festive for the party.

Fitz acted *mostly* normal, but Dawn still wasn't convinced that she was only 'a little tired.' She watched Fitz struggle to keep up the happy, carefree facade as more and more people arrived. When Tessa got there, she and Fitz secluded themselves in the corner of the kitchen. Fitz seemed to let her guard down with Tessa. Her joyful mask fell away to reveal a more strained expression. They both looked serious, faces pinched as they talked in low voices. Dawn stepped closer.

"Hey, Dawn, Tessa got Christine's ex added to the roster as a sub," said Fitz.

"Barely in time—roster-adds closed this week," Tessa added.

"So that's it. If she doesn't work out, we're going to be looking at a lot of tiring games." Fitz frowned and chewed her lip.

Is this what's keeping Fitz up at night? Somehow Dawn suspected there was more to her somber gaze than the team's dearth of subs.

"Oh em gee, Dawn!"

Dawn turned abruptly at the sound of Nikki's voice.

"Is that *hotdish?*" Nikki made a high-pitched squeal as she entered the kitchen. *I'm going to assume that was a happy noise.* "God, I haven't had real Minnesota hotdish in ages! Colorado *casserole* just isn't the same, I swear." Nikki immediately grabbed a plate and queued up for food.

"You're from Colorado?" Christine asked as Nikki helped herself to a large portion of the tater-tot topped dinner.

"Yes and no. I grew up here until I was twelve—that's how I know Tessa—but my family moved to Denver, and I ended up sticking around the area, until about a year and a half ago when I moved back!"

"Why did you move back?" asked Dawn. Nikki was leaning against the far counter, shoveling the piping hot food into her mouth.

"Divorce. I had to get the hell away from my ex and his crazy family asap." Nikki shook her fork at the group. "I tell you ladies, if you get even the whiff of divorce, get the hell out as fast as you can. That shit sucks. No matter how you get into it, it all ends up nasty. Men are the literal worst." Nikki looked around the room. "I guess I'm saying this to a bunch of lesbians. I don't know what it's like to fight with your girlfriend or wife or whatever—probably dramatic as hell."

"You have no idea." Christine laughed, as did Tiffany.

Dawn bobbed her head. *Women can be crazy.*

"But men, ugh," Nikki continued. "Men are so emotionally stunted. They're like dogs: give them a *bone* and they're happy; try and take away that bone, and they'll bite your arm off. I swear, men have three moods: happy, horny, and pissed the fuck off. Hey, Fitz, you married one. You know what I'm talking about, right?"

All eyes turned to Fitz. She shrank back, her face visibly reddening, even under the layers of makeup.

"Uh, yeah, I guess..." she stammered. There was an awkward silence.

"Hey, is everybody here?" Tessa interjected. "Who are we still missing? Just Jess? Emily?"

Dawn nodded, quickly jumping in to help move the conversation along. "Emily can't make it. Jess said she'd be running late, but once she's here, we can start the game. Can I get anybody drinks in the meantime?" Dawn walked across the kitchen.

"Let's do shots!" said Nikki.

"Yes, shots!" Tiffany agreed.

Dawn reached into the cupboard for the Fireball. When she turned back around, Fitz and Tessa were gone. *Escaped to the family room, no doubt.* Two rounds of Fireball, a pan of hotdish, and one too many of Christine's crazy-ex-girlfriend stories later, Jess arrived, and the whole group stumbled from the kitchen to the family room to start the White Elephant game.

Dawn joined Tessa and Fitz, already sitting on the sofa. Dawn's big gray cat jumped up onto the arm of the sofa as soon as she sat down.

"You have a kitty cat!" Christine exclaimed, reaching to pet it. "I suppose you did say that your house had cats in the Evite, but I hadn't seen one yet. Oh, look at you! Aren't you sweet!" Christine cooed. The cat sniffed at her hand once and then stepped forward, presenting himself for petting and chin scratches.

"We have three cats. This one is Lust, Sloth is probably hiding, I think I saw Anger in the kitchen. He'll likely come over for attention as well." Dawn reached over and gave Lust a few quick scratches on his back.

"Anger, Lust, and Sloth?" asked Nikki. "Based on the rest of your, uh, *decorations*, I would have thought they'd be, like, Spock and Kirk, or something."

Dawn laughed. That did seem like the type of thing she and Sharon might do. Although they were clearly a Next Gen family. *Worf would make an excellent name for a cat.*

"There's a story behind that," Dawn began. "A few years ago, Sharon talked me into us fostering a pregnant cat. The cat was a mean old thing: she would bite and scratch and hiss. Her real name was like Violet or something, but we called her the Devil. The Devil ended up having seven kittens, and as a survivor of a Catholic upbringing, naturally, my first thought was to name them for the seven deadly sins: Anger, Lust, Sloth, Greed, Gluttony, Pride, and Envy!"

"Wow, seven cats is a lot of them!" Tiffany exclaimed.

How is she already drunk? Dawn shook her head. "We only kept Anger, Lust, and Sloth. The rest were rehomed, as was the Devil herself."

"That's awesome," laughed Andy. Nikki scratched Lust's chin.

"Can I go first?" Tiffany had found the game dice and was shaking them in her one uninjured hand.

"Sure, why not, boo-boo."

The Darts began to unwrap the mystery gifts. There was quite a mix of things, some of which people might actually want (like the chocolate and scratch-tickets Fitz brought), and some gifts nobody would ever need or want (like Andy's Big Mouth Billy Bass or Nikki's crocheted TP holder—'a family white elephant tradition,' she'd claimed). They were about half-way done, and having a lot of fun when the front door banged open.

"Hello, bitches!"

Oops, I forgot Michelle was coming. Dawn stole a glance at Fitz and Tessa. Neither looked particularly happy. *I probably should have told them.*

190

Michelle

Saturday, December 30th

Michelle stood at Dawn's front door, hesitant to open it. *Was coming here a really stupid idea? Does anybody even want to see me?* She shifted the bag she was carrying from one arm to the other. She hadn't talked to any of the Darts—save for a few texts with Dawn—since the day she'd stormed off the ice. She knew she was going to have to apologize. She knew it was going to be awkward. Michelle hated awkward. *Get your shit together and get in there.*

"Hello, bitches!" The door banged open more forcefully than she'd intended. *Nobody can say I don't make a fucking entrance.* "Can I get a hand? I brought a fuckton of shit!"

"It's so great to see you, boo-boo!" Dawn bounded up to the doorway, smiling; she looked genuinely glad to see her. "What's all this?" Dawn took the heavy bag from Michelle's arms.

"My mocktail ingredients. The hubs says it's good with vodka too." Michelle brushed off the snow and shrugged out of her coat.

Dawn's house was warm and homey and quite unique. *I didn't know adults decorated with spaceships and dragons. Huh.* Michelle stepped through into the living room. Her teammates were all settled in, looking comfortable and happy.

"Michelle's back!" cheered Nikki, drink in hand.

Tiffany jumped up to give her a hug. "Oh my gosh, Michelle, I can't believe you're here!" Tiffany cooed.

"Believe it, bitch!" Michelle looked over the rest of them. "Hey guys, there's something I'd probably better say before I join the party." They all looked back at her expectantly. All except Fitz, who was staring into her drink. *Come on, Fitz, at least look at me.*

Michelle cleared her throat. "I just want to say I'm sorry. I'm sorry that I blew up, and I'm sorry that I just fucked off and didn't

191

call or anything. And although I stand by my belief that the Ice Queens were being a bunch of assholes, I didn't need to be such a dramatic bitch about it. And I certainly shouldn't have said some of the things I said to you, Fitz."

Fitz did look up then; she smiled thinly. *She's not going to forgive me that easily. Well shit.* Michelle took a deep breath. "So, yeah, I'm sorry for being such a bitch. But I'm still paying for the fucking ice, so you're stuck with me. Some of you bitches owe me money, by the way."

"Ah, there she is. Good to have you back, boo-boo." Dawn hugged her. There was a chorus of general agreement. Michelle felt some relief; she knew it wasn't all smoothed over, but she'd made the first step, and that took the edge off. Looking around the room, she could tell that they'd already started the white elephant game. Michelle had come prepared. She put her own wrapped gift on the pile of unopened items before squeezing in next to Nikki, who gave her the rundown on what had happened at the party so far.

"Jess brought wine? Wait, why didn't I think of bringing booze? Fuck my stupid pregnant brain." Michelle thumped herself on the forehead.

Dawn picked Michelle's gift from the pile. "Oh, it's a book, I like books."

Michelle smirked as Dawn ripped open the shiny blue wrapping paper to reveal a cover on which a shirtless muscular man leaned over a woman whose gravity-defying breasts were barely covered by a wisp of silk.

"A romance novel? I should have known better than to expect a real book!"

"It may not be a prize-winning work of literary fiction, but it gets the job done." Michelle winked.

Dawn shook her head. "Of course you *would* bring something like this." Dawn flipped through the pages, skimming them with her eyes. "Oh, my," she said in a slow, deep voice. "*Ohhhh, my.*"

Michelle laughed out loud. The book was passed around the room so that everybody could take a peek and giggle at the smut. Michelle followed Tessa to the kitchen to make herself a drink.

"Hey, Tess."

"Hey." Tessa looked at her awkwardly. "How are you... doing?" Tessa asked, gesturing in the general direction of Michelle's abdomen.

Michelle rubbed her still mostly flat belly. "About as well as can be expected for having a goddamn human parasite."

Tessa looked mildly disturbed by that response. Michelle laughed. Tessa didn't *get* pregnancy.

"Pregnancy is the actual worst. My morning sickness has finally abated, *thank God*, but I seem to have lost half of my mental faculties, so that's *fabulous.*" Michelle shook her head. "I swear I don't remember it being this bad last time. Maybe it's a compound effect. It really is a stupid way to propagate a species."

"Yeah, it doesn't sound fun," Tessa muttered.

"Understatement of the century." Michelle finished mixing her drink. She leaned against the counter. "Hey, Tessa, can I ask you something?"

Tessa looked at her curiously.

"Is Fitz, like, super fucking pissed at me?" Michelle asked.

"What? Oh, no, I don't think so." Tessa wasn't very convincing.

"Really, because she looks so... upset." Upset didn't quite cover it. *Crabby maybe?* "She seems tense as fuck."

Tessa sighed and looked back in the direction of the family room. "I think she's just worried about the team." Tessa lowered her voice. "It hasn't been going great. We're like three, seven, and two." That wasn't great, but it wasn't exactly catastrophic either.

"There's still a lot of season left to play," Michelle said. "Fitz shouldn't worry so much."

"You know how Fitz is; this is important to her." Tessa shrugged. "And ever since Tiffany broke her finger—"

"She did what now?!" Michelle walked briskly back to the family room. "Tiffany!" Michelle exclaimed. Tiffany looked up, startled. Michelle looked at her. Sure enough, her hand was bandaged up, with her middle finger splinted straight out. "Your hand! How did I not see that before?" Tiffany held her damaged hand aloft. The way the cast had been set made it look like Tiffany was flipping her the bird. Michelle began to giggle. "It looks like you're..." She pointed. More giggles.

"Yeah, it's already gotten me into trouble," Tiffany grinned. "Some guy flipped me off at an intersection when I was driving downtown, and I was confused until I realized he probably thought I flipped him off first." Michelle laughed harder. It wasn't really that funny, but she just could not stop laughing.

"I'm sorry," she managed between giggles, "but I can't believe that all this time sitting here, I didn't notice. And you've been here with that cast-thing, flipping people off all night long." She tried to stop, but the laughter won out. "Oh my God. It must be the pregnancy hormones because that is the funniest thing." More laughter. "It's like... I told everybody to fuck off and quit playing..." Tears streamed down Michelle's face as she laughed. "Now, you can't play and are stuck telling everybody to fuck off!"

Several other people were laughing now too. Including Tiffany. But not Fitz. She wasn't even smiling. Her arms were crossed. *Definitely crabby.*

"Come on, Fitz," Michelle said when she regained her breath. "Don't you think the irony is at least a little funny?"

"No, I don't. We had to play our last game with only seven skaters." She was dead serious.

Come on, it's just hockey. If Tessa was right and Fitz was this disgruntled about a less-than-stellar season...

"Jesus, Fitz, you are so uptight, sometimes I think you really just need to get laid." Michelle started to laugh again, but stopped dead when she saw Fitz's face.

"You're such an insensitive cunt sometimes, you know that?" Fitz turned and ran out of the room.

"Fuck." *I am such an asshole.* Michelle went to follow her, but Dawn held her back.

"Give her some space."

"Is she really this upset over losing some fucking hockey games? I mean, I know it was a dick move for me to... but... shit."

Dawn shook her head. "I wasn't at the last game, but no, I don't think that's what's really bothering her."

"The only good part of that last game was that there was this one crazy lady in all pink," said Nikki, clearly oblivious to the tension in her drunken state. "I mean, pink helmet, pink gloves, pink socks, it was quite a statement. And she played like she thought she was God's gift to hockey. I mean, she was the best on their team, but every time she got the puck, she'd try to take it in for a goal. Every. Fucking. Time. And when she was on the ice, her team would just give her the puck, give her the puck, give her the puck. Which was easy to pick up on given that her pink gear already made her stand out like Donald Trump at *Lilith Fair.*"

"The best part was," Christine picked up the thread. "Once we realized we were going to lose anyway, I decided to just shadow her. Just follow her around all shift every shift, just tap at her, block passes, strip the puck any time I could. And *Pinkie Pie*—oh, that's what we started to call her—anyway she eventually got really pissed off and just turned around and shoved me right on my ass, right in front of the ref. When he called the penalty I laughed so hard. They still trounced us, but man that was funny as hell."

Michelle smiled weakly at them. At another time, that story would have had her in stitches. She looked at Dawn and Tessa. They weren't laughing; Michelle didn't think they were even listening to the others. They were both still looking past the group to where Fitz had disappeared. Michelle's gaze followed theirs. *Oh, Fitz. What the fuck is going on with you, girl?*

Fitz

Saturday, December 30th

"Jesus, Fitz, you are so uptight, sometimes I think you really just need to get laid." Michelle started to laugh. Fitz's entire body went cold. She felt like she was going to be sick.

"You're such an insensitive cunt sometimes, you know that?" Fitz had meant it to sound angry, but her voice cracked, and she knew that she was going to cry. She quickly turned and ran out of the room. She shut the door to the bathroom and immediately began sobbing.

Fitz sank to her knees on the soft bathmat and buried her face in her hands, trying to muffle the sound of her crying. Her whole being ached with sadness. Everything felt bleak and impossible. *How can this be my life? Crying on the floor of Dawn's bathroom when I should be laughing and having fun. How did I get here?* She felt like an idiot, but that didn't stop her tears.

'You really just need to get laid.' Michelle had said it, but when she thought of those words, Fitz saw Tom, heard *his* voice and the things he'd said to her as he pushed her, night after night.

'*Come on, Belle, I thought you were going to keep putting in an effort.*' But it wasn't effort she'd given him, it was resignation. She was resigned to putting herself in her own emotional cage and letting Tom have his way, just to... *Just to what? Avoid one more fight?*

She sobbed harder, her body shaking all over. Her heart burned in her chest. *How did I get here?* She asked herself again. *Why is everything falling apart? Why am I falling apart right now?* What Michelle said may have set her off, but it wasn't Michelle's fault; she couldn't have known. *It's my fault.* Fitz pounded her fist on the floor until it hurt. *It's all my fault, and I have no idea how to fix it.*

Fitz didn't know how long she sat, crouched on the floor. After some time, her knees began to ache, and she forced herself to her feet. Her sobs had dwindled to small choked gasps, but tears still streamed from her eyes. She looked at herself in the bathroom mirror. Her eyes were swollen and red, her cheeks streaked with tears that ran through her makeup and made her look like a wax figure that had been left out in the sun.

I am so ugly when I cry. Fitz choked back another sob. *Maybe if I let Tom see me like this, he wouldn't want to touch me. If I didn't try to be pretty, maybe, he wouldn't love me anymore at all. That might be better.* Fitz looked into her own eyes, pleading with herself to stop thinking about him. The woman who stared back at her was so sad. So pathetic. Fitz couldn't look at her anymore.

Fitz washed her face. She scrubbed off all her makeup until her skin was raw and pink and matched her bloodshot eyes. As she dried her face, she heard a soft knock at the door. She took a deep breath, reassured herself that she wasn't going to cry if she tried to speak, and opened the door. She didn't know exactly who she expected to find on the other side, but it certainly wasn't Sharon, Dawn's wife.

"I'm sorry, I—" Fitz began, but Sharon shook her head.

"Don't be sorry. Never be sorry for being sad." Sharon looked up at Fitz. Her face was round and pale, and there were rings under her eyes. She looked as if she too had been crying not long ago. She gave Fitz a small, encouraging smile. "Would you like a hug?"

Fitz surprised herself by nodding and then letting this woman, who was barely more than a stranger to her, engulf her in a big warm hug. Fitz's eyes burned, and she worried she was going to cry again.

"Come in here and sit down awhile." Sharon released her from the embrace and led her into the bedroom across the hall. It was packed almost floor to ceiling with baskets and bags of miscellaneous junk. Sharon led her carefully around the laundry and toys and sat her down on the large plain bed. "I'm sorry that your heart is hurting right now. Heartbreak is never something you get used to."

"How did you know?" Fitz wiped tears from her eyes. Sharon inclined her head in the direction of the bathroom.

"The sound of ultimate suffering." She smiled to herself. Fitz squinted, confused. Sharon rubbed her back. "I am all too familiar with feelings of overwhelming despair. You can't hide the signs of heartbreak and helplessness from a lifelong depressive. I know too much about sadness." Sharon continued to rub her back. Fitz sagged, the heaviness in her chest drawing her down.

"I've never felt this way before," Fitz admitted. "I've never felt this lost. I don't know what to do."

"I know what you mean. And I wish I knew how to help." They sat silently for a while until the door opened, and Dawn stepped inside the room.

"You okay, boo-boo?"

"Yeah," Sharon and Fitz replied in unison. Fitz felt her face get hot. *Of course, she was talking to her wife.* Would there be any end to her embarrassing herself tonight?

"We'll both be alright." Sharon squeezed Fitz's shoulder. "Nobody stays sad forever, even if it feels like it sometimes."

"My wife is a wise woman." Dawn touched Sharon's face so tenderly. Fitz's eyes filled with tears. Before she could stop herself, she was crying again. Dawn sat down beside her.

"Oh, baby girl, what's wrong?" Dawn held Fitz's hand as Fitz told her everything—every sordid detail about her and Tom and his needs and what she'd been letting him do. All her feelings of helplessness and uncertainty came out in a gush. Fitz couldn't believe she was telling anybody this, let alone Dawn and her wife, whom she barely knew. But she found once she'd started, she couldn't stop. When she was done, Dawn opened her arms, and Fitz fell into her, exhausted.

"Oh, Fitz, you don't deserve that. Nobody does, baby girl." She stroked Fitz's hair like a mother stroking her child. "Why don't you stay here tonight, boo-boo."

"What will I tell Tom?" Fitz whimpered. She was so drained; she didn't want to go home. *Will I ever want to go home?*

"Tell him your teammates got you drunk, and you had to sleep it off?" Dawn suggested.

"Tell him to go to hell." Michelle's voice. Fitz sat up suddenly. Michelle was standing just inside the doorway. Fitz had no idea how long she'd been there, but apparently, it was long enough. "Or better yet, I'll tell him. Right before I fucking kill him."

"Michelle don't—" Dawn started, but Fitz put a hand on her shoulder, and she stopped. Fitz looked up at Michelle. Emotions warred within her. On the one hand, she wanted Michelle to go away, leave her alone. Fitz wanted to tell her that she couldn't possibly understand, that it was complicated, and that things weren't as bad as she'd made them sound. But a small voice in the back of her head whispered, *yes they are.*

"Fitz, I am so sorry. I just..." Michelle shook her head. "There's no excuse. I am an insensitive cunt sometimes." Michelle had never sounded more sincere. She didn't smile, didn't smirk. "You have every right to hate me, Fitz. Every cause to punch me right in the face. Just promise me you'll save the next punch for Tom."

Fitz stood up, threw her arms around Michelle, and hugged her.

"I'm sorry too, Michelle. When you got pregnant I—"

"Don't say another word about it." Michelle rubbed her arms. Fitz shook her head; she had been feeling so guilty over their fight back in November.

"I was too focused on losing a player when I should have been supporting my friend." It felt good to say it out loud. It was true; she was so worked up over the details of the team that she wasn't really seeing the big picture. *I haven't been seeing much of anything right lately.* "I've been way too focused on the hockey, it's like I forgot about the rest of life. Tom was right about—"

"Tom's wasn't right about shit. Fuck that guy," Michelle snapped. "Right, Dawn?"

"Michelle's right, Fitz." Dawn stood up from the bed. "He needs to learn that what he's doing is not okay. It's abusive."

Sharon nodded along as Dawn spoke. Fitz felt the sting of tears starting to form again.

"But it's not like he's hitting me or anything." Fitz didn't know why she suddenly felt the need to argue. She fought back her tears.

"Fitz, he's basically *raping* you," Michelle said.

Fitz swallowed hard. "But he's my *husband.*" She could barely get the words out.

Michelle hugged her again. "That doesn't matter. He doesn't have a right to your body just because he's your husband."

"But I love him," Fitz whispered. She did. Somehow deep in her soul, she knew it was true. *It would be so much easier if I didn't love him.*

"If you aren't actively consenting, then it's fucking sexual assault, and you deserve so much better." Michelle pulled back and looked Fitz dead in the eye. Fitz sniffed. Michelle's expression was stern yet warm. "Trust me, I'm really fucking smart, and I'm a fucking good lawyer. He needs to stop, or I will nail his ass to the wall. Literally and figuratively."

Fitz couldn't help but smile at Michelle's fierce defense of her. She considered what Michelle was implying. Fitz thought about what it would be like to leave Tom. She pictured his face when she told him she was going. *He'd be so upset.*

Fitz hung her head, shaking it slowly. "I can't leave... I just can't."

"I'm not going to tell you what to do," said Michelle. "But I need to know that you're going to do *something*. It can not keep going the way it is. If you're going to stay with him, he needs to change his behavior. You need a plan to get that to happen. Promise me you won't go back home until you have a plan. Okay?"

Fitz nodded.

"We're here to help," Dawn added. "Anything you need, baby girl."

"Thanks," Fitz managed a small grateful smile. *I am so blessed to have friends like these.*

Michelle linked arms with Fitz. "Now, come on, girl, you need a drink."

Fitz let out a small laugh. "Yeah, I really do."

Tessa

Saturday, December 30th

Tessa sat in the living room, awkwardly fiddling with her white elephant gift: a candle from Dawn that looked and smelled like a puck. Fitz had been gone for a long time. After a while, Dawn had disappeared after her, followed in short order by Michelle. Tessa felt uneasy inserting herself into whatever was going on. Fitz was one the people Tessa cared about most in the world, but there were aspects of her life that Tessa would never understand. *I wish there was something I could do to help.*

Nikki and Tiffany had passed out upstairs; Christine, Andy, and Jess had all gone home. Tessa was the only one left sitting alone in the quiet house. She looked around. The shelves in the family room were stuffed with books and DVDs, and scattered amongst them were little trinkets and toys. Action figures, dice, legos... It was somewhat cluttered and chaotic, but in a way, not dissimilar to her mother's bookshelves with their porcelain cats and hummels. Tessa liked it.

Tessa picked up her beer can. It was still empty. Just like it had been last time she'd picked it up. She put it back down. *Should I just go home?* Tessa shook her head, and the world moved hazily around her. *I can't drive yet.* She didn't want to take a *Lyft* or something and then have to come back for her car. Dawn lived too far away. *I guess it's the sofa for me.*

Tessa couldn't go to sleep yet. She needed to wait for the others to come out and tell her what was going on. *I might as well have another beer then.* Tessa had only just stood up when Fitz and Michelle re-entered the room, arm in arm. Fitz looked like she'd been crying. She'd washed off all her makeup, and her face was fresh and pink and strikingly beautiful in a sad sort of way.

"Are you okay?" Tessa asked as they walked past her, clearly intent on their destination.

"Fitz needs a drink," Michelle called back.

Dawn stepped up beside Tessa. "Fitz is going through some pretty tough stuff with her husband," she said quietly. "She just needs her friends right now."

Tessa nodded, understanding without needing to really understand. Dawn started toward the kitchen and beckoned Tessa to follow her. In the kitchen, they each got a drink and sat around Dawn's kitchen table. Tessa opened her beer and looked over at Fitz, who was stirring something pink and fizzy garnished with a lime. Fitz sipped at it cautiously.

"You're having one of Michelle's mocktails?" Tessa asked, curious.

Fitz took a bigger sip and coughed. "Oh no, not mocktail, this one is fully loaded. Michelle poured the vodka herself. Based on the amount she gave me, she *really* misses her booze." Fitz put her arm around Michelle. They looked so close. *What happened in there?*

"Don't you know it, bitch." Michelle smiled. "And speaking of bitches..."

That phrase is getting a little too familiar.

Michelle raised her glass. "A lot of shit might suck right now, but there's nobody better to help you ride out a storm than your hockey bitches. Right, Fitz?" Fitz nodded. "Would you do the honors?"

Fitz smiled gratefully at Michelle. "Cheers, bitches."

"Cheers, bitches!" they repeated together.

Saturday, January 6th

Tessa set off for the first game of the new year brimming with optimism. She blasted her favorite pre-hockey playlist on the long, slow drive to the rink. It had snowed last night, and although the larger roads had been plowed, the small street that ran by her parents' house had barely been passable. And now the wind was pushing the light white dusting across the highway, making the asphalt disappear from view. It was inconvenient, but on balance, Tessa liked snow. She appreciated the way it turned the gray dead winter landscape into something beautiful and bright.

Tessa had left extra early so she wouldn't be stressed about getting to the game on time. Unfortunately, not everybody had as much forethought. When she was dressed and ready, Tessa counted heads. They were still missing somebody. Two somebodies: Jess and Brooke. Tessa checked the time. There were only four minutes left before the start of warm-ups.

"Hey, has anybody seen Brooke and Jess?" Tessa hoped that she'd just missed them, and they were waiting out by the ice, but nobody'd seen them.

"Text them?" suggested Fitz. Tessa fished around in her coat pockets and pulled out her phone. She had a missed text from Brooke.

"Shit, guys, Brooke's not coming. Her landlord plowed her in or something. Crap. So much for having a full bench for once." Tessa sighed. "No word from Jess though. Hopefully that's a good sign?"

They were playing Bad News today—the team they'd played drunkenly during the summer tournament. Tessa had been looking forward to a solid rematch. *We could win this game. But with only eight?* She frowned.

"Don't worry, boo-boo. Jess gets dressed super fast," said Dawn.

"And there's still warm-ups, she could make it on time, I'm not worried yet," Christine added. Tessa wished she could say the same. Missing one person was one thing, but losing two would mean throwing out her line plans entirely.

"I just hope she's okay. The roads are terrible," Fitz said. Tessa stood up and made for the door, but before she got there, it opened, and Michelle came crashing through. Her cheeks were flushed from the cold, and she was smiling an excited, happy smile. She clapped her mittens together with a dull thump.

"Hey, bitches! Your team mascot has arrived!"

The team greeted her with warmth and some amount of bewilderment. Michelle wasn't the type to come to games when she couldn't play.

What the fuck happened at Dawn's? Tessa had never gotten an answer about that. But it had to have something to do with Michelle showing up today because she immediately walked over to Fitz.

"Hey, how are you doing?" Michelle searched Fitz's face, her own expression clouded with worry. Tessa also looked at Fitz.

"I've had my period all week," Fitz answered.

What? That seemed to mean something to Michelle. She nodded.

"Okay, but you're going to have to talk to him eventually, you know." Michelle looked intently into Fitz's eyes. "You promised me."

"I know." Fitz looked down, "I will. I mean, I'll have to. I can't have my period forever, right?" She looked back at Michelle.

Michelle sighed and gave her a quick hug. Tessa was so confused.

"Okay, but if you need back-up or anything, you know I'm there and ready to..." Michelle punched the air.

"I appreciate that, but I've got it." Fitz smiled. "I just want to focus on the game now, okay?"

"Okay, the game it is." Michelle turned. "What can I do to help with the game?" She asked the room at large.

We're actually talking about hockey now, right? "You could open the back door for the D," offered Tessa.

"Oh my God, *phrasing!*" Michelle squeaked. Several people giggled.

"What?" Tessa was so flustered by the missing players, and the whole thing with Fitz, it took her a minute to realize what she'd said. "Oh, fuck you all. Let's get on the ice."

Warm-ups started and ended with no sign of Jess.

"The goalie doesn't look great." Tessa shared with the team before the start of the game. "She goes down easy and stays down."

"That's what she said!" Michelle interjected.

"So take a lot of shots and go high with rebounds." Tessa scowled at Michelle. "I'm going to try and get a lot of shots from the point to give you guys chances for rebounds."

"So, you're saying the D should go hard in their end?" Dawn said with a barely straight face. Michelle giggled.

"Will they have the stamina to keep pounding it in so hard?" Nikki chimed in. "Or should the D pull out more?"

Michelle was laughing hard. Tessa looked at Fitz. If the goofing around and innuendo bothered her, she didn't show it. Her face was impassive.

"With a short bench, we have to play smart," Fitz said. "Let's get some goals early before we get worn out. And take short shifts." Fitz gave Michelle a sideways glance and smirked. "Michelle's here, so she can help everybody get off."

"You're killing me, Fitz," Michelle howled.

Not Fitz too. "Okay, okay, don't waste all your energy being a bunch of perverts," Tessa shook her head. "We only have eight skaters—"

"Nope, nine! Jess is here! I just saw her go into the locker room." Andy pointed.

Oh, thank God. Jess looked flustered and frustrated when she finally took her place on the bench.

"Sorry, sorry, sorry! I am so pissed that I'm late, you guys. There was this plow, and ugh, I thought I was going to die for a minute there, but I didn't, and now I'm here, and whew." Jess shook herself as if shaking off the stress from the journey. "I'm ready to kick some ass. I feel like I've got some goals in me today. And maybe a couple penalties."

Jess was not kidding when she said she had some goals in her. Her very first shot sailed over the goalie's shoulder and into the net. It was the first in a string of goals that earned the Darts a decisive victory.

Almost the entire team went to the Dart after the game to celebrate their first win of the new year, and to avoid the roads as the snow continued to fall.

"It's so hard to watch and not play, but it's easier when you win, and that was a great game," said Michelle.

"I think that was the best game we've had since you left, so it must have been because you were there," said Fitz.

Michelle flipped her hair back theatrically. "*Obviously!* I knew it wasn't my hockey skills that helped us win games but my *charismatic personality.*"

"Well, whatever it is, we're glad to have you back on the bench. Even if you can't play, I'm glad you can come," Tessa said.

Michelle chuckled softly under her breath. "Yeah, I do like to *come.*" Michelle winked.

For fuck's sake. Tessa made a face at her.

"But really, I'm glad I was here today too," Michelle added. "And I think my husband is glad I'm out of the house. I'm pretty sure he's really sick of me bitching and crying all the time."

"Oh, come on," said Fitz. "That man worships you. Besides, you? Cry? I don't believe it."

Come to think of it, Tessa couldn't think of a time when she'd ever seen Michelle cry.

"Believe it! Cuz, bitch, I'm pregnant!" Michelle pointed forcefully at her barely-there baby bump. "Wine commercials are the worst. I cry every time. I mean, what kind of monster brings Woodbridge to a dinner party?" Michelle put her hand over her heart. "It brings tears to my eyes just thinking of those poor people, fully able to drink real wine, and yet forced to drink that swill." She sniffed.

"Oh, that reminds me, Jess," interjected Nikki. "I have been meaning to ask: since you don't drink, what made you bring wine as your white elephant?"

"Was it that bad?" Jess ducked sheepishly.

Nikki laughed. "It wasn't the *worst* I've ever had! I mean, I drank it. I'm just curious since you never drink."

"Well, a few weeks ago at my internship, we had this workshop where we were put into groups, and we had like thirty minutes or something to design a targeted product and marketing campaign aimed specifically at thirty-five-year-old mothers. The workshop wasn't just interns, it was all sorts of people from the company, there were like sixty to eighty people there, so you'd think there'd be a lot of variety in the pitches, but every single group—like, every. Single. Group. Had designed a product involving alcohol, mostly wine."

"Ha! Of course, they did," said Michelle.

"So, since getting something for the team targets a similar demographic..." Jess shrugged.

Similar demographic. Tessa snorted.

"Well, you pegged the demographic," Nikki agreed.

"That story calls for another round of drinks," Fitz declared. They all ordered dinner as well as drinks. Just as their dinner plates were being cleared, the snow stopped. Most of the team took that as a sign and left for home. Tessa hung back. There was no way the roads to her house would be clear yet. But if she waited a while longer, there might be a fighting chance, assuming the snow was done falling for the night. Fitz stayed back with her.

"Do you realize the season is officially halfway over for us after tonight?" Fitz asked, swirling the remaining beer in her glass. Their season was only twenty-six games long. Tonight was lucky number thirteen.

"Yeah," Tessa agreed. "It's gone by really fast in some ways, and in other ways, the first game seems like a lifetime ago."

"If we keep playing like this, we should be safe from probation. This was a big win today," said Fitz.

Tessa nodded. With this win, they would be in the middle of the pack. It was the bottom half of the middle, but the middle nonetheless.

"Now, if we could pick it up a bit," Fitz went on, "we could have a chance at making the playoff tournament."

"*Playoffs? Playoffs?*" Tessa did her best Jim Mora impersonation. "*Don't talk about playoffs!*" Tessa smiled ruefully and shook her head. "Seriously though, let's not go crazy, we should just focus on winning as many games as we can, securing our spot in the division," Tessa paused, "and having fun."

Fitz shrugged one shoulder. "Just sayin'. A girl can dream, can't she? It would be so cool... And it would prolong the season. I guess I'm already dreading the end. I don't want it to be half over already! I don't want it to be over ever." Fitz frowned. She drained the last of her beer. "I suppose that should be my last drink..." She sighed. "I don't even want tonight to end... I should wait a bit and drink some water before I go home, though."

Tessa looked closely at her friend. The mention of going home put tension in Fitz's posture. She'd looked happy if wistful when talking about hockey, but now her eyes were unfocused, and she seemed almost afraid.

'*Fitz is going through some pretty tough stuff with her husband.*' That's what Dawn had said.

"How are things... with your husband?" Tessa asked tentatively. Fitz let out a sharp, bitter laugh.

"Trust me, you don't want to know." Fitz shook her head as if shaking away a bad memory. "Let's just say it's not the *snow* that's keeping me here."

Tessa didn't know what to say. She had no reference point for marriages aside from her own parents. She remembered times when they had fought. It happened most often when her dad didn't have enough work and money was tight; or when he had too much work and he barely came home. She wasn't sure which had been worse, because as a kid, they were both gut-wrenching.

At some point, the big fights had stopped, and life moved on like they had never happened at all. Tessa didn't know what changed. Maybe it was when her brother had moved out. Perhaps it was just not having little kids to worry about anymore. Tessa wondered about Fitz's kids. Did they notice the fighting? They probably did. Tessa felt for them.

"How about you? How's the new job?" asked Fitz. Tessa tried to remember the last time she'd given Fitz an update. It had been a while. Tessa had been at the new job for just under a month.

"It's... interesting."

"Interesting bad?"

"No, no, it's good. It's just... challenging in new ways." Tessa scratched her head. "I really love my new boss, and the atmosphere is awesome. It's just a lot of different processes and technical aspects to get acquainted with while also getting to know my team. It's a little more than I was prepared for, I guess. But I think maybe that's because I expect a lot out of myself. I'm good at the technical stuff, generally speaking, but I'm not an expert on medical devices, specifically, like the people on my team are. Maybe it's just imposter syndrome."

Fitz blinked; she didn't seem to be following. Tessa took a deep breath and tried to think of a way she could convey how she was feeling without sounding like so much of an engineer.

"It's like, the best analogy I can think of is that at my old job it was like I was playing hockey in a beginner men's league. I was super confident in my skills at playing the game, so I got promoted to captain or coach or something, but I felt like I was bumping up against this gender barrier that skill alone wasn't helping me break through. Like if the guys were all, 'sure you can out-skate me, but why does that mean I have to listen to you about the breakout?' And so I thought moving to this new company would be more like coaching women's hockey, but it's more like coaching women's... soccer or something. The team is great, and they listen to me, they respect my understanding of 'the game' and how to work together, but I'm still struggling with, like, coaching somebody with better foot skills than me, so to speak. I know I need to keep my focus on the 'team play,' but I also want to amp up my skills, so I don't look like an idiot at 'practice.' This analogy is getting away from me, but do you know what I mean?"

"Yeah, I think so." Fitz still looked a little lost, but Tessa didn't know a better way to describe it.

"So yeah, no, it's good, it's just, it's taking some getting used to." Tessa stretched her neck. She was stiff from sitting for so long. "At least I'm getting to hang out with Dragon more again."

"I don't see the connection, but that's good?" Fitz tilted her head.

"He was having a hard time being around me when I was at the old job, I think. He's been my friend since forever, but he can't deal when I'm ranting about men being dumbasses."

"But men *are* dumbasses," Fitz said pointedly.

"Oh, I know, trust me, I know." Tessa sighed. "Dragon's generally a good dude, love him to death, but he can get a little 'not all men' sometimes."

"Yeah, I get it." Fitz nodded. "Just because we love somebody doesn't mean they're perfect." Her voice had suddenly gotten very soft, her eyes downcast.

Tessa looked down into her empty glass. It was hard to see Fitz hurting, but Tessa didn't know what she could do. *If she wanted to tell me what was going on with her, she would.* Tessa glanced at her watch. It was later than she'd realized. They'd been at the Dart for hours.

"I should be getting home." Tessa stood up and began putting on her jacket and hat. "The roads are probably as good as they're going to get tonight. Are you going to be alright?"

"Yeah, I'll be fine. I should get home, too, I suppose." Fitz nodded, but she didn't make a move to get up. Tessa hesitated, but Fitz waved her off. "You go ahead, I'm going to go to the bathroom on my way out. See you soon."

"Okay." Tessa started to leave. "Hey, Fitz, good game."

Fitz smiled. "Yeah, you too, Tess."

Fitz

Saturday, January 6th

"Where the *hell* have you been?" Tom was waiting for her when Fitz got home. It was the opposite of what she'd wanted. She'd hoped staying out might mean finding him asleep when she got home.

I should have known better. Fitz felt jittery. Her heart started to race the moment she saw him.

"I went out with the team after the game. I guess we lost track of time." She brushed past him and started up the stairs.

"Lost track of time? Your game ended *five hours ago!*" Tom followed her up.

"Shhh, the kids are sleeping."

"Yeah, I know, *I put them to bed myself. Again,*" Tom growled, but he kept his voice down until the door to the bedroom was shut behind him. "I mean, come on! You've been gone since three! It's after ten! What the hell?"

Fitz took a few deep breaths. *Stay calm.* "It's snowing, the roads are bad." She tried to go into the bathroom, but Tom held the door, blocking her way. She flinched.

"No shit, the roads are bad, I was worried about you!" Tom didn't sound worried, he sounded pissed. Fitz avoided looking at him. Her ears were ringing, her head spinning.

"I'm sorry, I should have texted. But I'm fine, so can I please shower now?" It took effort to keep her voice steady. She really didn't want this fight tonight. *Please, God. Please.*

Tom released his hold on the door and Fitz locked herself in the bathroom. Slowly, as slowly as she dared, she got undressed and took her shower. She didn't turn off the water until it was ice cold. Shivering, she crept out from the bathroom. Tom was sitting on the edge of the bed, waiting for her. He watched her like a hawk as she readied herself for sleep. He didn't say anything, but Fitz could sense his eyes on her as she moved about the room. She was trying to act natural, but her heart was going a mile a minute, and she could hear Michelle's words echoing in her ears.

'*He's basically raping you.*' She shuddered.

"Come on, Patricia, what's wrong?" Tom stood up, placing himself between Fitz and her side of the bed.

She shied away. "Tom, I just want to go to sleep." She tried to move past him, but he put out his arm and stopped her.

"What is going on?" Tom demanded. "You come home late, you can't even *look* at me. You've been like this all week! You're avoiding me."

"No, I'm not," she lied.

Tom's nostrils flared in a brief moment of unhidden anger, but he quickly regained control of his expression. His mouth twisted in a faint smile that didn't reach his eyes. "Okay then, let's go to bed."

Instead of stepping out of her way, he put his hand around her waist, drawing her close. She tried to step away but he held her fast.

"Come on, *Belle.*" His voice was low in her ear. "Let's go to bed. Together."

Fitz shook her head. She couldn't breathe. "Tom, I'm not—"

"You're not on your period anymore, right?"

I can't be on my period forever. "No, I just—"

"You're what? You said you're not avoiding me." He cupped her chin in his free hand, forcing her to look at him. His eyes were intensely focused on hers, she felt herself shrink in his arms. "Are you?" he asked.

"No."

"Good." He kissed her. She let him kiss her.

What's a kiss? Just calm him down. We don't have to go through this tonight. He dropped his hand from her chin, and it brushed her chest. Fitz sprang backward, out of his embrace.

"Can we just go to sleep?" She folded her arms across her body.

Tom frowned. "I knew it, you are avoiding me! Jesus, Patricia! What happened to working on us? I thought you were going to keep *trying*."

"I don't feel like... like..." Fitz searched for words that would be clear without being upsetting. The last thing she wanted was to make anything worse. "I just don't want to make love tonight."

Tom narrowed his eyes. That wasn't enough. He wasn't giving up. *He wants this fight.* Heat burned in Fitz's chest, her heart was hammering so hard she could see her pulse in her vision.

"It's been a long week," Tom growled, taking a step toward her. "I was expecting you to put in some *effort*—"

"You were *expecting* me to let you *rape* me again—" Fitz was surprised to hear herself say it, but she was even more surprised by the slap. She froze, her skin stinging, her jaw jarred by the impact of his palm. There was a heartbeat, a flash, the briefest moment of time where she looked at Tom, and both of them just stared, disbelieving. Then shock flipped to rage and she began to shake. Fitz wanted to hit him back, and worse—she wanted to stomp the life out of him.

"Get out!" she screamed louder than she had ever screamed at him before. He hesitated. "Get the fuck out of my room, Tom, or I swear to God!"

He left. Fitz locked the door behind him and fell to her knees, sobbing. Her chest ached, pain like she had never known struck through her heart. Unbelievable, inescapable pain.

How is this real? She touched her hand to her cheek. It was warm where he had hit her. Fitz felt like she was outside of her body. Tom had *hit* her. Her husband. The man who was supposed to love her.

Why did he do that? She knew why. *I told him he'd raped me.* Pain throbbed in her chest, a hundred times worse than the pain in her jaw. *Why did I say that?* The pain radiated deeper with each breath she took. *Because it's true.* She couldn't breathe. *Oh God, what is happening to me?*

Sunday, January 7th

> Fitz: I won't be able to make it to the game today. Can you call a sub? I'm sorry.
> Tessa: Sure. Are you ok?

Michelle

Sunday, January 7th

"What do you mean she's not coming? Where is she?" Dawn's voice was sharp, sharper than usual, and filled with distress; it caught Michelle's attention immediately. They were standing outside the locker room as the Zamboni circled the ice.

"Who's not coming?" Michelle asked, afraid she already knew the answer.

"Fitz."

Shit. Michelle's mind flooded with concern.

"Where the fuck is she?" Michelle practically jumped on Tessa.

Tessa flinched. "I don't know, she just asked me to call a sub, but I couldn't get one in time." She scowled at Michelle.

Michelle gritted her teeth. "When?"

"When what?"

Fucking hell. "When did she ask? Last night at the bar?" Michelle grilled her.

Tessa's dark eyes blinked rapidly, her brow knitted. "No, she texted me this morning."

Shit.

"Why?" Tessa asked, uncomprehending.

Michelle looked at Dawn. Dawn looked scared. A hot burning flame of rage kindled in Michelle's chest.

"If that mother*fucker* has so much as *touched* her." Michelle pulled out her phone. She called Fitz. No answer. She tried again. Nothing. Michelle's blood was boiling, white-hot like it was going to burn right through her skin. Her hands shook with anger as she texted.

> Michelle: Where are you? Are you ok? What's going on?
> Michelle: If you don't call me back I'm riding to the suburbs with a fucking shotgun

"Do you even *have* a shotgun?" Tessa asked, looking over her shoulder.

Michelle snatched her phone away from Tessa's prying eyes. "No, do you?"

"Yes, of course, I do," Tessa smirked. It wasn't a cute look on her.

"Can I have it?" Michelle hissed through clenched teeth.

"What for?"

Michelle took a deep breath and exhaled slowly through her nose. Why the hell was Tessa looking so smug? *Stupid little pug face.* Didn't she have any idea what was going on with her friend? *I thought she and Fitz were tight.*

"Just in case I have to kill Fitz's husband," Michelle explained slowly in case Tessa was, in fact, just stupid. *Jesus fucking Christ.*

"What?" Tessa's smirk vanished into a bewildered stare. Michelle gave Dawn a help-me-out-here look. Dawn drew Tessa away and quietly tried to explain while Michelle called Fitz again. This time it didn't even ring, it just went straight to voicemail. Michelle almost threw her phone against the wall in frustration.

"Do either of you have her address?" Michelle asked. Tessa nodded and began searching through her phone, but before she found it, Michelle's phone chirped.

Fitz: Calm down. I'm at church.

Michelle allowed herself a small breath of relief. Emphasis on *small.*

Michelle: If you're at church send me a picture of you with Jesus or something

She waited. She couldn't wait.

Michelle: I'm serious, pics or I'm coming over

Michelle: We have your address and Tessa has a shotgun, bitch don't test me, I will fucking shoot him

Michelle was ready to head for the door when Fitz texted a picture of herself glaring at the camera, a large cross clearly visible behind her. Michelle let herself breathe.

Fitz: Satisfied? Now leave me alone, you're not helping. I'll see you next week.

Michelle wasn't entirely satisfied, but the fires of rage and alarm within her were abating. *Why would Fitz miss hockey for church?* Fitz never missed hockey. *Doesn't she go to one of those stupidly big churches with a million services?* Michelle didn't know shit about church, but she knew Fitz. Fitz didn't miss hockey.

Michelle: Fine, but you'd better really be ok, I mean it, I will come over there

"She'll be okay," Dawn tried to reassure Michelle. Tessa looked like she was going to be sick. Dawn must have told her everything. Tessa didn't have the stomach for sordid details.

"How do you know?" Michelle asked.

"I don't, but I don't think threatening her is going to help." Dawn put her hand on Michelle's shoulder.

I was threatening him, not her. But Dawn had a point.

Michelle: I'm just saying we're here for you because we care about you

"Better?" she asked.

"Better." Dawn nodded.

"I still feel like we should go see her or something. Make sure that she really is okay." Michelle narrowed her eyes. "Because if she is otherwise, I shall be very put out."

Dawn stared at her. "Did you just make a *Princess Bride* reference?" she asked.

Michelle shrugged, the tension beginning to dissipate. She rolled her shoulders. "Ben and I just introduced Ella to *The Princess Bride*. It's *totally* over her head, but she digs it, and even on endless repeat, it beats that Nick Junior shit hands-down."

Dawn looked completely dumbfounded.

Michelle gave her a lopsided grin. "Don't let our good looks fool you, Dawn, deep down my husband and I really are giant fucking nerds."

"You surprise me every day, boo-boo." She squeezed Michelle's shoulder.

"So we're confident that Fitz is okay?" Tessa asked. She still looked queasy.

"Confident? Hell no. But I guess we have to trust her." Michelle punched Tessa in the shoulder. "Come on, you need to get ready to play hockey."

Michelle tried to focus on the game and stay positive, but it was hard, especially given the beat-down they were handed by the Royals. Tessa encouraged the team not to lose heart—that the Royals were the top-ranked team in the league. But it didn't make the loss any less of a loss. And they all felt the lack of Fitz's presence. They went out to the Dart, but they didn't stay long. This time 'just one beer' actually meant 'just one beer,' even for Tessa.

Later that night, Michelle was watching TV with Ben in bed, half falling asleep, when her phone chirped.

> Fitz: How did the game go?
> Michelle: Shitty. We got killed.
> Michelle: How are you??
> Tessa: We lost 4-0
> Fitz: That sucks, I'm sorry I wasn't there
> Tessa: What happened? You NEVER miss hockey

No response. Michelle scowled at the phone. *Fitz can't just start talking about hockey all casual and ignore us when we ask how she is.* Michelle's delicate emotional state couldn't take shit like that.

"What's going on, babe?" Ben nudged her shoulder. Michelle only grunted in response. She had told him everything when she'd first gotten home. *Obviously.* But she didn't feel like giving him a play-by-play at the moment.

Michelle tapped her nails on the phone screen impatiently. *For fuck's sake, Fitz.*

> Michelle: Be honest. You missed today because of your worse-half
> Dawn: We're worried about you

There was another maddening delay before Fitz finally answered the real question.

> Fitz: Ok, Tom and I had a fight. I'm sorry.
> Michelle: Don't be sorry! OMG!
> Dawn: Are you ok?
> Fitz: I don't really want to discuss it on text

That sent alarm bells ringing in Michelle's head. Why wouldn't she want to discuss it on text? Was it just because she was a fucking phone call type person, or was she worried about Tom realizing she'd told them about what he'd done? Michelle picked up a pillow and threw it off the bed in frustration. Ben raised an eyebrow at her.

"Shut up, I'll explain later."

> Michelle: Fine. IF YOU SAY SO
> Michelle: But why tf were you at CHURCH?
> Fitz: We're talking to our pastor, working on getting some counseling

Michelle had to admit, that was a fairly reasonable reason. She couldn't think of a better one for going to church after a fight. *Maybe for Tom's funeral.* She was skeptical about the whole concept of 'talking to their pastor,' though. She didn't have high hopes that doing so was going to do any good for Fitz.

Michelle didn't have a lot of personal experience that led her to trust religious institutions to do what was in the best interest of women. What she expected out of organized religion was an agenda that emphasized obeying one's husband and avoiding divorce at the cost of a wife's personal happiness. But it probably wouldn't do much good to share that perspective with Fitz at the moment.

> Tessa: Will you be at hockey this week? Tiffany's coming back you know.
> Fitz: I wouldn't miss it. I'm sorry I made y'all worry
> Dawn: Nothing to be sorry about, baby girl. You know we just care about you.
> Michelle: We've got your back, bitch
> Fitz: I know. Thanks I appreciate it. Really.

It's her marriage. She'll deal with it the way she wants, I suppose. Michelle snuggled up closer to Ben. *I should really appreciate what I have more.* Ben wouldn't pull the kind of shit Fitz seemed to expect from Tom. And he would never, *ever* touch her without consent.

When she thought about the way that Fitz had talked about Tom, about her tears as she described how he used the whole 'prove that you love me' bullshit right out of a sexual assault PSA, it almost made Michelle want to cry. *Why the hell is she with that guy?*

"I'm so lucky I'm not married to a giant douche-nozzle." Michelle nuzzled Ben's arm.

"Luck has nothing to do with it, babe." Ben kissed her forehead. "There's no way you'd put up with an asshole like that. You're way too strong to let somebody get away with that crap."

Michelle sat up and away from him, suddenly pissed. "Fitz is fucking strong, Ben," she snapped at him. "It's not her fault she fell in love with that jackass. His bullshit behavior has *nothing* to do with how strong she is."

"I'm sorry, babe, I didn't mean it like that." Ben put his hand on hers, but she pulled it away.

"Yeah, well, you shouldn't say shit like that." Michelle's eyes stung with frustrated tears. *Fuck these goddamn hormones.* "People say shit like that too often, and it's just another form of victim-blaming. It perpetuates the idea that women are responsible for keeping themselves from being abused." She sniffed.

"I know, babe, I'm sorry. You know I don't think it's her fault."

Michelle took a few deep breaths. She knew she was lashing out at him because her emotions were so fucked up by the baby. But that didn't mean she wasn't right. People did say shit like that and mean it. And it wasn't right. *I've probably said the same thing. I am the insensitive cunt here, right?*

"I know you didn't mean it, babe. Just don't be a tool of the patriarchy, okay, asshole?" She sniffed again and managed to smile thinly at him.

He put a hand on her cheek and smiled back. "Don't be a tool. Got it." He kissed her. "Now, maybe we should get some sleep."

Tessa

Saturday, January 13th

"It's good to have Tiffany back," Andy said as they sat with Tessa on the bench during their first game against the Surly Wenches.

"Uh-huh," Tessa replied absently. The game was far from the first thing on Tessa's mind. She was watching Fitz and trying to reconcile the strong, intense, amazing woman she saw with the victim Dawn had painted her to be. *It doesn't make any sense. Why would she stay with somebody who did those things?*

"I think she's being more tentative with her poke-check, though, don't you?" said Andy. "Uh, Tessa?"

"What?" Tessa turned and refocused her attention on her defensive partner. "Oh, Tiff? Yeah, she does seem nervous with her hand. I wonder if it still hurts..." Out of the corner of her eye, Tessa noticed Michelle move to stand behind Fitz on the bench. Tessa strained to hear their conversation.

Michelle was good at asking questions without asking them. On the surface, Fitz was acting like nothing had happened, but from the little bits that Tessa could hear and understand, it sounded bad. Tessa knew Fitz and her husband had issues, but they were nothing like she'd envisioned. Tessa had pictured yelling and crying. That was a fight. That's what marital problems were supposed to look like. What Tom was doing went beyond her comprehension. Tessa was grateful she'd never met the man because she didn't want to picture it any more vividly than she already had. It made her sick.

"Sorry about that pass to the point," Fitz said to Tessa after a shift together. "I should have looked."

"Oh no, I should have been there. I'm off my game today," Tessa replied. It was hard to look Fitz in the eye. *Does she know that I know?*

"I think we all are." Fitz sighed. "But at least we have Tiffany back!"

"Yeah, she looks happy to be back," Tessa said. "I'm glad her finger healed so fast."

"I think Emily is even happier," Dawn added.

Michelle snorted. "Oh, I know there's a good fingering joke somewhere in there, I just can't find it." Michelle laughed. "I guess I'm off my game too."

"Shut up, Michelle, don't be gross." Tessa scowled at her. Michelle smirked. Michelle could be so crude, but she was also showing Fitz a hell of a lot of caring too, in her own way.

"So, how's *'church?'*" Michelle asked, resuming her casual interrogation of their captain. "There'd better be some serious *repenting* going on."

"Yes," Fitz said. Tessa looked out to the ice and tried to focus on the game.

"There's a lot to *atone* for," said Michelle.

"We'll be going to *'church'* every week," Fitz replied. "We do have a lot to pray about."

"You think it'll help?"

"I'm keeping faith that it will."

On the one hand, Tessa wished Michelle would leave Fitz alone, but at the same time, she listened intently for each answer.

"Just promise me he's not..." Michelle trailed off.

"No, he's not," Fitz said firmly. "I promise. I'm fine now, okay? I'd like to just play hockey, please."

"Fine. But you know I'm always going to be here, right?"

"On the bench?"

"Yeah, right here on this fucking bench. Forever, bitch." Michelle laughed. Tessa stole a glance at the two. To her surprise, Fitz was smiling.

Tessa felt the urge to say something to make sure Fitz knew that she was there for her as well. *What would I say?* Tessa looked at the game clock. The third period was almost over. *So much for focusing on the game.* The Darts lost two to one.

Sunday, January 14th

The Darts played the Surly Wenches again the very next day. Michelle was there, but she didn't bring up Tom or 'church' on the bench, and Tessa was better able to concentrate on the game.

"That was a good game," said Andy in the locker room afterward; the Darts had beaten the Wenches four to two. "You played awesome."

"Thanks. You too. I'm sorry I was a little out of it yesterday." Tessa glanced unconsciously over to Fitz.

"Yeah, you seemed pretty distracted. Is everything okay?" Andy asked. Of course, they had noticed. They were Tessa's D partner, and Tessa had barely spoken to them on the bench all game yesterday. Tessa felt bad about that.

"Yeah, just a lot going on with work and stuff." *Stuff like finding out my friend's husband is an abusive asshole.* "Please yell at me if I'm zoned out like that again. We should have won that game."

"Will do." Andy grinned. "It helped that Tiffany played more normally today too."

"Yeah, for sure. I was worried for a minute, but I feel better going into next week now." Next week they were facing the Ice Queens again for the first time since Michelle had lost her shit and stormed out.

"I am *not* looking forward to playing the Ice Queens," Andy groaned.

"I still can't believe you played with them," said Tessa. The Ice Queens were, as Michelle said, 'the literal worst.'

"Yeah, it pretty much sucked to be on that team." Andy frowned.

"Are they as big of bitches off the ice as on?" Tessa asked.

"Not exactly." Andy shrugged. "Like I said before, they really do think playing cheap is a good strategy. With the right refs, it does actually work sometimes. They can draw a lot of penalties. Off the ice, I don't know. They're not really *mean*, but they are pretty stupid." Andy sighed. "Or at least ignorant enough to be offensive for no reason."

"Yeah?" Tessa asked. "Like how?"

"Well, the team did pretty well with my pronouns actually. I had to shut down a couple overly personal questions at first, but overall, they acted friendly to me. But sometimes they would say things around me that were like, *seriously?*"

"Like what?" Tessa hoped she wasn't prying too much. Andy was a pretty private person, but they were getting closer as friends.

"Like they'd call something 'gay' or make a joke that they really had no place making. And I don't really like to call people out. I'll talk to somebody I know one-on-one, but I just don't have the energy to be the gender professor everywhere I go, you know?"

"I can imagine." Tessa thought about all the sexist bullshit she'd let slide at Hill House for the same reasons. "Stuff like that gets really old really fast."

"Yeah... when my teammate's boyfriend made a transphobic comment, and she didn't say anything," Andy shook their head, "I knew I could never hang out with them outside of the rink."

"I'm sorry you have to deal with assholes like that." Tessa sighed. Life seemed hard enough as a woman who didn't fit the social standard of husband and kids and whatever. There were always people who didn't seem to get that she wasn't looking for a boyfriend or husband, and certainly did not want to be 'set-up.' People lost their minds when she told them that she never wanted kids. "People suck."

"Yeah, well, I'm glad I left." Andy grinned. "The Darts are much better. Not perfect, but seriously, worlds better."

"No, certainly not perfect." Tessa's teammates sometimes tested her patience with their innuendo and jokes about her 'man-friend,' but at least she felt like she could talk to them if anything really bothered her. She hoped Andy felt the same.

"Please tell me if I could do anything to help anything," Tessa said.

Andy nodded. "Let's just kick the Ice Queens' asses."

Tessa grinned. "Sounds like a plan."

Michelle

Saturday, January 20th

"I'm like, *stupid* nervous for this game." Michelle zipped up the side of her boot, and Ben helped her up.

"Still worried about Fitz?"

"No. I mean, yes, but no. I'm being more self-absorbed today. We're playing the team I rage-quit against. The team I screamed my crazy-ass head off at. So yeah, I'm stupid nervous about that. Like, it's literally making me nauseous." Michelle frowned. Memories from the game back in November kept resurfacing. *Psychos.*

"But you're not even playing." Ben pointed out.

"Yeah, I know, shut up. It's those motherfucking Ice Queens. I just can't even with them, they are the literal worst." Michelle pulled on her coat; it felt snug as she zipped it. This second baby had recently begun making her extra poochy. She rubbed her belly. "I just have this bad feeling." She looked at Ben. "Is it really still cool with you that I'm going to all these games? Even though I'm not playing?"

"Of course! I've got Ella, and when she's asleep, I've got video games that are just begging me to play them. Those Nazis won't kill themselves, you know." He kissed her. "Have fun. Good luck against the Ice Queens." He kissed her again. "And try not to lose your shit this time."

"Mmm, fuck you."

When Michelle arrived at the rink, she ran into Tessa's man-friend. It felt like it had been a while since he'd been at a game, so when she saw that he was in the box setting up his tablet to play music, she got excited. *This game will be more fun with music.* She stopped by the box to request a few songs.

"Hey, bitches!" She popped into the locker room. The team was almost ready to head to the ice. "Now ladies, and Andy!" She put one hand on her hip and stared hard at the team. "Today, you are playing the Ice Queens, and we know from experience that they are some of the worst excuses for hockey players and human beings you've ever faced off against. However!" Michelle paused for dramatic effect. "Let's not have anybody here 'pull a Michelle' and lose their shit on the ice today. They are *not* worth it. Trust me." Michelle stole a glance at Fitz. *Think of all that I missed out on because of that bullshit.* "To that end, I brought you all a little something that I think you ladies, and Andy, have been missing lately. A little *fire.*"

Michelle pulled out a large bottle of *Fireball*. She cracked open the top and took a whiff; the warm spicy scent filled her nostrils. *It almost covers up the stench of the locker room.* She savored the smell for a moment, as it was the closest she was going to get to a drink of her own. Michelle held the bottle out to Fitz. For a heartbeat, Michelle worried she wouldn't take it, but Fitz shook her head and, with a wry smile, accepted the booze.

"Michelle is right, y'all! Keep your heads up, don't retaliate, and let's have some fun!" Fitz put the bottle to her lips. She took a large swig, wincing as she swallowed. She grinned at Michelle as she passed it along.

"Now, let's play hockey, bitches!"

As if on queue, *'Welcome to My House'* began to play, and the team burst out of the locker room together. Michelle took her place on the bench, feeling lightheaded and giddy, almost as if she'd drunk the *Fireball* too.

The Ice Queens were as cheap and aggressive as before—only this time, the Darts were ready for them. They weren't perfect, the Darts were human, after all. Emily had to be reminded a few times to keep her head up and be safe along the boards, and Tessa let a few frustrated four-letter-words slip out. But for the most part, the Ice Queen's attempts at provoking them either failed or resulted in power plays for the Darts. The referees were calling a tight game; they weren't putting up with anybody's shit. Michelle wondered how different her life would have been if they'd had these refs last time.

The Darts only got charged with one penalty: Andy had moved to cut off a pass when an Ice Queen skater charged at them; Andy planted their feet and dropped low, sending the opposing player flying over their back. The Ice Queen skater got up quickly, ego bruised more than anything, and Andy went to the penalty box, grinning sheepishly.

Michelle leaned over into the box. "Daaaamn, bitch flew right over you!"

"I know I probably should have just sidestepped her, but," they shrugged, "the look on her face was worth the two minutes."

Michelle laughed. Andy almost never socialized and rarely spoke loud enough to be heard from more than two feet away. As a teammate, they had been practically invisible to Michelle. But now that Michelle was watching games instead of playing in them, she was getting a new perspective and was appreciating things about her team that she never had before. One of those things was what a badass Andy was.

"Totally worth it," Michelle agreed. "*Fireball?*"

Andy shrugged again and took the bottle. "Thanks."

"Any time, my friend, that's what I'm here for." *I am the money and the Fireball.*

At the end of the second period, the Darts were up by three goals. Fitz called the team's attention, her eyes bright with eagerness and delight.

"I wasn't going to tell y'all, because I knew this game was going to be stressful, and I didn't want to add any pressure but since we're playing so great, I figure it's probably okay, now that we're up by three..."

"Tell us what?" asked Dawn.

"Yeah, spit it out, captain," added Michelle. Fitz bounced on her skates.

"If we win this game, it will guarantee that we won't end up last in the division. We win today, we survive to play another season!" Fitz beamed.

"That's awesome!" Emily cheered. There was a chorus of agreement.

"Oh my God, Fitz, do you not understand jinxes, or are you trying to kill me?" Tessa shook Fitz violently.

"Sorry, Tess, I just couldn't keep it to myself." Fitz laughed.

"Have some Fireball and chill your shit, Tessa." Michelle handed her the bottle. "You know we got this."

"Okay, but if we lose, we know it's all your fault now, right?" Tessa chided and downed a large gulp of whiskey.

Fitz laughed again. "Fine," she agreed. "But we're not going to lose!"

The Darts not only won, but did so with the greatest goal differential of the season. They destroyed the Ice Queens, and had fun while at it. Michelle enjoyed cheering on her team, but when the game ended, she realized that something in the back of her mind was still bothering her. Michelle rubbed once more at the small bump in her middle. *Just fucking enjoy the win, bitch.*

Dawn

Thursday, January 25th

"Hey, sweetness, did I tell you that the Darts are safe from the chopping block?" Dawn said as she sat on the end of the sofa opposite her wife, entering the Darts' game stats online. "It'd be nice to win more, of course. A second year of probation would be no fun. But it's good to have the worst threat gone."

Sharon wasn't listening. She was on her own computer, working on the final touches of her book. Dawn turned her eyes back to her screen. She was done entering the stats and didn't have anything else she needed to do online. She scrolled casually through the league website.

"Oh, hey, the Hot Shots are playing directly after us next week, on the same ice." Dawn hadn't spoken to Connie since the scheduling meeting, but she had sent her a Christmas card and received one in return. That simple exchange was meaningful to Dawn; it made her feel like the rift between them had been partly mended. "Seeing Connie would be nice, and it might be fun to watch my old team play... Maybe I could even go out with Connie after. What do you think?"

"What? Sorry, I'm almost done." Sharon's voice was distracted. *She didn't hear a thing I said.*

Sharon shut the laptop and rubbed her bloodshot eyes. "And I'm spent," she yawned.

Dawn took the computer off Sharon's lap and drew her into a hug. "My poor queen of squirrels."

"I'm okay," said Sharon, settling into Dawn's embrace. "Now tell me all about the hockey drama." Dawn ran her fingers through Sharon's soft hair and smiled.

"No drama this time, sweetness. I was just saying that I might stay and watch the Hot Shots play next week and catch up with Connie."

"Just you?"

"I assume so. Tessa and Fitz aren't really on good terms with them, and Michelle will want to go out to the bar."

"Really? I always hated going to the bar when I was pregnant." Sharon made a sour face. "I can't believe she goes to games either. That sounds cold and exhausting even when you're not pregnant."

Dawn laughed. Sharon was the opposite of Michelle in almost every way; it was no wonder that they would handle pregnancy differently.

"Yeah, well, I doubt Michelle is spending her evenings curled under her blankets, eating *Cheetos*, and watching *Serenity* for the fiftieth time, even though she knows it's just gonna make her cry again," Dawn teased.

"Oh hush, you." Sharon squirmed in Dawn's arms. "I did not."

"I am a leaf on the wind, watch how I eat all the *Cheetos*," Dawn cooed.

"Too soon," Sharon pouted.

"Baby, that movie came out in 2005."

"It'll always be too soon." Sharon nuzzled back into Dawn's arms. "And I did not watch it fifty times. Only, like, five. Maybe."

"Ok, fine, sweetness, whatever you say." Dawn rested her chin on Sharon's head. "I bet Michelle hasn't even seen *Serenity* once."

"I don't see how you can be friends with somebody like that."

"Hockey makes friends out of the most unlikely people." Dawn smiled.

"Speaking of friends, how's Fitz?" Sharon tilted her head back so that she could look at Dawn.

"The same as last time you asked. She says she's going to counseling, but won't say so much as a syllable more. Michelle asks about her *jackanape* husband every game, but Fitz won't say boo.

I hope Michelle's persistence isn't driving Fitz to be more secretive."

"It comes from a place of love," Sharon said. She was right; Michelle's brand of love was just a little more intense than some people were ready for.

"Yeah, sweets, I know. And I love how *fiercely* Michelle cares. I just also worry about Fitz. She's a much more private person." Dawn sighed. "You have to read between the lines with her."

"And what are you reading there, love?"

"Right now, Fitz is all hockey all the time. It's like nothing else in the 'verse matters," Dawn said.

"And that worries you?" Sharon asked.

"Yeah..." Something *was* worrying Dawn, but she couldn't quite put her finger on it.

Sharon nudged her. "You're a good woman," she said.

"Well, I'm alright." Dawn smiled down at her wife. "I know it's late, but let's watch TV for a little while anyway. I'm suddenly feeling in an 'aim to misbehave' type mood."

"Yes, sir, cap'n tight pants." Sharon leaned into her. "Promise to say hi to Fitz and Michelle for me next game, would you?"

"I promise."

Sunday, January 28th

Michelle didn't show for the next game. Dawn had grown accustomed to having her there; the bench seemed lonely without her. It was a tough game, but the Darts played well.

During the third period, Dawn looked up to see that Connie and a few other Hot Shots were watching through the glass. They wore matching sweatshirts and placid expressions. Dawn looked from the Hot Shots to the Darts. The Darts were panting and smiling; they were skating hard and getting shots on net. Dawn was proud of her new team.

"Seeing the Hot Shots was a little awkward," said Tessa in the locker room after the game. "The last thing I need is to look up and see Jackie's stupid face on the other side of the glass." She shuddered.

"Yeah, but at least they got to see us win," said Fitz. "Not only that, I think we looked good tonight. It was a close game, and much faster paced than any we ever played with the Hot Shots. I don't mind rubbing their noses in that a little."

"Hell yeah," Tessa agreed.

Dawn would have preferred to enjoy their success without the 'stick it to the Hot Shots' attitude. On balance, Dawn still felt more guilt over their departure than anger over the Hot Shots' reaction to it. *I might be alone in that sentiment.*

"I'm going to stay and watch the Hot Shots play," said Dawn, and then more tentatively, "Anybody wanna join me?"

"Nope, nope, all the nopes." Tessa shook her head. "I'm still on team *Fuck Those Guys* after what Jackie pulled."

"I'm with Tessa there. Sorry," said Fitz. "It's too bad Michelle isn't here, she might have stayed."

"Maybe... Has anybody heard from her, by the way?" Dawn asked. Nobody had. *That's mildly concerning.* Michelle had disappeared for weeks at a time in the past, Dawn reminded herself—missing one game was no great cause for alarm. *She's not Fitz.*

"I'll stay for a little while," Jess offered, "but not too long. I have a date night with Matt."

"Ooh, so that's still going on! It's been a few months, hasn't it?" asked Nikki. Jess nodded. She looked happy.

Once they were dressed and out of the locker room, Jess and Dawn found seats on the cold metal bleachers. The Hot Shots moved more slowly than Dawn had remembered. Their passes were a bit less sharp, but they clearly knew where each other were. They played like a team.

"It is slower, isn't it?" Jess said aloud what Dawn had been thinking.

"Yeah." Watching her old team was making Dawn simultaneously sad and happy: sad that she wasn't out there with them, but happy when she realized that, although she did miss the Hot Shots, she felt more at home with the Darts. Dawn knew she had grown as a player, and she was closer with her current teammates than she'd ever been with any of the Hot Shots, even Connie.

"So tell me about Matt. How's that going?" Dawn asked, nudging Jess with her shoulder.

"It's good, for the most part." Jess kept her eyes on the ice. She smiled. "We're thinking about moving in together."

"That's a big step, baby girl. Are you ready?"

"Yes, I *so* am," Jess said without hesitation. "The hardest part about dating is finding time when our schedules work. It's been causing some problems. Everything will be so much easier once we're living together." Her voice was firm with the certainty of youth.

"Oh, my sweet summer child," Dawn smiled and shook her head, "I can promise you it won't make everything easier."

Dawn put her arm around Jess's narrow shoulders. Jess was about the same size as her daughter Annabelle. Dawn felt a kind of motherly love for the young woman.

"Just make sure you're both going into it with your eyes open. Living with the person you love can be the best thing in the world, and it can be the worst. Either way, it's going to change things. Take it from me, I had a few relationships that imploded as soon as we moved in together."

"A few? You lived with people before your wife?" Jess seemed genuinely surprised.

"Oh, baby girl, haven't you heard the classic joke?" Dawn chuckled. "What does a lesbian bring to a second date?"

"What?"

"A *U-haul*!" The joke was as old as time, but it always tickled Dawn to share it with oblivious straight girls. "Oh, boo-boo, you've got to go into something like that with your eyes open. Even with Sharon, I think we 'broke up' a week after moving in together. It didn't stick, of course, but it wasn't always happy, happy fun times either."

Jess's expression hovered somewhere between amusement and concern. Dawn rubbed her back.

"Don't worry, child of summer, if you put in the work and it's meant to be, it'll be grand."

At the end of the second period, Jess left. And by the end of the third, Dawn was more than ready to get out of the rink too. All the warmth she'd generated from playing hockey was gone, leaving her damp and cold. Her teeth were chattering as she greeted Connie.

"Hey, Dawn! It's great to see you! Thanks for watching the game." Connie was literally steaming with heat.

Dawn shivered and shoved her hands in her armpits. "Yeah, it's good to see you. You guys played a great game!"

"Thanks, we're having a pretty good season. We should make the playoff tournament if we keep it up." Connie gave Dawn a warm look. "We miss you, though. How's your season going? I watched a little bit of your game. You looked good."

"Yeah, it's good. I doubt we'll make the playoffs, but we aren't in last place, so that's good."

They both nodded. It was friendly but noticeably awkward.

"So, I've been meaning to say..." Connie hunched down closer to Dawn, "I heard that there were some rumors about your team going around, and I just wanted to let you know I *always* stand up for you when I hear them."

Dawn didn't know what to say. There was an uncomfortable feeling in the pit of her stomach. *Doesn't Connie realize where those 'rumors' originated?* Brooke had long ago confirmed their suspicions that Jackie had bad-mouthed them in the locker room after the assessments. Either Connie didn't know that, or she was acting *incredibly* passive-aggressive. Dawn wanted to believe the former.

"Oh, uh, thanks?"

"Of course! I mean, just because the split was a little rough, I know that was mostly Tessa and Fitz. It doesn't reflect on your whole team. I mean, *you* came to me right away, and I've always appreciated that, you know." Connie smiled. Dawn was trying to process all the implications of what Connie was saying.

"Well, I should get changed." Connie gestured at the locker room. "Some of us are going out to The Ole College Bar, if you're interested in joining us."

Dawn shook her head, clearing her thoughts. "Oh, thanks, but I should be getting home." Dawn had intended to go out with the Hot Shots, but it didn't feel appealing anymore. The Hot Shots chapter of Dawn's life was closed now. It was time to move on. She and Connie said their goodbyes.

Dawn walked out into the cold, dark parking lot. The steam from her breath caught the moonlight, forming a white cloud. The cold air pricked at her lungs as she took slow deep breaths. Something in her chest loosened—something she hadn't even realized was tight. *I don't miss the Hot Shots anymore. And I don't think I will again; it's not my team.* There wasn't even a hint of the gut-stabbing guilt she'd once felt. Not one little twinge. She smiled to herself.

On impulse, Dawn pulled out her phone. She suddenly needed to reconnect with her Darts teammates. She'd only just seen them, but not all of them.

> Dawn: missed you at the game today. The bench was too quiet without you. Where you at baby girl?
> Michelle: I'm in the hospital
> Dawn: are you ok? Is the baby ok?
> Michelle: I don't know
> Dawn: Anything I can do?

Dawn: I work tomorrow, can I come see you?
Michelle: sure
Dawn: ok, take care

Michelle

Monday, January 29th

Michelle stared hard at her reflection, barely recognizing her own face. Such a sad, grotesque creature stared back at her. *God, I look like shit.* Her dark hair hung limp around her chalky pale face. There were dark circles under her bloodshot eyes. *I look like something out of a horror movie.*

Her eyes stung. She squeezed them shut until she saw spots and felt the hint of moisture at the edges of her lids. She opened them again and blinked a few more times. No use, her eyeballs still felt like they'd been rolling around on the surface of the sun.

Refocusing, she glared at herself. *Get your shit together.* She slapped her damp cheeks. She knew she had to prepare for the worst. *Nobody gets stuck in the hospital this long when everything is fine.*

It had started with a bad feeling, a gut intuition that something was not right. Michelle had been retaining water, her stomach expanding but without any of the little fluttery sensations of a kicking baby. It wasn't like it had been with Ella. It felt wrong. Michelle called and insisted on moving her ultrasound up a week. *What's one week for a little peace of mind?* If they just took a peek, saw the wiggling arms, heard the heart beating, then surely, she'd be able to sleep again.

The ultrasound tech did find the heart, and the arms, and something else she couldn't, or wouldn't, share. Something that made her call Dr. Peterson right away and kickstarted a series of increasingly invasive and seemingly endless exams. There were so many needles, so many machines, and way too many doctors. Almost two days later, and still Michelle and Ben knew nothing. The bad feeling had expanded inside of Michelle, like a balloon of fear and anxiety.

Michelle shuffled back into the hospital room that had been her prison for these past thirty-odd hours. Ben was watching her intently. Michelle dropped her eyes down to her feet. Her big white socks looked ridiculously large on her, and the hospital gown barely reached her knees, exposing her thin, unshaven legs. She hated the sight of them. They were the legs of somebody old and weak—some sad, sickly thing.

Every part of Michelle's body ached from the prodding and poking. She was exhausted from the stress of not knowing, and the effort of keeping hope in check. She could sense Ben's gaze on her as she gently lowered herself into bed. She quickly drew the blankets over her unsightly limbs.

"Should you be out of bed for that long?" Ben had wanted Michelle to call for the nurse just to go to the bathroom. Michelle looked up at him. Her first instinct was to snap at him, to say something sarcastic. She wanted to tell him that it was her body and to mind his fucking business.

But the look on his face stopped her, and she swallowed her words unsaid. Ben looked as bad as she did. *He looks even worse that I do.* His face was drawn and ashy, and his broad shoulders slumped. Michelle could see her own fear mirrored in his eyes.

"It's fine, I'm okay." Michelle reached for his hand and pulled him down to the bed. "I can go to the bathroom when it's fucking three feet away, okay?"

"Okay." He leaned in and kissed her. Michelle closed her eyes and focused on the soft, warm touch of his lips against hers. She held his face in her hands and pressed her lips harder against his. He was her touchstone, her safe harbor in the storm.

Michelle heard a soft cough and opened her eyes. Dr. Peterson had slipped into the room unannounced and was standing there, quietly watching them. Ben jumped up from the bed. A dark cloud of annoyance and fear rumbled through Michelle. *Sure, fine, don't tell us you're coming in, it's not like you've told us anything anyway.* Michelle glared at the doctor.

"I'm sorry for having kept you waiting for so long," Dr. Peterson's voice was soft—*too* soft. Michelle had to remind herself to keep breathing while she waited. Dr. Peterson flipped through Michelle's chart. "We needed to get all the results to be certain." There was a maddening pause while Dr. Peterson continued to flip through papers. Michelle clenched her jaw and waited.

"Well?" Ben snapped—apparently he couldn't wait. "What the hell are the results then?" His tone was uncharacteristically sharp.

The doctor looked up, her eyes flashed in momentary annoyance before settling into a sympathetic look. "I'm sorry, there's no easy way to tell you this. But there's nothing we can do at this point."

A numb tingling sensation washed over Michelle.

"What do you mean there's nothing you can do?" she heard her husband ask.

Please no.

"The fetus's condition is incompatible with life outside the womb. The safest course of action for you would be to terminate the pregnancy."

This can't be happening.

"What?" Ben's voice cracked. Dr. Peterson tried to explain but her voice sounded far away.

Michelle's chest felt empty, her head light. She couldn't process what the doctor was saying. The words 'incompatible with life' rattled around in her brain, drowning out all other words. She gazed down at her abdomen, vision blurred by tears. The balloon of hope and fear had burst and left her insides shredded. Pain, anger, sadness, helplessness, all these emotions swirled within her, each fighting for dominance.

She didn't want to feel any of those things. But she was trapped, held hostage by the emotions she didn't want to have, inside a body she didn't want to inhabit anymore. And inside that body with her was... was what? What was it if it wasn't her baby? Would never be her baby? Never hers to hold and raise. She clutched her arms across her belly. *What is it that I'm holding on to?* Michelle felt like she was going to throw up.

"What about Michelle? Is she going to be okay?" she heard Ben ask.

"Yes, she'll be okay. She needs a simple procedure to remove the fetus, and she should start feeling well enough to go home within a day."

"Just like that," Michelle whispered. "*A simple procedure.*"

"I'm sorry, I know this is hard—"

"Is it an abortion?" Michelle asked pointedly, looking up. The doctor nodded. Michelle dropped her eyes back to her arms, wrapped around her midsection.

"Yes. Technically it's a surgical abortion."

"And there's no chance the baby..." Ben's voice was scratchy with emotion. Dr. Peterson continued to explain. Michelle couldn't sit there and listen to the doctor describe in detail just how everything had gone wrong.

"How soon can we do it?" Michelle interrupted. She didn't need to hear about the potential side-effects of prolonging a doomed pregnancy.

"Pardon?"

"How soon?" she snapped, not bothering to look up.

"This afternoon."

"Okay. I'd like to sleep now. Please leave." Michelle shut her eyes. She rolled to her side and curled into a ball. Michelle knew she wouldn't be able to sleep, but she needed quiet. She needed solitude.

Dr. Peterson and Ben stepped out of the room. Michelle continued to lay curled on her side, letting the silence of the room fill her. There was nothing she could do. The situation was hopeless. All that was left was to survive.

Michelle had let go of hope, but wasn't ready for grief. She was in between. In the quiet of this emotional no-man's-land, details of the physical world seemed to stand out stark and bright. Almost hyper-real.

The cheap white sheets rustled when she moved. The rail of the bed let out a hard plastic creak as she pulled herself to a sitting position. The blinds tapped lightly at the window sill, moved by the soft circulation of air in the room. If Michelle could stay focused on these surface things she could avoid everything lurking deeper. Stay in the quiet place. Keep the grief at bay. The door opened and closed.

"Are you... babe, what are you feeling?" Ben's voice was pleading, desperate, and powerless. Michelle looked up at Ben; he was running trembling fingers through his hair. She reached for his hand and squeezed it. It was cold and clammy. Or was that her own sweat she felt?

"I'm okay." The words came out automatically. On some level, she knew she wasn't okay, but she didn't *want* to know that.

"Let me know what I can do to help. I'll do anything, babe."

"I know." She stared at Ben; Ben stared back. His eyes were filled with the emotion she didn't want to feel. Then suddenly, like the crack of lightning signaling the start of a thunderstorm, the quiet inside her broke, and grief poured over her in sheets. Michelle began to sob.

Immediately Ben's arms were around her. Michelle clung to him like a liferaft, as wave after wave of sorrow crashed over her. Ben shook as he cried with her. The sea of grief surrounding them seemed endless. *We'll get through this together. We have to; we don't have a choice.*

Time passed in a haze. Michelle tried to forget the events of the day, even as they happened around her. Dawn visited, as did her mother. Michelle wouldn't let them bring Ella; she couldn't let Ella see her so broken. Just thinking about Ella made Michelle cry even more. The little girl didn't need to see that.

Michelle didn't know what time it was when Ben finally took her home, but it was dark, and the nanny had already put Ella to sleep. With help from Ben, Michelle showered, scrubbing off the stink of the hospital, and climbed into bed, not knowing how she could possibly ever have the energy to climb back out again.

Dawn

Monday, January 29th

It was late into the wee hours of the morning when Dawn finally got home. Sharon was on the sofa in front of the TV. She was curled in blankets, head resting on Falkor, eyes vacant and glazed. *Why isn't she asleep?* Sharon didn't stir when Dawn entered the room. Dawn watched her silently. The light from the TV flickered across Sharon's face, giving her skin a pale blue tone. *She really should be asleep.*

Dawn rubbed at her own weary eyes. She'd stayed at the hospital until Michelle was sent home. She didn't need to, but she'd wanted to make sure Michelle had been taken care of. *Poor Michelle.* Dawn didn't know how she was going to tell Sharon. She studied her wife's face. Sharon blinked now and then but otherwise didn't move, her aspect eerily calm. She didn't react to the action on the screen or Dawn's approach. *Where are you at, baby girl?*

"Hey, sweets. How are you doing?" At the sound of Dawn's voice, Sharon slowly raised her eyes from the TV.

"Oh, hi. You're home."

"Sorry. It's really late. You didn't have to wait up for me," Dawn told her.

"I didn't mean to." Sharon's voice was soft and flat. Her gaze floated back to the television.

I should have come home sooner. Dawn turned off the TV; Sharon blinked but didn't stir until Dawn pulled her up by the hand.

"Come on, let's get you to bed, baby."

Sharon let herself be led away to the bedroom.

"Did you eat tonight?" Dawn asked.

"I... I think so. I fed the kids, but I don't know."

DAWN

"Are you hungry?"

"I can't tell." Sharon frowned, a crease forming between her brows as she rubbed at her stomach thoughtfully. "I feel... empty, but not like, hungry..." Her voice trailed off. Sharon would get this way sometimes when her depression was bad. Able to function and care for the children, but often forgetting to care for herself.

She wasn't waiting for me, she just failed to go to bed. I hope she didn't fail to eat. "I can get you something if you'd like." Dawn stripped off her scrubs and pulled on her PJs. Sharon crawled into bed, shaking her head.

"It doesn't matter. It's late. I should just sleep anyway."

"Okay." Dawn was too tired to force the issue. *Sharon can eat in the morning, she won't starve to death tonight.* Dawn had barely eaten today herself. She'd used all her breaks to check in on Michelle and Ben. *Poor Michelle, I can't imagine how she's feeling tonight.*

Dawn snuggled up next to Sharon, hugging her tightly and burying her face in her wife's tangled hair. She took a deep breath.

"I should tell you," Dawn whispered, "Michelle lost the baby today." She could feel a knot forming in her throat. She squeezed Sharon tighter.

"That's sad." Sharon's voice was soft and detached.

"Yeah." Dawn closed her eyes as tears crept out from their corners.

"I'm sorry." It almost sounded like a question: like Sharon knew that she should feel sad, but couldn't remember how. Sharon wasn't going to process this news emotionally in her current state—she was too far down the tunnel of depression to feel the full effect of those words.

It'll hit her tomorrow, or maybe the next day. And when she did feel it, it would hurt, because Sharon was sweet and loving and deeply empathetic. When her brain would let her be. Dawn kissed the back of Sharon's neck.

"Yeah, me too... Now let's get some sleep, sweetness. I love you, Shar."

"Love you too, Dawn."

Tessa

Tuesday, January 30th

> Dawn: Michelle lost the baby. She said I could tell you.
> Fitz: Oh no!
> Tessa: That's terrible!
> Fitz: Is there anything we can do?
> Tessa: What happened? Is she ok?
> Dawn: She was just released from the hospital last night. She's in rough shape emotionally but physically she'll be ok in a day or two
> Fitz: Maybe we can put together a gift for her?
> Dawn: That's a good idea
> Tessa: Will she be able to play hockey again before the end of the season?
> Dawn: If she wants to
> Fitz: Poor Michelle. I'll put something together for her and get a card for the team to sign

Tessa put down her phone. *Wow, that really sucks.* Part of her couldn't believe it. She hoped asking about hockey wasn't insensitive. It probably was. *Stupid.*

"You okay?" Sheryl's voice made Tessa jump. Tessa hadn't noticed her boss standing there beside her desk.

"Yeah, oh, no," Tessa stammered, "my friend just, um, suffered a loss...?" *What do you even call it? Is it still a miscarriage?* "She was pregnant. I just found out."

"Oh, I'm so sorry," Sheryl said sympathetically. "Do you need some time? Feel free to take off if you need to be there for her."

"Oh, no, it's okay, she's just someone from my hockey team." It felt wrong as soon as Tessa said it. *'Just someone from my hockey team.'* Her teammates were more than that. But she wouldn't expect Sheryl to understand.

"Oh, alright, then. Have you seen Peter Cunningham in the office today?"

Tessa shook her head. "No, sorry."

"Ah, well. He is so hard to pin down, sometimes I wonder if he even exists." Sheryl glanced around the office and sighed. She looked back at Tessa, eyebrows slightly raised, like she was waiting for something. Tessa stared blankly back.

"I was just about to head to the conference room for the heads-up meeting. Do you want to walk with me?" Sheryl asked.

Tessa jumped up, nodding, and clumsily gathered up her notebook and laptop. Sheryl was a great boss, but she was intimidating as hell. She was so smart and confident—a force to be reckoned with. She was just the type of person Tessa hoped to be one day.

"So you've been here a few months now," Sheryl said as they walked, "how do you feel like things are going with your team?"

"Good," Tessa replied automatically. "It was an adjustment at first," she added slowly and with more thought. "But I really feel like I've gotten a handle on things now, and I think the team is responding well to my leadership."

"I'm glad you feel that way," Sheryl smiled back at her as they entered the conference room.

You're glad I feel that way? It wasn't the most reassuring response. Tessa's phone vibrated loudly in her pocket. Sheryl looked at her somewhat impatiently. Tessa felt her face get warm as her boss watched her look at her phone.

> Fitz: Are y'all free to go to see Michelle after the game Sunday?

Tessa didn't respond. She quickly put her phone on silent, stuffed it in her pocket, and sat down for the meeting.

Sunday, February 4th

"AJ is a lesbian too? Oh my God, this team is super gay isn't it?" Nikki's loud, high-pitched laugh made Tessa look up. Nikki had the attention of most of the locker room.

"I've been on gayer," said Dawn. "In fact, Wisconsin has a whole gay league, so I'd say this team is pretty normal in its gayness."

"Really?" Nikki shook her head. "I thought softball was the lesbian sport."

"Oh, we like that too," confirmed AJ. "I played softball before I started playing hockey."

"I have *no* gaydar," said Nikki. "Like, seriously none." She looked around the room and tapped her finger on her chin. "How many lesbians are even on this team?"

Tessa didn't like where this was going. Sure enough, Nikki began to point to each person, counting them off. Dawn, AJ, Christine, Tiffany, Emily...

"Actually," Emily interrupted her, "I'm not a *lesbian*."

Next to her, Tiffany chuckled.

"It seems like your girlfriend might disagree," said Christine, but Tiffany shook her head.

"I'm not disagreeing, I'm just laughing. I'm Emily's *first*." Tiffany batted her eyes at Emily, who blushed.

"Just because you're inexperienced doesn't mean you're not gay, baby girl," said Dawn. Emily's blush deepened.

"Oh, I just meant I'm her first girlfriend, because she's bi." Tiffany put her arm around Emily and kissed her pink cheek. "Sorry if I embarrassed you," she whispered.

Tessa looked away; her own face felt warm.

"Well, either way, you're with a girl now. Congratulations on escaping men. I wish I could." Nikki laughed and continued her count. "Brooke, you're straight, right?"

"Yup."

"And Jess has a boyfriend, and Fitz is married to a man, Andy's..."

"Not straight, you can leave it at that," said Andy sharply. They clearly wanted no part of this conversation. Neither did Tessa. But it was too late—Nikki was looking at her.

"What about you, Tessa?" She was the last one to be categorized.

Great. Tessa's face burned. Unconsciously she looked at Fitz. Fitz looked back at her; her bright blue eyes seemed to echo the question.

What about you, Tessa?

Tessa looked at her lap.

"I don't... I never..." Tessa didn't want to talk about it. She didn't want to tell a room full of people that she'd never dated, never even had a *real* kiss.

"Alright, leave her alone," Fitz said to Nikki.

"Whatever, I'm just saying this team is *super gay*."

With that, the topic was dropped, and the room went back to its usual mix of small conversations. Fitz slid closer to Tessa until their shoulders bumped.

"It's okay, you know," Fitz said softly, "if you haven't slept with anybody before. It doesn't change who you are. You don't have to sleep with anybody ever if you don't want to."

"It's not that I don't want to, exactly." Tessa swallowed. Her mouth was dry. Her heart was hammering against her ribs. "It's just that the person I'd want to isn't—isn't somebody who I ever could..."

Tessa finally looked back up from her lap and Fitz's eyes locked with hers. There was something there, in her expression: an understanding Tessa never expected to see. Tessa froze. Time seemed to stand still as Fitz put her hand on Tessa's cheek. It was so soft, so warm. Slowly she leaned closer.

The moment that their lips touched it was like Tessa's heart exploded with joy. She closed her eyes, leaning into the sensation, and when she opened her eyes again she was by herself, in her room, in bed—panting and sweating and utterly alone. She sat up. *Holy shit.* It had felt so real. Tessa's eyes filled with tears.

"Fuck," she whispered. *Fitz.* She fell back onto the bed and closed her eyes. The image came rushing back. Fitz's face. The touch of her lips. It felt so real. "Fuck." Tessa pounded her fist on the bed. *What does this mean?* She knew what it meant. She'd never felt this before, but she knew. *Just forget about it.* She couldn't. *Goddamnit.* Tessa wasn't going to get any more sleep tonight.

She looked at her watch. Four a.m. It would be four hours until her parents woke up, six until her hockey game. In less than six hours, Tessa would see her. *Fitz.*

Fuck. Tessa threw back the covers and stood up. She shuffled out of her room to the kitchen and started for the coffee machine. *No, I can't make coffee.* The smell would wake up her mom.

Tessa leaned against the counter and closed her eyes. *Oh God, Fitz.* The corners of Tessa's lids were damp with tears. *I didn't ask for this. I don't want this.* Tessa licked her lips. They still felt warm. Why did they feel warm when it wasn't even real? *It felt real.* Tessa buried her fingers in her hair and shook her head. *Just stop thinking about it. It was just a dream, it doesn't matter. It could never be real.*

Tessa opened her eyes and opened the refrigerator. She grabbed a beer and sat in front of her laptop. The beer slowed her heart rate. The work distracted her mind. The second beer dulled her mind and she switched from work to *Facebook* until the sky started to get light and the time came to switch to coffee.

Tessa made herself black coffee and toast with peanut butter. She turned on the TV and slumped onto the sofa. One hour until she would have to leave for hockey, ninety minutes until she'd see Fitz. Tessa's heart rate picked up as she sipped the dark bitter beverage. *Forget about it. It was just a fucking dream.*

Ninety-five minutes and one-too-many cups of coffee later, Tessa arrived at the rink. When Fitz pulled her aside in the locker room, Tessa's pulse quickened, her insides suddenly tight with anxiety. *It was just a dream*, she reminded herself. *Fitz can't read your mind.* Fitz wanted to confirm that Tessa would be joining them to visit Michelle after the game.

"Oh, right, yeah. I'm sorry, I guess I forgot to respond." Tessa ducked her head. *How could I have forgotten about that so easily?* "Sorry."

"Oh no, it's okay, I just wanted to make sure. We aren't going to invite any more people from the team along—I don't want to overwhelm Michelle—but I wanted to make sure you were coming." Fitz's bright eyes scanned the room. "Dawn is going to tell everybody about the baby today before the game."

"Before the game? Don't you think that might make it hard to concentrate on playing?" Tessa asked.

Fitz frowned and slowly shook her head. "No, I feel like they should know. And we have to get them all to write in the card." Fitz sighed. "I feel so bad for Michelle. I keep trying to remind myself that God has a plan, but some days it's hard to see it. I want to do anything we can do to help her."

Tessa wondered how much good a sympathy card from her hockey team would really do for Michelle. *At least she'll know we're thinking of her.*

"Are you ready?" Fitz asked Dawn. She nodded. "If everybody could just stop dressing for a minute," Fitz called the room to attention. "We have some bad news we need to share with the team." She looked over at Dawn.

When everyone was quiet, Dawn spoke, her voice soft and sad. "Michelle lost the baby this past week."

It was deathly quiet as they all absorbed the news. Tessa fidgeted awkwardly with the edge of her sleeve. The emotion in the atmosphere was so heavy, it made Tessa uncomfortable.

"How is she doing?" asked Nikki.

"About as good as can be expected," answered Dawn. "She's been home for almost a week now."

Has Dawn been talking to Michelle? Or does she know this because she's a nurse?

"Is she going to come back to hockey?" AJ asked.

Dawn shook her head. "I don't know. I'll try to keep the team updated."

Slowly the players got back to the business of getting dressed for hockey as the card made its way around the room.

"I think Emily's crying," Fitz whispered to Tessa. She looked over. Emily was sitting with her head in her hands, shaking slightly. Tiffany was rubbing her back and talking to her in low tones. When Tessa and Fitz got up to take the ice, Tiffany caught them at the door.

"Emily's going to sit out for the moment," she said quietly.

"Is she okay?" Tessa peered over Tiffany's shoulder. Emily's head was still in her hands.

"Yeah, she's just sensitive about stuff." Tiffany ushered them out the door, leaving Emily alone in the locker room. "She'll be okay in a few minutes, but she'll probably be embarrassed, so maybe don't make a big deal out of it, okay?"

"Yeah, okay, no problem." Tessa's mind immediately went to numbers on the ice. "We'll just have you play up at wing until she's ready. Does that work?"

Tiffany nodded. Her face was somber, concern evident in her expression. *Is anybody going to be able to focus on hockey today?*

It was one of the tougher games of the season, and the Darts struggled to get the puck out of their zone. The A-Team was a talented and cohesive group. AJ kept them in the game by blocking shot after shot. When Emily didn't come out of the locker room by the end of the first period, Tiffany went back to check on her. Tiffany returned to the bench, shaking her head.

"She's too worked up," Tiffany reported. "She wouldn't be able to help us out much with this team anyway, so she's getting undressed. Sorry guys."

TESSA

"Well, that sucks," Tessa said. She wasn't angry, but she was getting tired from playing on a three-D rotation. *How can she be too sad about somebody else's baby to play hockey?* That was a level of empathy beyond Tessa's comprehension.

"Alright, y'all, let's get the centers helping more in the corners and in front of the net," said Fitz. "Maybe we can try to get some long passes out to our wings."

Fitz was in captain mode. Tessa knew she was hurting deeply for Michelle, on top of whatever shit was going on in her own home, but she didn't let any of that get in the way of leading the team. Tessa admired that. *She would make a good manager.*

The Darts put up a decent fight, but ended up falling to the A-Team three-to-nothing. They were now seven, twelve, and two. Tessa did the math in her head as they rode the elevator up to Michelle's apartment. Fitz's pipe dream about playoffs was probably out of the question now, but they still had a shot at getting off probation.

"Maybe next time we can at least hold them to a tie," Tessa thought out loud. "That third goal doesn't really count since it was an open-netter."

Neither Dawn nor Fitz responded. They both looked very solemn as they walked down the hall to Michelle's door. Tessa didn't know what to expect on this visit, she had no idea what she would say to Michelle. Her mouth felt dry; she missed the beer that would have awaited her at the bar.

"You told her we were coming, right?" Fitz asked Dawn for the second or third time.

"Yes, she knows."

Michelle's husband opened the door. "Hey, come on in." He beckoned them inside.

Tessa was not prepared for how large and open the apartment was. She blinked in astonishment. It looked a little like Tessa's office building, with the polished concrete and large windows.

Tessa couldn't imagine living somewhere so industrial and cold. It was more like a showroom than a home.

Michelle was standing in the kitchen, leaning against the countertop, a glass of wine in her hand. She didn't look particularly pleased to see them. She didn't move as they entered, she just watched them, her eyes dark.

"How are you doing, baby girl?" Dawn asked.

Michelle shrugged.

"It's hard, but we're moving forward." Ben put an arm around Michelle. "Right, babe?"

"We'll be able to *move forward* when we can get back to our lives without all this... whatever the fuck all this is." She gestured at Fitz and the giant gift bag in her hands.

"Babe, don't be an asshole." Ben squeezed her shoulders. "Thank you, Fitz."

"We just wanted to check in on you." Fitz set the gift on the counter. "And to let you know we're thinking of you."

Michelle swirled her wine and didn't say anything for a long moment. She looked like she hadn't slept in days. Her nose was red and her mascara was smudged like she'd been crying not long ago—although her current expression was more angry than sad.

"So everybody knows now, huh?" Michelle threw back the last of her wine and swallowed. She set the glass down hard on the counter and the sudden sharp clink of glass on granite made Tessa flinch.

"I told the team, yeah." Dawn nodded.

Michelle snorted. "I should thank you, I suppose. It's a fucking awkward thing to tell people. People are always so..." Again she gestured at Fitz. "I don't need all this fucking pity, you know."

"Don't confuse sympathy with pity." Fitz put a hand on Michelle's shoulder but Michelle shrugged her off.

"Well, I don't need that either, thank you," Michelle snapped.

"You're being an asshole again, babe."

"Oh shut *up*, Ben," Michelle turned on him. "I don't *need* their fucking sympathy!"

Tessa felt her face get hot. *Maybe we shouldn't have come.* But to Tessa's surprise, Ben smiled.

"Yeah, well, Fitz probably didn't *need* you to threaten to kill her husband with a shotgun, did she?" Ben put his hands on her shoulders. "But you did."

Tessa glanced over at Fitz. Her face was pink, she looked flustered. *It's gotta be weird to hear this guy so casually mention her husband like that.*

Fitz quickly regained her composure. "You know, a smart lady once told me, 'when shit sucks, there's nobody better to help you than your hockey bitches,'" said Fitz.

"That sounds like somebody I might know." Ben leaned his forehead against Michelle's. "Come on, babe, it's your turn to shut up and let your friends care for you."

The rigidity in Michelle's posture softened as the fight seemed to slowly drain out of her. "Fine, I'll try not to be an asshole."

Ben kissed Michelle tenderly, and Tessa looked away. She suddenly felt like she was intruding on a personal moment. Seeing her teammates outside of hockey always felt a little strange, but seeing one of them in such an emotional show of affection as that kiss was too much.

A flash of memory from Tessa's dream sent hot blood rushing to her face. *Don't think about kissing.* She looked at Fitz. *Ah! Don't look at Fitz!* She turned to the countertop. *Oh hey, they have the same coffee maker as we have at the office too.* Tessa fidgeted with the edge of her sleeve.

"Can I get you all something to drink?" asked Ben. Tessa turned back. Ben and Michelle had parted.

"Thank you, Ben, but no, first Michelle has to open her gift." Fitz pushed it across the counter, closer to Michelle.

Michelle shrugged. "You're the captain." She reached in the bag and pulled out a pint glass and a handle of Fireball. She raised an eyebrow. "A whole *pint* of Fireball might be a bit much, even for me, Fitz."

"Look at the glass."

"*Cheers, bitches,*" Michelle read. She smiled faintly. "Where did you find this?"

"Power of the internet." Fitz grinned. Dawn pulled three matching glasses and a six-pack of beer from the innocuous brown bag she'd been holding.

Michelle shook her head. "You bitches are too much."

"I think I'll leave you 'bitches' to it." Ben kissed Michelle again, this time chastely on the forehead, and left the kitchen. Fitz poured beer into Michelle's glass and held it out to her.

"Okay, fine." Slowly Michelle took the glass from Fitz. "I guess I promised not to be an asshole. So thank you."

"Cheers, bitches?" said Fitz. Dawn and Tessa raised their glasses to Michelle.

"Cheers, bitches," Michelle repeated. She drank. Tessa drank. It wasn't *Coors Light,* but nonetheless, Tessa was happy for it.

"We missed you at the game today," Dawn said when she'd put down her glass.

"Yeah? How did it go?" Michelle asked.

"We got spanked pretty hard." Tessa was relieved to be talking hockey.

"I wouldn't say we got *spanked,*" said Dawn. "I thought we played pretty good, they're just a really tough team."

"It felt like a spanking." Tessa shrugged. She looked cautiously at Michelle. "Do you think you're going to be able to play anytime soon?" *I hope it's not too early to ask.*

Michelle shook her head. "Do you even have space for me? What about *Christine?*" She rolled her eyes as she said 'Christine.' *I guess Christine hasn't won Michelle over.*

"Come on, are you kidding? This is *your team*, Michelle," said Fitz earnestly. "As soon as you're ready to come back, we're ready to have you."

Michelle seemed to consider for a moment. "Fuck Christine then, huh?" Michelle smirked. "It would probably do me some good to get out on the ice again. I'm going to give it another week, but yeah, I'll play."

"I'm so glad." Fitz gave Michelle a quick side-hug. "I've missed you on my wing. We'll keep Christine on as a sub, though, so you might have to play with her."

"Seriously?" Michelle scowled. "Come *on*, Fitz, Christine is the *queen supreme* of unwanted commentary. I can usually deal with a lot of shitty things people say, but not right now." Michelle shook her head. "It's like, I swear to God if one more person tells me that God has a motherfucking *plan,* I will stab them in the eye with a screwdriver."

Tessa glanced sideways at Fitz, but Fitz didn't react.

"So really it's for her own good that I not spend time with Christine, because if she were to say one solitary *fucking* word while I'm armed... bam!" Michelle fiercely jabbed her hands forward, demonstrating a crosscheck that would have caught Fitz across the neck had she been holding a stick.

"Okay, we get the picture, baby girl," said Dawn. "I'm sorry you've had to deal with those types of comments."

"Yeah, well, it's just part of the shitty hand I've been dealt, isn't it." Michelle took a deep breath and a big gulp of beer. "Speaking of being dealt shitty hands, how are you doing, Fitz? You kick that bastard out yet?"

Does Michelle really not see the irony in complaining about other people commenting on her problems when she turns around and does the same thing?

Fitz hunched her shoulders. "Only out of the bedroom." She shook her head. "We're going to counseling. Praying a lot. I don't know if it's helping. But I have to keep faith. I want to be optimistic."

"Well, if you ever need to get out of that house, I've got a guest room and a shit ton of booze. Come over any time," said Michelle.

"Thanks." Fitz smiled. "Your place is gorgeous, by the way."

"Yeah, I know, right? It's fucking amazing. Did you see the view?"

Fitz

Sunday, February 11th

Fitz kept glancing at her watch; she had promised Tom she wouldn't stay too long. Fitz was having a hard time focusing on Nikki and Tessa. The game today had been brutal—a six to zero loss against the A-Team. Only the three of them had bothered to go out at all. While the other two recounted the failings of their game, Fitz was distracted thinking about her husband and about the upcoming holiday. *Valentine's Day.*

Things were so delicate right now. She and Tom had been going to counseling; they were trying to pick up the pieces of their shattered relationship and somehow put them back together. It was slow and difficult. Fitz couldn't tell if they'd made progress or if she'd just found new ways to stay in denial about how bad things really were.

The events of that horrible night, when everything had come to a head and Fitz's world had come crashing down around her, were no longer spoken of. It was the fear and anger and pain of those events which had sent them running to their pastor, begging for counsel, but now it was almost like it never happened. Tom had hit her barely over a month ago, and yet it was like it belonged to a different lifetime—somebody else's lifetime.

In counseling, Fitz never used the word '*rape*' again, as she had that night. She tried to explain to Tom how it felt when he didn't wait for her consent to touch her or to make love to her. Tom swore he had no idea how much he had hurt her. He promised never to do it again. He made a lot of promises.

Fitz didn't know how to feel about the things Tom said in that room, on the faux-leather sofa, under the eyes of their church counselor and the large painting of Christ that hung above his desk. The counselor was good at getting Tom to open up. Tom discussed his feelings in ways Fitz had never heard him do before. He would talk; she would talk. They would make promises to each other. Then they would go home and barely speak.

They hadn't shared a bed in over a month, although Tom made no secret of the fact that he wanted that to change as soon as possible. He wanted her to feel *safe* with him, he said. He wanted her to demonstrate some level of trust to show that she hadn't lost all faith in him as her husband.

Fitz wanted to believe what he said. She wanted to trust him. But her mounting anxiety over Valentine's Day proved that she wasn't there yet. Valentine's Day with Tom used to be romantic. He could be incredibly charming. However, at some point the charm of Valentine's Day had begun to feel forced. Instead of being a celebration of love, it was an obligation to be fulfilled. There were *expectations*. Fitz wasn't ready to play her usual part in the ritual, and she didn't yet trust Tom to understand and respect that. Valentine's Day would be a test—one she wasn't prepared to take.

"Are you looking forward to next week?" Tessa asked.

Fitz started. "No!" she reacted before she realized Tessa was talking about next week's game and Michelle's return, not about the world's most hated holiday. "Sorry, I was thinking about something else. I am looking forward to our next game. I cannot wait to have Michelle back on the ice."

"Oh good, I was afraid you and Michelle were fighting again there for a second," said Nikki, wiping her brow.

"What? Michelle and I weren't fighting," Fitz said defensively.

Nikki laughed. "Um, I'm pretty sure I heard you call her a cunt at the holiday party. I mean, I was pretty drunk, but people don't roll out the *C-U-Next-Tuesday* all that often, so that made it kind of memorable."

"Oh, I was just—that wasn't really..." Fitz stammered. She hadn't forgotten about that exactly, but so much had happened since then. It was embarrassing to think about. "Actually, sorry y'all, I really do need to be getting home. I promised my husband."

"Come *on*, Fitz." Tessa scowled.

"Please don't, Tessa, I'm tired." Fitz looked pleadingly into Tessa's face. Tessa's big brown eyes held Fitz's gaze for a long moment before she looked away in resignation. Fitz knew Tessa was worried about her. But she was grateful that Tessa didn't say any more about it. Fitz said goodbye and left for home.

Friday, February 14th

"Good morning, Belle."

Fitz squinted and rubbed her eyes. Tom was sitting on the edge of the bed. "Happy Valentine's Day," he said.

"What time is it?" Fitz sat up groggily.

"It's early, but I wanted to see you before the kids woke up." Tom put his hand under her chin. "Happy Valentine's Day," he repeated.

"Happy Valentine's Day," Fitz echoed.

There was so much anticipation in his eyes, it made her heart race. He leaned forward and gave her a brief, soft kiss. She didn't resist; the kiss was sweet and unintrusive.

When he pulled back, he handed her a small rectangular box, and her heart sank. *More jewelry.* It was the annual tradition; he gave her something shiny and expensive, and she thanked him by giving him herself. It was trite and cheap and right now, it scared her a little.

"Open it," Tom said impatiently. Slowly Fitz unwrapped the box and lifted the lid. It wasn't jewelry.

"Tickets?" Fitz looked closer at the unexpected gift. "*Wild* tickets?" She was stunned; she looked at Tom. He smiled his little self-satisfied smile. He was enjoying her response.

"For the game tonight. My parents are going to take the kids overnight," he said. She stared at him.

"You do like hockey, don't you?" he asked. She nodded. He cupped her chin again.

"Then it's a date. I'll pick you up at six." He kissed her once more. "Happy Valentine's Day, Belle."

That night, Fitz and Tom walked together through the gates into the Xcel Energy Center in downtown St. Paul. Fitz was still in shock over the surprisingly thoughtful gift.

"What made you think of doing this for Valentine's Day?" she asked. "I feel like anytime I mention hockey, it makes you upset."

"Your hockey. Come on, don't ruin this," he said tensely, but then he caught himself and smiled at her. "I'm sorry, I mean, let's try to have a good time. Tonight is about us. Don't you remember when I brought you here way back when? When I took my sweet southern Belle to her first-ever real live hockey game?"

"Oh... Oh, wow." Fitz put her hand over her heart. "I haven't thought about that in a long time." Fitz's mouth curled up as the memory came back into focus. "Spring break, senior year."

It felt so long ago. She and Tom had been newly engaged and were apartment hunting in preparation for their move to Minnesota. They'd left the beauty of North Carolina in springtime to come to the land that spring forgot. She'd had her reservations, but Tom was determined to make Fitz see past the sloshy snow and freezing rain, and help her find something to love about their new home.

"Right. The Wild beat Calgary four to two that game, and you asked a million questions." Tom laughed. "You didn't know anything about hockey." He stopped and looked at her. He pushed a stray strand of hair back from her face. "You were so beautiful. I remember feeling like the luckiest guy on God's green earth."

Fitz's face burned with heat.

"Those are both still true, you know," he added. She smiled at him. *He can still be so charming.* She leaned forward and kissed him on the cheek.

"Thanks, Tom." She took his hand, entwining her fingers with his. "Come on, let's get some hotdogs."

Tom seemed to appreciate her G-rated show of affection. He smiled warmly at her as they got food and found their seats. Fitz felt a warm glow inside. *This is the man I married.* He looked so handsome tonight; he was always more attractive when he was happy and at ease. *Where does this Tom go when we're at home?* Tom put his arm around her, and she leaned into him. *I wonder if he's thinking the same thing about me.*

Fitz relaxed and enjoyed the game, and the time with her husband. The Wild lost but the game was exciting, and Fitz and Tom left the Xcel Center in high spirits. However as they rode home, their SUV felt deathly silent and cold in comparison to the crowd of excited fans they'd left behind.

"That was a great game," said Fitz as Tom drove. She chewed her lip. "We out-shot them. It's too bad they had the stronger goalie." *We're lucky AJ is a strong goalie, although it'd be better if we were getting more shots too.* All night Fitz's mind had been wandering back to the Darts. Although the NHL game was so much faster and rougher, it was still hockey.

"Dubnyk is normally a strong goalie," said Tom. "I still think the Wild actually have a shot at the Stanley Cup playoffs this year." The mention of playoffs also reminded Fitz of her team.

"I was looking online the other day, and the Darts might have a chance at making the playoff tournament if we win our remaining games." She smiled. It was such an amazing turnaround from the start of the year. "We could do it too; we have some easier matchups coming up—"

"Jesus, Patricia, you take that shit too seriously," Tom snapped. Fitz fell silent. She'd let down her guard too much. Tom took a breath. "It's not exactly the pros, you know." He tried to sound light-hearted, but his words had already stung.

"I know. I'm sorry for bringing it up," Fitz muttered.

Tom sighed. "No, I'm sorry. Can we just forget it?" He glanced over at her. "I had such a good time with you tonight, Belle."

"I did too." Fitz had been happy at the game, but now the reality of their current relationship weighed on her again. *Focus on the happy times. A cheerful heart is good medicine. Tonight's happiness can only be healing if we open our hearts to it.* She smiled at him. "Thank you, Tom, this was a wonderful idea for Valentine's Day."

"You're welcome, Belle."

That night Fitz let Tom back into her bed. She wasn't ready to make love, and although he was clearly disappointed, Tom respected her boundaries. It was a small step, but Fitz went to sleep with more peace of mind than she'd had in a long time.

Michelle

Saturday, February 17th

"Did my bag get heavier, or am I just that out of shape?" Michelle dragged her hockey equipment into the apartment. Ben leaned against the wall, watching her. "You could offer to help," she said.

"Yeah, right, like you'd take my help carrying your hockey gear. You'd probably castrate me for even asking." Ben rolled his eyes.

"Fair point." Michelle stretched. "Fuck, I'm sore."

"How was your first game back?" Ben stepped behind her and began to rub her shoulders.

"It was alright." She sighed as Ben rubbed. "We tied."

"And how did it feel?" He asked. "Was it... okay? Being back?"

She stepped away, jerking her shoulders out from under his touch. Ben was so fucking concerned about her feelings. It was aggravating. "Yes, it was fine—I'm fine, Ben," she snapped. He put his hands up in surrender.

Shit. Michelle sighed. "Sorry. It's fine. I'm going to go shower."

"Yeah, you probably stink," he said playfully.

"Fuck you," she replied, the words coming out less playfully than she'd intended. She'd been doing that a lot lately. Too much. *You're not angry at Ben, stop being a bitch.* She put her arms around his neck.

"Sorry, babe," she said. She smiled. It was easier to smile when she was looking into his eyes. "Come on, I don't smell that bad."

He wrapped his arms around her waist and squeezed her tight. "Sorry, babe," he parroted, "but you kind of do."

"Alright, asshole." She gave him a quick peck on the lips. "I get the message. I don't want to upset your *delicate sensibilities*. I'll go shower." She smirked at him.

"Want company?" Ben raised an eyebrow.

"No," Michelle shook her head, her smile falling. They hadn't had sex since before the hospital. That fact saddened her, but she just hadn't been able to get in the mood. How could she? With the shadow of grief following her around, often out of sight, but always there?

I haven't really tried, have I? How am I supposed to get in the mood if I don't try? Ben never pressured her. He seemed almost as timid about sex as she did. *Come to think of it, is this the first time he's even asked since the hospital?*

"Okay, I'll let you wash my back," Michelle said, smile returning. "But that's it. Got it, horn-dog?"

"You're the boss." He let her lead the way to the bathroom. Inside the large double shower, Ben gently scrubbed her back and shoulders. The hot water, combined with Ben's touch, relaxed her senses. When Ben kissed the back of her neck, she felt a tingle in her toes that she hadn't experienced in some time. Michelle turned and kissed him. She ran her fingers down the length of his bicep and back up. She softly brushed the stubble on his cheek as she kissed him.

"I thought I was just here to wash your back," Ben murmured between kisses.

Michelle pulled back. "Well, now I'm offering to wash you. Do you accept?" she asked. Ben nodded. Michelle kissed him again, her hands continued to wander Ben's wet body, moving south.

"That's not my back," he sighed.

"I never said anything about your back."

Fooling around in the shower wasn't quite the same as a good fuck, but it still put a real smile on Michelle's face. She realized something while her body was pressed, naked and wet, against Ben's. She realized she didn't want to have sex—hadn't been able to 'get in the mood'—because she was afraid of getting pregnant again.

Fear. It was just another emotion she'd been trying to avoid, but that sat inside her always. Along with the sadness, pain, and grief. All these emotions together created that shadow, that dark presence that had been haunting her. She didn't want to see it, to touch it—but sometimes it touched her. And sometimes it consumed her.

Today the touch of fear had been light but powerful. Michelle was terrified by the possibility of getting pregnant. It seemed so obvious once the thought had crystallized. She didn't know why she hadn't figured it out weeks ago. *Maybe because I'm avoiding thinking about my feelings? Duh?*

Dried and dressed, Michelle snuggled up to Ben on the sofa. "Ben?"

"Yeah, babe?"

"I don't want to get pregnant again," she said. Michelle could hear his heartbeat as she leaned against his chest, waiting for him to react. "Are you gonna respond?"

"Okay," Ben said.

"That's it? Just, 'okay?'" Michelle pulled her head back so she could look at him.

"Do you want me to go out and buy condoms or something?" Ben asked. Michelle smacked him on the arm.

"Come on, I'm serious! Is it really okay with you that I don't want to get pregnant again?" She watched his face for any hint of sadness or disappointment.

"Yes, it's okay with me," he said. She continued to stare, unconvinced. Ben sighed. "Does it make me a little sad? Yes. But only a little. I don't need another baby to be happy, I just need *you.* And if what you need right now is to take that off the table, I am more than willing to do that."

Michelle looked into his eyes. She had to be sure.

"I'm serious babe, I will go to Costco and get the biggest box of condoms you have ever seen." *He means it.*

Michelle smiled and laid her head back on his chest. "Condoms suck, I'll make an appointment with my doctor to get an IUD or something."

Ben chuckled softly. "I love you," he said. He kissed the top of her head. "I love you, and I love Ella, and I love our family just the way it is."

"I love you too." Michelle fiddled with the collar of his t-shirt, brushing her fingers against his chest. "I hate how shitty things have been. I'm ready to be happy again. Like, not just avoiding being sad, but I'm ready to be actually fucking happy."

"Me too, babe."

"Thing is, I don't think I was before *just now*. I don't think I've been letting myself enjoy things, you know? Like hockey today. It was like I didn't want to have fun. Like I shouldn't have fun." Michelle was thinking aloud. Recognizing that she hadn't been giving herself permission to be happy was a big revelation. She'd avoided positive emotions as much as she avoided the negative ones.

"I can see that," Ben said thoughtfully. "I think maybe I've been doing the same thing."

"Well, we need to cut it the fuck out." Michelle sat up. "Because we deserve to be happy, dammit!"

"Hell yeah, we do!" Ben agreed.

"So how the fuck do we do that?"

"I have no fucking idea. I thought you knew."

Michelle laughed. "Nope. Not a fucking clue." She shook her head.

"Well then, I guess we'll have to wing it."

"I guess so." Inside, Michelle could feel something else she hadn't felt in a while: hope—actual, real-life, 'the sun will come out tomorrow' optimism. And that felt almost as good as happiness.

"God, I love you." Michelle sank back into Ben's arms.

"I love you too. So much."

Saturday, March 3rd

Michelle's second game back was more fun. It was amazing the difference a week of determined optimism could make. The Darts won. She had a good time at the bar with her friends. And Michelle went home to her family feeling more like her old self than she had in ages.

Michelle must have made hockey sound a little *too* good though, because the next thing she knew, Ben had invited himself and Ella along to today's game.

"Hock-ey, hock-ey, hock-ey!" chanted Ella from the backseat of the car.

"I'm not so sure about this." Michelle glanced at her daughter in the rear-view mirror as she drove. "It's like you guys are invading my personal space."

"Come on, Ella wants to see her big tough mama play some hockey! Kick some butt! Right, Ella?" Ben looked back at their daughter.

"Kick butt, kick butt!" Ella repeated.

Michelle rolled her eyes. "Oh, for fuck's sake," she muttered under her breath. "Thanks for that."

"You're welcome." Ben was smiling—he looked quite pleased with himself.

"The game is so not going to hold her attention, you know that. I don't see what you're trying to accomplish here."

"Who says I'm trying to accomplish anything, babe?" Ben grinned. She squinted at him. He shrugged. "And so what if I am? What's so bad about wanting to show our daughter what a badass you are?"

Michelle rolled her eyes again. Being a strong role model for her daughter was important to Michelle. But did that mean they had to actually come with her to hockey? *Couldn't he just tell her that I'm a badass?*

"Whatever. I'm going to play like shit—you are totally fucking up my pre-game routine."

"Naw, babe, we're your good luck charms, you're going to kill 'em tonight." Ben was so stubbornly upbeat.

"Tessa would kill you if she heard you say that, you know," said Michelle. "If we lose, I'm holding you personally responsible. Got it, asshole?"

"Fair enough."

Michelle turned up her music and tried to ignore them the rest of the drive to the rink. When they arrived, she stubbornly refused to let Ella follow her into the locker room. Ella cried and threw herself on the nasty rink floor.

"Ella! Get up right now! People walk around here on skates! Do you want to get your finger sliced off?" Michelle said, sternly. Ella did not get up; she *did* cry louder.

"I wanna go inna rocker room!" Ella screamed.

Michelle glared at Ben. "I told you this was a bad idea. I need to get ready, this is your problem now." If Michelle had to deal with Ella's latest tantrum for one more minute, she was going to punch somebody—probably somebody on the ice, but still, she didn't need the penalty minutes.

Ben nodded. "As you wish," he winked at her. Michelle rolled her eyes as she watched Ben struggle to pick the flailing toddler up off the floor.

"Hey, now, let's calm down," Ben cooed. "Do you wanna go get a snack, princess? I think I saw some vending machines over there!"

Michelle turned and walked off before she could see if his bribery tactic worked. Once she was in the locker room, she was finally able to focus and get into game mode. By the time the game got underway, Michelle almost forgot that Ben and Ella were there. *Almost.*

From the bench, Michelle watched Ella climb over and around the bleachers. *See, I knew it wouldn't hold her attention.* But the next time she looked up, Ben was holding Ella up to the glass, pointing at Michelle. They waved. Michelle waved back.

"Is that your daughter?" asked the woman Michelle was facing off against.

"Yeah, it is."

"She's adorable! I bet one day she'll play hockey just like mommy." The woman smiled warmly at Michelle—until the puck dropped, and she roughly shoved her shoulder into Michelle's chest, knocking her to the ice.

This league is so weird. On the sidelines, Ella clapped her hands and giggled at her mom, sprawled on the ice. *My daughter, ladies and gentlemen.*

The Darts did win, three-to-one. After the game, Michelle acquiesced and let Ella follow her into the 'rocker room.' The women on the team cooed over the little girl.

"She is so cute! Look at her eyes!" Nikki swooned. "I'm dead. She's such a beauty."

"Did you like watching your mom play hockey?" Dawn asked. Ella nodded. "Are you going to play hockey when you get big?" She nodded again.

"What did you think of the game, Ella?" Fitz asked.

"So fast!" Ella jumped up and down excitedly.

"Your mom is very fast, isn't she?" Fitz's eyes were bright with laughter. Ella began to run around the room, chanting, 'fast fast fast!' The team didn't seem to mind the loud little girl. They all smiled at Ella as she passed by them.

"It must be so nice to be able to bring your family," Fitz said wistfully. "My kids have never seen me play. It's such a testament to you that your family wants to be here."

Michelle didn't know what to say. *I just got lucky: I got Ben, while poor Fitz got Douchey McAssface.* Fitz blushed, and Michelle realized she must have been staring at her.

Michelle coughed. "Yeah, well, who knows if she got anything out of it, or will even remember it by tomorrow."

"She watched a lot of the game for such a little one! I kept looking up and seeing her staring at you," said Dawn. "She really looks up to you, doesn't she?"

Michelle grinned to herself, a warm blossom of pride blooming in her chest. Ben was right, bringing Ella to the game was fun.

"You should bring her more often," Dawn said. "Maybe we should do a family game day sometime, get all our kids out here. I know Annabelle would just love to look after this little munchkin." Dawn tickled Ella as she ran past.

"Michelle, are you bringing your family to the bar?" Nikki asked. Michelle did the mental math. If they went out now by the time they got drinks Ella would be precariously close to the pre-bedtime meltdown zone. That could suck, but she didn't want to miss going out either. *Ella might be able to handle a later night.* Ben would know.

"I don't know. I guess I should talk to my husband." Michelle scooped up her daughter. "What do you think, Ell? Do you want to go to the bar?"

"I wanna go to a bar," said Ella seriously, as if she had any concept of what she was talking about. Michelle laughed.

"Well, of course, you do! You are my daughter, after all!"

Dawn

Friday, March 9th

"I might stay a little extra long at hockey tomorrow, since it's the last game of the season," Dawn reminded Sharon as they cuddled up on the sofa for their traditional Friday night *Netflix* binge. The kids were asleep, or at least pretending to be, which was good enough for now. There wasn't much on the schedule tomorrow aside from the Darts' game.

"I can't believe it's already almost over. With all this cold and snow it feels like it should be the middle of the hockey season, not the end," said Sharon. "It's like Winterfell out there."

"Yeah, it's gone by really fast." Dawn cracked her neck. "Especially since Michelle came back, it's like I blinked, and suddenly we're down to the last game."

"How *is* Michelle doing?" Sharon snuggled up close, pulling her TARDIS blanket up over both of them. It was *stupid*-cold for March.

"Michelle seems like she's doing a lot better. She's been acting like her usual self these last couple games. She's making jokes, playing hard, swearing a lot. She's Michelle."

"Are you sure she's not just putting on an act? She seems like the type of person who has a hard time being vulnerable. Sometimes the ones who put on the biggest show are the ones who are hurting the worst. Never forget Robin Williams and Anthony Bourdain. I think about them a lot when I'm feeling depressed and start envying the people who look so *furiously happy*. You know?"

Dawn understood what Sharon meant. She kissed her wife on the forehead as she considered the point. Michelle certainly knew how to put on a show. But she did have some 'tells' when she was upset. Subtle ones, but they were there. Dawn wondered if she'd missed any the last time she'd seen her.

"I know what you're saying, sweetness, but I really do think she's doing well. When she's upset, her sarcasm tends to trend away from humor and gets a little… pointy. I don't think I've heard her snap at anybody." Dawn laughed. "Except this one time at Christine, but that was kind of funny. Christine was going on and on about how the other team didn't have any fast skaters, and eventually, Michelle was like, 'If they're so effing slow why are they beating you to the effing puck, *Christine*?'" Dawn chortled. "Only she didn't say 'effing.'"

"Just keep an eye on her, okay?" Sharon gave Dawn a pleading look.

"Okay, sweetness, I will." Dawn patted Sharon on the knee. She appreciated Sharon's concern. The brief interaction Sharon had with Michelle and Fitz at the holiday party had made a lasting impression.

"And how about Fitz?" Sharon asked.

Fitz was a more difficult question to answer. Dawn chewed her lip the way Fitz did when she looked upset. *How is Fitz doing?* She certainly talked as if things were getting better, but Dawn and Michelle both still had grave concerns.

"I worry about her," Dawn answered truthfully. "She says things are getting better. And honestly, she might believe that they are, but some of the things she says… To me it sounds like her husband is just manipulating her, and she's going to end up right back where she was a couple months ago. Or worse."

"Like what does she say?" Sharon asked.

"It's little things, you know? Like how *charming* he was at Valentine's, or how he's *letting* her go to hockey without picking a fight. She's sleeping with him again, and the fact that she mentioned it at all, it just seemed like she still isn't sure that it's what she wants. She let slip that he was the one who convinced her not to go to individual therapy. He doesn't see a reason for it, since they're in marriage counseling already. That really made me worry, but she swears it's what she wants too. I don't know, sweets. I just get the sense that she's still not comfortable really talking to him, she almost seems kind of... scared of him?" Dawn frowned. When she said it all aloud, it sounded worse than it had in her head. *Should I say something to Fitz?*

"Sleeping with him or, like, 'sleeping' with him?" Sharon was visibly alarmed.

"I don't know." Dawn shook her head. "Although it's really none of our business."

"No, I suppose not. I just worry." Sharon entwined her fingers with Dawn's and laid her head on her shoulder.

"Me too, boo-boo." She kissed Sharon's hand. "I'll check in on her. Okay?"

"Thank you." Sharon kissed Dawn's cheek softly. Dawn turned her shoulders so that she could kiss her wife properly.

Sharon's kisses were warm and inviting and Dawn felt a swell of happiness and awakened desire. She put both hands on Sharon's face as she kissed her faster and more deeply. The world faded away behind her, and nothing mattered at that moment except for Sharon. Dawn wanted nothing else but to consume this beautiful creature in front of her.

"Yuck, mom, please stop!" Mari's voice echoed from the top of the stairs.

Dawn collapsed on the sofa dramatically. "No! What? Child? Why?" She groaned.

"Go back to sleep, sweetie," said Sharon.

"I'm thirsty."

So am I, kid.

"So get water and then go back to sleep." Sharon's voice was sweet but impatient.

She's thirsty too. Mari's feet plodded down the stairs toward the kitchen. Dawn listened to the sound of water running as she filled a glass.

"Hurry up, or I'm gonna start making out with your mama again!" Dawn threatened. Mari ran off with a squeal. Sharon tilted her head at Dawn disapprovingly, but Dawn only laughed.

"Come, my lady," she said, standing up from the sofa and extending a hand to her wife. "There is naught but troublesome interruption to be found here. Let us adjourn to the boudoir."

Sharon snorted. Dawn pulled on her and Sharon let herself be led away.

"You're such a dork." Sharon giggled. Dawn pulled her close, pinning her against the wall outside their room and kissed her.

Mmmmmm. She slipped her hands under Sharon's shirt. Sharon pushed her off and dodged out of reach. She stuck out her tongue. "Save it for the *boudoir.*" She disappeared through the doorway.

"As you wish." Dawn followed close behind.

Tessa

Saturday, March 10th

Tessa stepped into the arena for the last game of the season. *The last game.* It was hard to believe it was already here. It didn't seem like it should be the last game already. Tessa looked around. *This rink really does feel like home now.* She'd miss it—hot, sweaty locker room and all. It had been good to them.

"Psst, Tessa," Dawn called from the doorway to the locker room. "Have you seen Fitz yet?"

"No, is everything ready?"

Tessa, Dawn, and Michelle, along with the rest of the team, had cooked up a little surprise for their captain.

"Almost, Michelle just said to stall her another couple seconds if—oh, there she is!"

Fitz bounded up to them, electric with energy. "Hey y'all, do you realize that if we win this game, we could go to the playoffs?" She was overflowing with excitement.

"What?" Tessa blinked, confused. Fitz grabbed her arm and pulled her close. A shiver went up Tessa's spine, and she felt her heart skip a beat. She didn't need to stall Fitz—Fitz had stalled *her.*

"If we win this game, we could potentially get a spot in playoffs," said Fitz, her bright eyes searching Tessa's.

What is she talking about? How is that possible? "Really? Are you sure?" Tessa breathed.

"I was looking at the website, and based on that, I'm sure that if we lose, we won't make the cut, but if we win we have a chance!" Fitz released Tessa's arm.

Tessa frowned; she thought that making the playoffs had been taken off the table weeks ago. But she might have been wrong. Tessa buried her fingers in her hair and scratched her head. *Wouldn't that be cool.*

"You spend too much time on that website, baby girl," said Dawn.

"But to have any chance, we absolutely need to win today," Fitz reiterated. There was fire in her eyes, her face set with stern, almost desperate resolution.

"Hold on a minute, boo-boo. I don't want to end this season the way we ended the last season with the Hot Shots, all stressed over the outcome. This is our last regular-season game. Let's just have fun. Okay?"

Tessa hadn't thought about the Hot Shots in a while, she realized. Fitz's energy was so intense right now, Tessa could easily see herself getting swept up in it. Tessa almost liked the idea of getting swept up in it, but she could sense the pressure that came with such intensity—the pressure to win. When Tessa thought about it that way, it did sort of remind her of the bad old days.

"Dawn is right, making the last game of the season stressful because of a potential playoff spot would be a real Hot Shots thing to do. Remember how miserable everybody was when Jackie would yell about how we'd better not fuck up our chances for playoffs?" Tessa said.

Fitz winced.

"Oh, no, I'm not saying you'd *ever* be *anything* like Jackie," Tessa added quickly, shaking her head. "But it's just not a great path to start down."

Fitz chewed her lip. "Yeah, okay, you're right. I won't make a big deal about it," she agreed.

"Great, now hold on just one second." Dawn poked her head inside the locker room. "Yup, we're good, come on in, Fitz."

"What's going on?" Fitz looked skeptically at Tessa. Tessa grinned and pushed Fitz forward into the locker room.

"Surprise!"

The team was all already there, wearing matching dark green sweatshirts: Darts sweatshirts. Michelle held one out to Fitz. Fitz's mouth dropped open, and her eyes went wide. She looked absolutely *floored*.

"We wanted to do something as a team to thank you for being such an awesome captain," Tessa explained, grinning. Fitz opened and closed her mouth wordlessly.

"Come on, take the damn thing." Michelle thrust it at her. "Tessa said you missed having a team hoodie."

Slowly Fitz took the sweatshirt from Michelle's hands. "Y'all, I just can't..." Fitz sniffed. "Thank you. But I didn't do that much."

"Yes, you did, boo-boo." Dawn wrapped an arm around Fitz.

"Really, Fitz," Tessa added.

"Come on, group hug for Fitz!" Michelle threw her arms around them and scooped Tessa in as well. Tessa felt both exhilarated and uncomfortable as the rest of the team piled on, squeezing them close together.

"It really was a group effort," Fitz said through tears when the hug broke apart.

"Yeah, but it never would have happened without you leading." Tessa looked up at Fitz and smiled. "You're amazing." Tessa nudged Fitz's shoulder with her own.

Fitz nudged her back. "Thanks, Tess."

The team dressed and took the ice for their last game of the season. After a quick team huddle and cheer, they all took their places on the ice. It all seemed quite ordinary until the face-off when instead of signaling to the goalies, as usual, the ref pointed at Tiffany and blew his whistle. Tiffany dropped her gloves and stick. She slowly approached Emily. Tessa had no idea what was going on until Tiffany pulled off her helmet and went down to one knee, all in one fluid motion. Emily's eyes went wide.

"Oh my God," Emily mouthed as she allowed Tiffany to take off her gloves so she could hold her hands.

"Emily, you are the light at the center of my universe. You are warm and kind and loving. You are creative and funny and clever. And you are a badass hockey player."

Emily smiled and even chuckled through the tears that had begun to trickle down her cheeks.

"You are also the most beautiful woman I have ever seen. I marvel every day at the wonder of being with you. These past two years have been an incredible, fantastic adventure. And now I'm asking..." Tiffany pulled a small box from the back of her breezers and opened it up to reveal a ring, "will you continue that adventure with me forever?" She held the ring up to her teary-eyed girlfriend. "Emily, will you marry me?"

Emily was nodding before Tiffany had even finished. "Yes!" she squeaked from behind her tears. Tiffany smiled and slipped the ring on her finger.

The bench went wild. All the players from both teams banged their sticks, kicked the boards, and cheered. Tessa wasn't usually touched by grand romantic gestures, but she felt her heart swell watching her teammates. *They look so happy.*

Tiffany stood up and Emily grabbed her for an embrace, Tiffany pulled back slightly and tapped Emily on the head. She was still wearing her helmet. She tore it off. Tiffany then took Emily's face in her hands and kissed her. Everyone around them cheered even louder. Tessa didn't look away; it was so incredibly sweet. Something inside of Tessa burned. *I wonder what that's like.* Tessa took a deep breath. *Don't think about it, we still have a game to play.*

Emily and Tiffany gathered up their things and got off the ice. Fitz followed them, her eyes red with tears. Tessa smiled and shook her head ruefully. *Is anybody going to be able to focus on hockey today?*

The team they were playing, the Blackbirds, played a very physical game. The distracted Darts did let one goal in early, but they got better and fought back. When they ended the first period one-to-nothing, it still felt like anybody's game.

"Let's not get ourselves down over one goal," said Fitz. "We just need to be more careful in front of the net. They're sneaky, but we can do this y'all."

Early in the second period Brooke answered back and scored one for the Darts.

"Consider it an engagement gift," Brooke said to Tiffany.

"Hey, can you get one of those for Emily too then?" asked Tessa.

"Get her one yourself!" Brooke shouted over her shoulder as she vaulted the boards. Tessa grinned. They were working hard and having fun. They were connecting as a team.

Tessa was cautiously optimistic when they finished the second period one-to-one. She tried really hard not to even *think* the word 'play-offs,' but it wasn't easy. *I wonder what would happen if we tie? No, don't worry about that, focus: we need more shots on net.*

Unfortunately, sometimes the puck just doesn't bounce your way. In the third period, a scuffle in front of the Darts net resulted in a goal for the Blackbirds. The Darts lost the last game of the season two-to-one.

Fitz

Saturday, March 10th

Fitz sat at the end of the Dart's biggest table. She looked at her teammates, decked out in their matching Darts hoodies. They looked good. Not just good, they looked happy. They were laughing, drinking, and having fun. Fitz was content sitting among them. She was sad that the season was over, but at the same time, she felt a calming sense of purpose. She was blessed. She had a wonderful team, great friends, and she knew that although it was the end of this season, it wasn't the end of everything. The Darts were only just getting started.

"A well-fought end to a great first season," said Tessa.

"It really was. I mean, I know we lost, but we played so well today," Fitz said. Around her heads nodded in agreement.

"So that's it, huh? The season is totally over?" asked Nikki.

Fitz sighed. "I'm afraid so. If we had won, we might have had a shot at playoffs..." She was hesitant to even bring it up, but since they no longer had a chance, there didn't seem to be any harm. "But you have to be in the top six, and we're not. But it doesn't matter. What matters is that I'm pretty sure we didn't end up in the bottom three. So we should be off probation for next season!" She grinned. Reaching that goal marker made the season a success, even if they didn't qualify for playoffs. They would be back to try again next year.

"Speaking of next season," said Emily, fiddling with her ring. Fitz cocked her head to the side. Emily glanced back at Tiffany, who nodded at her encouragingly. "I'm not going to come back to the Darts next year."

"What?" Fitz was shocked. Her thoughts went immediately to Tiffany; the Darts couldn't lose two players, and Tiffany was so good. She tried to control her expression. "Can I ask why?"

"It's not because this isn't a great team—it is! You guys are really fun!" she insisted. "It's just that I think this level is too much for me. I want to go back to feeling like I make a difference on the ice."

"You make a difference," Tessa said, unconvincingly. Emily was far and away the worst player on the team. On reflection, Fitz realized, playing on a team that rarely passed to you and often skated around you couldn't have been much fun.

"We'll miss you." Dawn squeezed Emily's shoulder.

"Thanks. But you'll see me." Emily looked again at Tiffany. "I'm gonna have to come watch my wife play."

Next to her, Tessa let out an audible sigh of relief.

"Oh, yeah, no, I'm staying," Tiffany added with a laugh. "The league would never let me drop back down, but I wouldn't want to anyway. I love this team."

"Awww." Dawn put her hands over her heart. "We love you too, boo-boo. We love both of you."

"Plus, I figure that once we're married, it might be good to each have a little bit of our own space," added Emily, looking at Tiffany with great tenderness. "You know, we don't have to do *everything* together."

Tiffany nodded and gave Emily a squeeze. An acute pang of jealousy ran through Fitz. The young couple was so smitten with each other, but they were also *friends*.

How sweet must it be to know you're marrying your best friend. Fitz loved Tom, but even at their best, they'd never had what Emily and Tiffany seemed to have. *I'm probably romanticizing their relationship. Every couple has their issues.* Fitz just couldn't possibly imagine these two going through the kind of trouble she and Tom were. *Could I have imagined it for myself when we were younger?*

"I guess it is time to start planning for next season." Tessa's voice brought Fitz back to the table.

"Yes, I suppose it is," agreed Fitz. "If Emily is leaving, that leaves room for Christine to play full time. Or do we want to look for somebody else?"

"We should confirm that everybody else is coming back first," said Tessa. "And we should do that tournament again."

"Actually, I heard of a charity tournament in April that might be fun to do as well." Fitz pulled out her phone and began looking up the tournament website.

"It never ends with you two, does it?" Michelle rolled her eyes. "Can't take a break, even for a minute."

Fitz grinned and put down her phone.

"I suppose it can wait a little, but what do you say, social captain, are you up for a couple off-season tourneys?"

"You can't fucking tailgate in April," Michelle pointed out. "Why bother if we can't party?"

"We could do a tournament up north, stay in a hotel, make it a whole girls weekend," Dawn suggested. "My kids get to do those trips, why not us?"

"That would be *amazing*," Tessa agreed.

"Girls' trip! Hell yeah! Okay, count me in for that." Michelle looked at Fitz and raised her eyebrows fractionally. "What do you say, captain? Will Tom be okay with you going away for a whole weekend?"

Fitz's face burned. She honestly didn't know what Tom would say. Michelle squinted at her.

"Don't tell me we're going to have to break you out at shotgun-point."

"No, no, don't worry," Fitz shook her head. "There's no way I'd miss it." She'd find a way. A trip up north with her 'hockey bitches' sounded like *heaven*. She smiled at Michelle, Dawn, and Tessa. "I couldn't let y'all have all the fun without me, could I?" Fitz raised her glass. "To the end of the first season, and the start of much more to come."

"Cheers, bitches!"

Coming in March, 2021

The Darts survived their first season, but the drama isn't over yet! Dawn's daughters are keeping her on her toes, Michelle is grappling with being mom to a preschooler, Tessa has an un-wanted crush on her best friend, and Fitz must decide what she's willing to endure in order to save her marriage.